Frederick Smith joined the RAF in 19▒▒ ▒▒ ▒▒▒▒▒▒▒ air gunner and commenced service ▒▒ ▒▒▒▒▒▒▒ Britain, Africa and finally, the Far Ea▒▒

At the end of the war he married an▒ ▒▒▒▒▒▒ ▒▒▒ several years in South Africa before returning to England to fulfil his life-long ambition to write. Two years later, his first play was produced, his first novel was published, the film rights to which were sold shortly afterwards. Since then, he has written twenty-four novels, about eighty short stories and two plays. Two novels, 633 SQUADRON and THE DEVIL DOLL have been made into films and one, A KILLING FOR THE HAWKS, has won the Mark Twain Literary Award.

Other novels by the same author:

Frederick E. Smith

Saffron's War

Futura Publications Limited

A Futura Book

First published in Great Britain in 1975
by Futura Publications Limited

Copyright © Frederick E. Smith 1975

ISBN 0 8600 72029
Printed in Great Britain by
Hazell Watson & Viney Ltd
Aylesbury, Bucks

For very special reasons that she will understand
I dedicate this book to Shelagh, my wife

Futura Publications Limited
49 Poland Street
London W1A 2LG

CHAPTER 1

Saffron sat staring at the sea and the sea stared back at him. Vast, blue-green, enigmatic. Two hundred yards away a dolphin arched gracefully into the sunlight. As it dived back, a second one appeared and was followed by three others of diminishing size. The effect was that of a proud father displaying his prodigy to the passing convoy but Saffron eyed the spectacle with some jaundice. All right. You've made your point. You're getting it regularly. I'm happy for you. Now eff off.

His gaze shifted. On every point of the compass ships were lunging southward. Some were less than four hundred yards away. Others were only smoke-stacks on the horizon. A vast target to make any self-respecting Kraut airman's mouth water. Or so you'd think, Saffron ruminated. He'd sat there, four hours on, four hours off, for nearly five days and apart from initial seasickness, his only reward had been a bird's-eye view of dolphins and wavetops.

Restless, he climbed to his feet. On the *Rangitata*'s forward quarter another troopship steamed purposefully forward with her cargo of meat. On her port side an oil tanker kept station with the grace of a wounded whale. Behind every ship an oil slick stretched out like a marker to the horizon. You have to believe it, Saffron thought. Those Krauts are even more stupid than we are.

The wind, chilled by the North Atlantic, made him shiver and pace round the six foot square of concrete. It was perched on scaffolding high up alongside the front funnel. In its centre a single Lewis on a swivel mounting pointed forlornly at the empty sky. Surrounding it were three-foot-high steel plates. The entire contraption was reached by a steel ladder from the quarterdeck.

In his RAF greatcoat, collar-and-tie and forage cap, Saffron was an incongruous figure. The *Rangitata*, carrying an RAF draft to a secret destination, had barely left Liverpool before a call had gone out for all armourers and air-crew gunners to man the anti-aircraft posts. That no combat gear, not even tin helmets, had been issued, reinforced the belief

5

of some, Ken Bickers in particular, that the war was a secret plot among the capitalistic states to cut down their surplus populations.

'Stands out a mile, doesn't it? They can't give us the chop themselves or we'd turn on the bastards. So they set us against one another and they're laughing. Like the first world war.'

Saffron's gaze moved to the gun-post one hundred feet aft of the funnel that Bickers was manning. Bickers, another incongruous figure muffled up in a blue greatcoat, caught his movement and waved an arm. He then jabbed a finger at his wristwatch. Reading his thoughts, Saffron grinned.

Bickers was a 23-year-old, self-styled Communist with lugubrious features and a gangling body that was all knobs and angles. Pipe-smoking and slow-moving, with woebegone mannerisms, he was the antithesis of the rabble-rouser. He and Saffron had met at West Kirby when the draft had formed and, in the way of the Services, had drifted together. Why, Saffron wasn't sure, unless Bickers's graveyard humour was the attraction.

He leaned over the steel plates. Below, a large flat deck was deserted except for half a dozen officers who were pacing its length for exercise. 'A' deck was reserved for commissioned ranks only. The egalitarian in Saffron bristled at the sight. Although the decks and holds below teemed with men and made sleeping a nightmare, the officers had turned down a request from the padre that their deck should be used for the nightly overspill when they retired to their cabins. Half a dozen Heinkels strafing the deck would teach them a lesson, Saffron thought and then smiled again. It was a reflection Bickers would find pregnant with promise.

A shout from the rear of the quarterdeck made him turn. A squat figure with tufts of fair hair sticking like straw from his forage cap was clumping towards the steel ladder. It was 'Lofty' Sellars, his relief. Until he had joined the RAF Saffron had never met anyone like Lofty. He had not even known the species existed. Now, as more and more Lofties were entering his life, Saffron discovered that self-posed questions were mounting. Only the previous evening he had discussed Lofty with Ken Bickers when they were off duty.

'I've known him ten days and in that time he hasn't said half a dozen words without effing. He stinks of BO and

6

halitosis and talks of nothing but beer and sex. Where the hell do characters like him come from? I never saw any before the war and now they're everywhere. What's even harder to understand' – Saffron's bewilderment had been totally genuine – 'what must the women be like who sleep with them?'

Bickers' pronouncement had been dark and damning. 'Pure bourgeois prejudice!'

'What?'

'You don't see, do you, that Lofty's BO and halitosis are the results of capitalistic oppression? If he'd received decent social services and education he'd be no different from you and me.'

'How do you know that? Why can't he just be a scruffy, lazy bastard who hates soap and water?'

Bickers' expression had turned even more scathing. 'You see! Bourgeois prejudice. It's that background of yours.'

'My background! A local grammar school and a clerk's job in the corporation?'

'Petty bourgeois,' Bickers had qualified disdainfully.

'You've a bloody nerve. What about that grammar school you went to?'

Bickers was not easily thrown. 'Some of us saw past our nose ends, mate. We could feel for the common man.' Pausing, he had scrutinized Saffron's fresh-complexioned face. 'Anyway, *you* look bourgeois. And act it too. An aircrew volunteer in the RAFVR, praying that we're going to Malta or Egypt so you can get another crack at the Krauts! As frustrated as a nympho in a monastery because the Huns don't attack us! How bourgeois can you get?'

Saffron had decided it was time for a counter-attack. 'Now the Jerries are going for Joe, I'd have thought your lot would have been as keen as anybody.'

'Come off it. If the Ruskies win, they get a system they believe in. If we win, we get another touch of the Lord Salisburys and the Lord Norfolks. I can't wait for that, can I?'

Thinking back, Saffron decided this was where he had gone sanctimonious. 'You've got politics on the brain. Don't you know that some men join up just because they don't like being pushed around?'

Bickers' laugh had been hollow. 'Pushed around? What

do those poofs on A Deck do to us? Why are you always bitching about them?'

'That's different.'

'Why is it different? That's what gets me about you, Saffron – for a clever devil you're as mixed up as a fruit cake. One minute you're playing hell about everything from class distinction to the moronic orders we get, and getting yourself into all kinds of trouble. In the next you're wanting to win the war all on your own. Why don't you decide which side you're on?'

Before Saffron could answer, Bickers' voice had sunk into a hoarse whisper. 'You're too brain-washed to see it but deep down you're one of us. Then break out, mate. Throw off the chains!'

'Chains?'

Bickers had glanced round before continuing. 'The chains of capitalistic indoctrination. You think I'm going to die so that Lord Norfolk can keep his half million acres? Not me. I'm playing the bastards at their own game and having the easiest war I can.' Leaning forward, Bickers had jabbed the stem of his pipe meaningfully at the brevet on Saffron's tunic. 'Think what they've done to you, mate. And get smart along with me.'

The reference had been to Saffron's drop in rank after being wounded on a mission over the Low Countries. Relegated to the ground staff until his health was fully restored, Saffron had been reduced from sergeant to corporal. The practice, standard at that time of the war, was bitterly resented by aircrews.

The clump of boots on the steel ladder brought Saffron back to the present. A moment later the squat figure of Lofty entered the gun post.

'How's it gone, Corp? All right?'

Saffron tried to keep to windward. 'Nothing's happened, if that's what you mean.'

'Who wants anything to effing happen,' Lofty grunted. He had a broad flattish face with clusters of blackheads, fleshy lips and three missing front teeth. Saffron watched him in fascination as he stuffed a half-smoked cigarette into his mouth and cupped a match behind two calloused hands. Sucking in smoke, he straightened.

'You know what Jock Wagstaff is sayin'?'

Jock Wagstaff was the draft's chief gossip. 'No. What?'

'He says we're goin' to Alexandria.' Lofty smacked his fleshy lips. 'Gawd, I hope so. They say the women out there are bloody marvellous. All bottom and tits. I'd an oppo once who went to one of them shows. He said the bint took a penny and . . .'

Saffron, who had heard the grisly details at least a dozen times, hastily picked up his gas mask and made for the ladder. 'Malta's a better bet. That's where all the action is at the moment.'

For a moment Lofty looked anxious. 'They've got women there too, haven't they?' As Saffron nodded he relaxed and made an obscene sound with his lips. 'I wish this effing old tub would get a move on. If I don't have a roll soon it's goin' to drop off.'

Saffron descended the ladder and made for 'B' deck. On the way Bickers joined him. Bickers' long face wore more than its usual aura of gloom. 'We're in trouble. Or at least you are.'

'Why?'

'It's that report you put in about the steel plates. McBride thinks it reflects on him.'

'Who told you?'

'Taffy Williams, my relief.' Bickers tried to resist the temptation and failed. 'I told you last night, didn't I, but you wouldn't listen.'

They pushed their way across the teeming deck towards a companionway that led down to the cabin Warrant Officer McBride, in charge of the gun-crew detail, was using as an office. McBride was a regular with red hair, red cheeks and red hands. There were some who swore he had red eyes to boot. He was lying on his bunk reading a paperback as the two corporals knocked and entered and Saffron caught a glimpse of a nude girl as he put the book aside and sat up. From the look he received before McBride concentrated on Bickers, Saffron knew there was trouble ahead.

'You two just come off duty?'

'Yes,' Bickers said.

McBride reacted instantly. 'Yes what?'

'Yes, sir,' Bickers said hastily.

McBride wasn't leaving it there. 'What's the matter? Don't you like saying "sir"?'

'I don't mind, sir,' Bickers lied.

He received a forbidding nod. 'I've heard all about you, Corporal. You're the one with Red ideas, right? Well, don't try those bloody ideas on me or I'll have your guts for garters. Understand?'

'Yes, sir.'

With his knife nicely sharpened, McBride turned his attention on Saffron. 'What about you – the clever one? What have you to report?'

'Nothing, sir.'

'Nothing, Corporal? You're quite sure?'

'Quite sure, sir.'

'I mean, there isn't any little detail you want to talk over with Squadron-Leader Jackson? Like no ammunition in the pits or anything of that sort?'

Saffron decided attack was the better form of defence. 'I mentioned the steel plates to you three days ago, sir. High angle fire would ricochet round inside them and cut a gunner to pieces.'

'And so when nothing was done, you went over my head to the Squadron Leader?'

'No, sir. He spoke to me last night and asked if everything was satisfactory. I couldn't very well say yes, could I?'

Saffron could now vouch that McBride's eyes did turn red. 'And how could I have the bloody things removed? Don't you know they're embedded into the concrete?'

'We could use oxy-acetylene, sir. I've checked they have the equipment aboard.'

McBride's breathing could be heard across the cabin. 'I've got a right couple of jesters here, haven't I? A bloody Red and a clever sod who knows everything. I'll tell you something, Saffron. If you go over my head again, you're for it. Both feet and from a great height. Is that clear?'

Before Saffron could answer there was a sudden, enormous clamour of bells. Frowning, McBride pushed forward. 'What the hell's that?'

Bickers looked scared. 'It's action stations.'

'Action stations?'

'An air or sub attack,' Bickers explained.

'Christ,' McBride muttered, throwing open the cabin door. The sound of the bells became louder and footsteps seemed to be running all over the ship. As Saffron and Bickers followed

McBride out into the companionway the bells ceased, bringing a moment of thick silence. Then, as the shouts and running footsteps returned, there was a thump-thump that sounded like a rubber hose pounding an empty barrel. It was followed by the distant hammering of Oerlikon cannon.

A shout through the tannoy came over the din. 'Action stations! Action stations! Close all doors and batten down hatches. At the double!'

Saffron threw a glance at Bickers. 'Come on.'

As he began to run a hand caught his shoulder and swung him round. 'Where are you going?'

It was McBride, looking both scared and malicious. Saffron tried to pull away. 'I'm going back to my post.'

McBride's hand tightened. 'Who says you are? Your stint's over. You're staying down here with the rest of us. Both of you.'

'But Lofty's only an armourer. He's had no combat experience.'

McBride glanced with dislike at Saffron's brevet. 'Then he'll get some, won't he? You want to be the only bloody hero in this mob?'

Saffron, whose tongue had got him into more trouble than he cared to remember, lost control of it again. 'Who the hell's trying to be a hero? There's an air attack and I'm volunteering to man a gun. You can't stop me.'

McBride stiffened. 'Can't I, by Christ! You move another step forward and you're in the brig. Faster than that.'

As Saffron hesitated, the shaft of sunlight at the end of the companionway dimmed and vanished. Giving Saffron a glare of triumph, McBride walked back into his cabin. The two corporals followed him to the porthole and tried to peer over his shoulder. The anti-aircraft fire was louder now and interspersed by heavy thumps. The shock waves could be felt through the *Rangitata*'s steel plates.

'Can you see anything yet?' Bickers asked breathlessly.

McBride shook his head. Two hundred yards away the oil tanker was pouring black smoke as the convoy tried to raise its speed. As Saffron leaned forward he saw a dark shadow sweeping diagonally across the blue-green water. 'Condors,' he muttered, 'Focke Wulfs.'

There was a massive thump and a column of water rose a hundred feet from the tanker. The *Rangitata* winced as if

11

struck below the belt. A second bomb made a hit just forward of the tanker's bridge. 'Christ,' McBride muttered.

The explosion cracked the long hull like an eggshell. The front half yawed to port, the rear half, still driven by its engines, began swinging the stricken ship in a circle. As flames sheeted along the deck, ant-like figures began leaping into the sea. Oil, gushing out like blood from a mortal wound, flattened the waves and engulfed the swimming men. While it choked their lungs, fire raced across the water and incinerated them.

His face pale, Bickers turned away as another black shadow swept across the sea. As the thin rattle of the *Rangitata*'s Lewis guns sounded through the roar of engines, Saffron let out a yelp of impotence.

'What the hell am I doing down here? It's bloody crazy.'

A massive explosion drowned his voice. The *Rangitata* rolled drunkenly to starboard and for a minute seemed unlikely to right herself. Then she reeled back, throwing the three men to the other side of the cabin.

It signalled the end of the raid. The hammer of pom-poms and thud of explosions faded and the smell of burning oil and flesh began to disperse as the convoy ploughed on. McBride, his eyes unnaturally bright, swung round. 'That seems to be it. Let's go and see what the damage is.'

As they hurried along the companionway a young AC2 appeared on the steps. Seeing McBride, he ran towards him. 'I've a message from Corporal Johnson, sir. He wants to see you right away. It's the No 2 post.'

McBride glanced at Bickers. 'That's yours, isn't it?' As Bickers nodded, McBride swung back to the white-faced AC2. 'What happened?'

The youngster looked uncertain whether to cry or be sick. 'They put a cannon burst right into it, sir. Williams was on the gun and . . .' Gagging, he turned away and sent a shower of vomit down the nearby wall. Bickers and McBride jumped back, Saffron stood his ground.

'What happened to Williams?'

Stained with shame and vomit, the AC2 lifted his ashen face. 'He got cut to pieces, Corp. From the waist down. It's a hell of a mess in there.'

*　　*　　*

12

Saffron was on the dawn watch the following morning. He saw the ships turn from dark smudges to silhouetted cut-outs as the sky lightened. One hundred feet aft the stricken No 2 gun-post could now be picked out from the superstructure around it. It was empty and covered by a tarpaulin. When Saffron had suffered his morning resurrection and crawled from his blanket, he had been greeted by a thankful croak from the brown mound alongside him that was Bickers.

'Good luck, mate. Mind you give 'em hell.'

The sky was cloudless. And empty. Unless Jerry had fitted extra fuel tanks to his Condors, the convoy was now out of range. Keeping the watch on sea and sky that had now become a habit, Saffron wondered if they would be ordered to stand down. He hoped not. There was a loner in him that loathed the anonymity of the lower decks with their stifling claustrophobia and sweat. With thirty minutes more to go on his watch, he was wondering what joys were awaiting him on the messdeck when the clump of booted feet made him glance down. A helmeted marine sergeant, all square jaw and bulging muscles, was leading a squad of six men across the quarterdeck. The two marines at the rear were carrying what appeared to be a gas cylinder. The sergeant reached the foot of the steel ladder and lifted his craggy face.

'Up there! You!'

'Me?' Saffron enquired.

'Who bloody else? You're relieved. Come on down.'

Saffron gazed down at the seven upturned faces. 'Did Warrant Officer McBride send you?'

The sergeant, wasting no more time on words, clumped up the ladder and swung into the pit as if taking an enemy strongpoint. 'What's the matter with you, lad? Don't you understand English?'

'Sorry but I'm lost,' Saffron confessed. 'What are you supposed to be doing?'

'What's it look as if we're doing – knitting socks for Santa Claus? We're taking over the ship's security, lad, that's what we're doing.'

Down on the quarterdeck men were bending over the cylinder. As a rotund shape began swelling beneath them the bewildered Saffron turned back to the sergeant.

'It's a balloon! They're blowing up balloons!'

13

He received a smirk. 'Target practice, lad. That's how my men keep their eye in.'

The truth came to Saffron like a thunderclap. 'You're the ship's gun crew, aren't you?'

He received a wink of pride. 'Professionals, lad. Been on this old tub for over a year and she hasn't had a scratch.'

Saffron's eyes moved from the marine's polished boots and white gaiters to his bellicose face sheltered by a tin helmet. He gazed down at his own greatcoat and then it all came up in a yelp of indignation. 'You mean we've been manning these bloody guns for over a week while you've been hiding below decks? And now we're out of range, you're taking over?'

The sergeant's jaw came forward like the prow of an icebreaker. 'You've a big mouth, lad. You'd better batten it or you'll be for the high jump. Now get the hell out of here and don't come back.'

Breathing hard, Saffron climbed unsteadily down the ladder. Beside it the squad of marines had now filled the balloon with gas. Floating it from his wrist like a child's toy, a man climbed up to the gun post and stood alongside the sergeant. Fascinated, Saffron watched the sergeant cock the Lewis and give the marine a nod. The balloon leapt upwards, to swerve sharply astern as it met the slipstream and the wind. A second later the Lewis began to chatter. The balloon grew rapidly smaller as it bobbed over the heaving sea. As the ship's superstructure intervened, the sound of the Lewis died away.

'Missed it,' Saffron said with loud malice. 'Can't even hit a bloody balloon.'

The satisfaction that all six marines felt at their sergeant's failure died under this attack from an outsider. Saffron received six threatening glances and a snarl from the only NCO in the group, a corporal. 'You looking for trouble, Brylcreem Boy?'

Saffron gauged his distance to the nearest companion-ladder before answering. 'It must be hell fighting those balloons. What do you get – danger pay?'

Before he got a reaction Saffron was down the ladder. On his way across the deserted officers' deck he met Ken Bickers. Saffron was too indignant to notice the Londoner's euphoria. 'Guess what's happened?'

'What?'

Saffron told him. Bickers looked aghast. 'They've been on the ship since we sailed?'

'Where else could they have been?'

For once Bickers looked too shocked for lucid comment. 'The bastards! Skulking in safety while we've fought for 'em. What a bloody outfit we're in. Didn't I tell you?'

A sudden burst of firing made the choking Bickers duck. 'It's all right,' Saffron reassured. 'They're firing at balloons.'

'Firing at what!'

Saffron pointed at a spherical shape receding into the morning sky. 'We can't let them get away with this,' Bickers said hoarsely. 'Someone has to be told.'

'Who?' Saffron asked.

Bickers was still watching the diminishing balloon. 'They're bloody poor shots, aren't they? Thank God we've got the Russians.' He turned back to Saffron. 'Never mind, mate. We'll find a way.' His earlier euphoria began to flood back. 'Maybe sooner than you think.'

Saffron eyed him curiously. 'What's that mean?'

Bickers' recovery was an indication of the magnitude of his news. 'Old Jackson gave us our posting this morning. That's what I was coming to tell you.'

Saffron took a deep breath. 'Is it Malta?'

'No.'

'Egypt?'

'No.'

'Stop buggering about and tell me. Where?'

Bickers gave a smug, infuriating grin. 'You're not going to like it.'

'You're not going to like your bloody face if you don't tell me. Where?'

'South Africa,' Bickers announced triumphantly.

Saffron's mouth fell open. 'South Africa?'

'Right. We're part of the Commonwealth Air Training Scheme.' Bickers' expression was ecstatic. 'Think of it, mate! Sunshine, bright lights, cheap booze, and girls, girls, girls.'

'It's a mistake,' Saffron said thickly. 'It has to be.'

'It's no mistake, mate. We've been given our postings when we arrive. I'm going to Number 99 Air School, Cape Town. You're going to some place up country for a course,

15

then you're posted to Cape Town too.' Bickers' eyes turned skywards. 'Someone up there must like us. You can't explain it any other way.'

Before Saffron could speak a querulous voice made both corporals turn. 'What are you two men doing up here? Get down to your deck at once or I'll take your names.'

A young Flying Officer, wingless and with down still on his face, was striding angrily towards them. Burning with rebellion at his posting, Saffron was about to answer back when Bickers caught his arm and dragged him towards the nearest companion ladder.

'Don't let poofs like that worry you,' the Londoner hissed. 'Keep in your mind we're heading for Utopia. And don't do anything to eff it up.'

CHAPTER 2

Kitbag on his shoulder, sweat pouring down his face, Saffron ran after the moving train. Ignoring the shout of the guard he fumbled for a door handle. A young South African soldier saw his plight and swung the door open. Heaving his kitbag into the compartment, Saffron jumped in after it. 'Thanks,' he panted.

The compartment was filled to overflowing. Half a dozen assorted civilians sat knee to knee down one side. Two middle-aged men and the young South African soldier stood in the space between the seats. Two beefy Royal Navy seamen sat on Saffron's left side. The three standing men momentarily blocked his view of the remaining seats but as one of the men shifted his stance, Saffron gave a start. A Great Dane lay luxuriously across the cushions. With legs outstretched it sprawled from the interior window to the second seaman's thigh, on which its massive head partly rested. It opened one eye at Saffron's abrupt entrance but as the corporal stared back its yellow eye closed again.

Saffron tried to identify its owner. The six seated civilians wore the embarrassed masks of those who knew they were in a delicate situation and wanted no part in it. The two middle-aged men, their faces buried in newspapers, were acting as if every day of their lives a Great Dane denied them

16

a seat. The two matelots, smelling strongly of beer, sat like inscrutable sphinxes. Even the youthful South African soldier's eyes turned quickly away when Saffron addressed him.

'Who owns that dog?'

The silence in the compartment seemed the quieter for the clatter of the wheels outside. Noticing the young soldier had thrown a split-second glance at the two beefy seamen, Saffron turned towards them and said loudly: 'It's a damn disgrace to let a dog take up four seats when people are standing.'

Still no reply. The two middle-aged men buried their faces deeper into their newspapers, the seated men and women tried to look even blanker, and the two matelots stared impassively across the compartment. The sailor against whom the dog was resting its head was imperturbably chewing gum. Glaring at him, Saffron leaned forward.

'Is it your dog?'

The man's only reaction was to turn his bucolic eyes on Saffron's face and to cease chewing. A couple of seconds later his jaws began their rhythmical movement again. Breathing hard, Saffron turned to his companion.

'Is he deaf?'

The second sailor, who was balding slightly, had a face like a turnpike. He contemplated Saffron a moment, then shook his head.

'Then why doesn't he answer me?' Saffron demanded.

The sound the matelot emitted was that of a file scraping rusted metal. 'You new to Cape Town, mate?'

'What if I am?'

'I thought so. Then belt up!'

'Belt up? When a dog's keeping four of us from a seat?'

The matelot's eyes travelled from Saffron's shoes, past his khaki shorts and smart bush-jacket, and ended on his RAF cap. His contemptuous nod said it all. 'You pansy mob are all the same. Never could mind your own business. That dog's got the same rights as you an' me.'

'What rights? Even if you've paid for it, it can't occupy seats when people are standing.'

The matelot leaned triumphantly forward. 'And that's where you're wrong, Clever Trevor. That dog's a member of the Royal Navy. A seaman with name, number, rank, ration card, the lot. Which means he's entitled to the same privileges as any other member of the Armed Forces. So why don't you run off and chase your tail?'

Prudence was never one of Saffron's strengths when he was provoked. 'A seaman? How bloody silly can you get?' His sarcastic eyes turned on the dog. 'Although I'll say this for him – he looks more intelligent than most of your lot. Who is he – your First Officer?'

The beefy matelot exchanged a glance with his gum-chewing companion and like one man they began to rise from their seats. Sensing mayhem only a few seconds away one of the standing civilians let out a cry of dismay. 'Gentlemen, please. There are ladies in the carriage. We don't mind standing for the dog. Do we?' he appealed to the second man who gave a hasty acknowledgement.

Saffron, who had regretted his sarcasm the moment he made it, blessed the intervention as the matelots sank reluctantly back. The gum-chewing seaman spoke for the first time.

'I'll tell you what, mate. You move 'im.'

'Why the hell should I?' Saffron demanded. 'He's your dog'.

The matelot's bucolic eyes glinted with malice. 'He ain't, mate. That's where you're wrong.'

'You mean you didn't put him on the train?'

' 'Course not. He was in the carriage when we got in.'

'You're telling me he travels on his own?'

'That's right. Knows the way to Simonstown like the back of his paw. Does the trip at least three times a week.'

All the fight had gone out of Saffron now. 'You're having me on.'

'He's not, Corporal.' It was the young South African soldier, relaxing at the fall in temperature. 'He's called Nuisance. Everyone knows him. He travels on the buses too.'

'And wears bell-bottom trousers and a suit of navy blue. Not forgetting his medals,' Saffron said sarcastically.

The youngster looked doubtful. 'I don't know about that, Corporal. But he does go round the pubs at night.'

Saffron groaned. Turning, he made his last attack on the Navy. 'If he's not your dog, why stick up for him like that?'

The gum-chewing seaman looked surprised. 'Why not? He's a matelot, ain't he?'

Saffron made a choking sound and pushed across the carriage. The dog's eyes were closed and its expression beatific. Conquering his trepidation Saffron prodded a finger into the animal's haunch. 'Get up!' As one sclerotic eye-opened. Saffron prodded again, harder. 'Come on. Get off that seat.'

The dog's tail began thumping the carriage door like a baton. His huge head lifted and stared benignly at Saffron.

'He thinks you want to play,' the gum-chewing matelot explained.

Feeling more confident Saffron caught hold of the dog's front paws and tugged. The huge body moved an inch and no more. Saffron glanced over his shoulder apologetically at the two civilians. 'May I have a bit more room?'

They stood obediently aside, fascinated by the drama. Saffron took a firmer grip of the huge paws and tugged hard. This time the dog began to slide towards the edge of the seat. His head lifted again as he recognized his danger and a growl like nearby thunder stopped Saffron in his tracks. As he stared into two rows of dripping fangs, he heard the gum-chewing matelot's guffaw. 'Go on, mate. You're not scared of losing half a dozen fingers, are you? Or maybe your hand.'

Humiliated, Saffron edged back to his place by the door. Coughs sounded from the civilians and behind Saffron the gravel-voiced sailor gave a derisive laugh. 'These Brylcreem boys are all the same, mate. All wind and, ladies present, you know what.'

Saffron dropped dejectedly on his kitbag. The young soldier leaned over him sympathetically. 'It's not your fault, Corporal. That's the one thing Nuisance hates, to lose his seat. Otherwise he's the best-tempered dog in the country.'

'I think he's lovely,' Saffron growled, lighting a cigarette.

The train stopped at Dryberg fifteen minutes later. As Saffron flung open the compartment door and dragged out his kitbag he saw the dog raise its head as if to check the station. With another groan, Saffron slammed the door and hurried away.

Kitbag alongside him, Saffron waved his thanks to the

driver as the vegetable truck pulled away. Opposite him was Number 99 Air School, Breconfield, a huge conglomeration of wooden huts, parade grounds, and distant hangars. To his left the road led towards the Cape Flats and to the sea, to his right it ran like a straight ribbon to the city suburbs that spread out beneath the blue-green heights of Devil's Peak. The sky was cloudless, the road empty of traffic, and the camp across the way strangely quiet and peaceful. As Saffron stood there the only sounds were the drone of crickets and the distant roar of an engine under test. The afternoon sun was hot and the total effect was one of pleasant lethargy. Saffron stood a full minute before shouldering his kitbag with a sigh and starting across the road.

On the train down to Cape Town Saffron had come to a decision of the soul. In the camp near Johannesberg where he had spent the last three months, he had investigated all possibilities of escaping from Training Command and had found none. Which to a rational mind – and Saffron prided himself on having a rational mind – meant he must now make the best of the situation. In Cape Town he would carry out orders to the letter, keep out of every kind of trouble, become in every way a model acquisition to the camp. Such behaviour would at least ensure he obtained every benefit his situation offered. In recidivist moments Saffron wondered if this decision was a sell-out, particularly as he knew it was one Bickers would heartily endorse. At the same time it was logical and Saffron intended to pursue it.

He made his way through the main gate and towards the guardroom where he impressed the Afrikander personnel with his friendliness and civility. He obtained his billet number and began tramping down the rows of wooden huts in search of it. His only impression of the camp so far was its apparent emptiness and the sand upon which it was built. His shoes sank into the brown grit at every step and he tried to push away the vision of insects and wind that it conjured.

He found his hut at last and dropped his kit into the small empty cubicle at its entrance that was reserved for NCOs. By the time he had drawn blankets from the store his bush-jacket was stained with sweat. He mopped his face in the washroom and then started down the dusty road that led into the heart of the camp. Wooden huts flanked it on either side but two hundred yards further on they gave way to a wide parade ground backed by huge hangars. Personnel were still at a premium but three khaki-clad figures were chatting in the centre of the parade ground and Saffron started towards them.

As he drew nearer he saw that two of the men were young South African Air Force pilots. The third man was a South African Warrant Officer. With his resolution firmly in mind, Saffron snapped up a crisp salute as he came within range. The two lieutenants, their eyes on Saffron's brevet, returned his salute and greeting somewhat diffidently. Conscious that he had a psychological superiority, Saffron was relaxing when the Warrant Officer let out an impatient bark.

'Well, Corporal. What do you want?'

The man's voice was more guttural and had a more pronounced South African accent than the two young lieutenants. In contrast to them, both of whom were fair-skinned, he had a beefy, swarthy face with close-set eyes and a surly mouth. He was wearing South African summer dress, brown boots, khaki shorts and bush-jacket, and a circular toupee. All were impeccably clean and his boots had a mirror-like polish. He was perhaps two inches under Saffron's six feet with a rotund body that looked as powerful as a bomb casing. Black chest hair sprouted through the V of his bush-shirt and his brown, stocky legs looked like the pillars of Hercules. Saffron, whose vivid imagination was already wondering how a gorilla could achieve such a rank, pulled himself together.

'I'm looking for the Chief Ground Instructor's office, sir. I believe his name is Flight Lieutenant Price.'

Before the Warrant Officer could answer, the taller of the two lieutenants broke in. 'Are you a new posting, Corporal?'

Saffron swivelled. 'Yes, sir.'

The officer's eyes were fixed on his brevet. 'What as – an instructor?'

'I understand so, sir.'

'Where have you come from?'

Saffron could feel the hostility of the Warrant Officer's eyes as he answered. 'I've been up country on a Senior Armourer Instructor's course, sir.'

The taller officer sounded impressed. 'This is Lieutenant

Wilson. My name's Davidson. We're a couple of the Joes who take the u/t observers up on their joy rides.' He indicated the frowning gorilla. 'Mr Kruger is the CFI's Admin Officer.'

'My name's Alan Saffron, sir.'

'Welcome to Breconfield, Corporal.' This time it was the other pilot. 'I see you've been on operations. In the Middle East or the UK?'

'The UK, sir. I came out here three months ago.'

From the corner of his eye Saffron was watching Kruger's impatience at all this camaraderie between officers and other ranks. Davidson was pulling out a packet of cigarettes, clearly preparing for a chat.

'We teach a mixed bag here, Saffron. Observers and armourers.' He offered the cigarettes to Saffron. 'With your qualifications you're certain to get observers.'

A sharp bark froze the tableau. 'All right, Corporal. This isn't a bloody tea party. Mr Price might want you for lectures this afternoon.' Raising a hairy arm, Kruger pointed across the parade ground. 'You'll find him in the Educational Block, straight ahead. Through the swing doors into the quadrangle and the third door on the right.'

The lack of protest by the two officers against the Warrant Officer's intervention had its message for Saffron. Thanking him and snapping another salute at the lieutenants, he turned away. He had not taken five paces before Kruger's guttural voice followed him.

'Man, you can't get away from these damned bluebottles these days. I had a dust-up with one in Cape Town last night. He made a pass at my girl and I knocked the bastard down. I wanted him to get up because he'd more coming, but these bloody roineks are all the same – once they're down they stay down.'

It should be recorded that Saffron tried. In another dimension his good intentions met his anger with protesting arms but the issue was never in doubt. Turning, he walked back to within two paces of the burly Warrant Officer.

'I heard that. And there's only one way to prove you're right, isn't there? Try knocking me down.'

The man's eyes filled with prurient lights. 'I thought I just told you to report to Flight Lieutenant Price.'

'You did. And then you insulted me. Why?'

22

Kruger glanced at the two young officers, read their expressions, and shutters closed over his malice. 'Eavesdroppers get what they deserve, Corporal. Like everyone else, I've got my opinions.'

'And I've got mine,' Saffron said savagely. 'Want to hear them?'

The look he received was almost thoughtful before Kruger turned to the two officers and said something in Afrikaans. His hand snapped up to his toupee, his boots thudded the ground, and he marched away with stiff, jerky strides. After half a dozen yards he halted. 'What did you say your name was, Corporal?'

'Corporal Saffron – sir!'

The man nodded and strode on. Behind him Saffron heard breath being released and turned aggressively. 'What the hell else could I do?'

His anger died at the officers' expressions. Both were showing acute embarrassment but while Davidson's face contained respect, his companion looked dismayed. 'He did it deliberately,' Saffron went on in disbelief. 'Why?'

'He did provoke you, Corporal,' Davidson admitted. 'I'd like you to know those were his opinions and not ours.'

Appeased, Saffron began to relax. 'What's he got against us, anyway?'

Wilson gave Davidson a warning glance. 'If I were you, Corporal, I'd go and tell Flight Lieutenant Price what's happened. He'll be able to advise you.'

Saffron stared at him. 'Advise me on what?'

Wilson cleared his throat loudly, effectively drowning Davidson's reply. 'We mustn't keep you any longer, Corporal. I hope you'll be happy here. In any case we'll see you around. Good luck.'

Summarily dismissed, Saffron made his way towards the Educational Block. Before entering it he glanced back. Davidson, who appeared to be arguing with Wilson, was gazing after him with concern. With the strong feeling there was more amiss than the incident warranted, Saffron pushed through swing doors, crossed a corridor, and emerged in a large inner courtyard. A sunken lawn decorated by flowerbeds was surrounded by a tiled path that gave access to a dozen or more classrooms. The effect was more that of a modern college than the kind of military establishments

Saffron was accustomed to, and the sight eased the Kruger incident from his mind.

The silence that had impressed Saffron earlier was not present here. With classroom windows open in the hot sunlight, the voices of lecturers could be heard against an unruly background buzz that made Saffron think of a power-station he had once visited. It took him a moment to establish the link. The menacing hum had suggested mighty forces straining against an insecure leash.

The third door on the right had the words Chief Ground Instructor stencilled on it. Saffron tapped on the glass panel and entered. At first sight the office appeared empty. A large desk, cluttered with papers, faced him. Two metal filing cabinets stood against the left wall, a large cupboard stood in the far corner. The walls were covered with cut-away diagrams of bombs, guns, and ancilliary equipment with an occasional security poster interspersed between them. As Saffron paused uncertainly, he heard a scrabbling noise, the clink of metal, then a muttered curse. A second later an oily hand fumbled at the desk, followed by a raised head. The voice that greeted Saffron was querulous.

'Yes, Corporal. What is it?'

'Are you the Armament Officer, sir?'

The man straightened. Capless, he had dishevelled hair and sharp, birdlike features. The sleeves of his shirt, with its twin-blue shoulder epaulettes, were rolled up, revealing skinny, oil-streaked arms. A jerkiness about his voice and movements made Saffron think of a perky house sparrow. Then, as the man moved and his skinny legs, clad in knee-length shorts, showed through the well of the desk, Saffron's opinion changed. This was the world's first commissioned gremlin.

The man was grinning ruefully. 'I *was* the Armament Officer this morning, Corporal. Now I'm not so sure. What do you want?'

'My name's Saffron, sir. I've just arrived and been told to report to you.'

'Saffron, eh? Oh, yes, I've got a report about you somewhere among all this bumph. Come in, lad, and close the door. Are you fixed up with a billet yet?'

'Yes, sir. That's all been taken care of.'

'Good, good.' The tiny officer was scrabbling among the

papers on his desk and leaving oil traces everywhere. 'If I remember right, you've just taken an SAI course, haven't you?'

'That's right.'

Price's head jerked up suddenly like a bird spotting an insect. 'Know anything about VGOs?'

Saffron hesitated. 'I ought to.'

'Then come over here.'

Saffron rounded the huge desk. Littered over the floor were the stripped components of a machine gun. Price frowned down. 'The bloody thing keeps on having stoppages. No one can find out why and so it's ended up with me. And I'm as knackered as they are.'

Saffron squatted on the floor and pulled the pieces towards him. 'What kind of stoppages?'

'Number One, mostly.'

'They've tried it with different magazines?'

Price's comical figure squatted alongside him. 'Yes. And it's made no difference.'

Saffron checked the feed piece and the firing pin. He then picked up the gas cylinder and held it to the light. As he lowered it he caught Price's eyes, bright with understanding. 'The bloody gas block! Think that's it?'

Saffron lowered the cylinder to the floor. 'It's badly fouled up. I'd say that was the trouble.'

Price smacked a tiny fist into a tiny palm. 'Lad, you've saved my reputation. Not a word of this or I'll have you shot.'

Grinning, Saffron moved back round the desk. Price followed him and began scrabbling among the papers again. 'I know that bloody report's here somewhere. Ah, what's this?'

He dropped into his chair and supporting his head with his hands began reading. A minute later he sat back. There was a fresh oil smear across one cheek as he gave Saffron a nod.

'I like it, lad. Damn good record. I see you were top on the SAI course. Is that how you got here, by exercising your preference?'

'No, sir. They just sent me.'

Price nodded, his gaze roving over Saffron's well-knit thirteen-stone frame. His question caught the corporal by surprise. 'You play football?'

'You mean soccer, sir?'

'Is there another game?'

Saffron grinned. 'Yes, I play.'

Price's eyes gleamed. 'Full back?'

'I can. Although I prefer centre half.'

In one movement Price was out of his chair and through the door. His shout echoed around the quadrangle. 'Sergeant Ainsworth!'

The buzz of voices died, startled faces appeared at lecture room doors, but no one came forward. A moment later Price returned, grinning diffidently. 'I'd forgotten. He's got his course on the Eerste Rivier firing range. You can meet him in the morning. If you're any good you'll be playing for us on Saturday.'

'Saturday?'

'Why not? You're fit, aren't you?' When Saffron nodded, Price went on: 'Our right back was posted last week and I want you in shape by the time we play Wingfield. They beat us three months ago and the bastards are still crowing. They've got a great little left wing but you're just the size to do him.'

With his absurd shorts flapping around his knees, Price returned to the desk. 'Right – that's settled. Now – where to place you. We're an odd set-up here – we take u/t observers, conversion courses, and armourers and that's quite an assortment.' The midget gave Saffron a puckish glance. 'Seen any of our armourers yet?'

'No, sir. I've hardly seen anyone.'

'That's because there's no flying today and everyone's at lectures. Don't worry' – Price was grinning – 'you'll see life before long.' He slid a hand under a buttock and scratched himself, a characteristic gesture. 'With your qualifications you ought to go straight on to aircrew. I suppose that's what you want?'

Saffron nodded happily. 'Yes, sir.'

'Pity, because I'm desperately short of instructors for the armourers.' Price paused, then continued with wicked smoothness. 'Or rather I'm short on men who can handle 'em.'

'Handle them, sir?'

'Yes. You see, they're a bit different from the lads we're used to. Straight from the bush, most of 'em, and a bit on

26

the wild side. Our chaps call 'em all kinds of names but they're just hard men, that's all. Which means they need hard men to handle 'em.' Price eyed Saffron up and down again, coughed, and nodded. 'I think you're probably right to want aircrew, Saffron.'

Saffron, who had some pride in his physical prowess, was frowning. 'I've handled hard men before, sir.'

Price lifted an innocent eyebrow. 'You have?'

'Of course I have.'

Price drummed his fingers on the desk for a moment. Then, with the air of one who had the gravest doubts but wished above all else to be fair, his face cleared. 'All right, Saffron, I'll give you a try. Perhaps an easy course to see how you get along. Now off you go. I don't want to see you until the morning. You parade at 06.30 hours.' At Saffron's start, Price gave his puckish grin. 'The CO believes in pre-breakfast exercises. You'll learn all about 'em tomorrow.'

Feeling he had been conned by a master, Saffron was at the door before he remembered. 'There's just one thing, sir. A Lieutenant Wilson said I should mention it to you.'

'Wilson? I know him. Go on.'

'I'd a bit of a fracas with a warrant officer he was talking to. Someone called Kruger.'

In the sudden silence a bellow of laughter could be heard in one of the classrooms, followed by an instructor's yell for silence. The start Price gave puzzled Saffron. 'You've had a fracas with who?'

'Warrant Officer Kruger, sir.'

'When, for Christ's sake?'

'A few minutes ago. Just after I arrived.'

'What happened?'

Saffron told him, finishing on a note of defiance. 'It was obviously meant as an insult. So what else could I do?'

'What were the exact words you used? Can you remember?'

'I told him to try knocking me down. That's about all.'

'Did he put you on a charge?'

'No. How could he? I had witnesses.'

'And all this happened a few minutes after you arrived?' Price's question, put over-casually, added to Saffron's bewilderment. 'You don't know what star you were born under, I suppose?'

27

'Star, sir? No, I don't.'

'Pity,' Price murmured.

Saffron decided there was a ghost somewhere that ought to be laid. 'What's so special about Kruger, sir? He's only a warrant officer. Why did those two officers let him talk that way?'

He found Price's switch in conversation unnerving. 'That settles it, lad. You work with me. If I can keep you, that is. All right?'

'Yes, I suppose so, sir.'

'There's one other thing.' Price was scratching his backside again. 'I like to look after my chaps, so if at any time you get into trouble, don't say a word until you've seen me. Don't argue, don't say anything. Got it?'

Saffron discovered his throat was turning dry. 'Yes, sir. But why should I get into trouble?'

Price was trying to look as innocent as his gnomelike face would allow. 'I talk to all my new men this way, Saffron. In case you haven't found out yet, things aren't quite the same here as in the UK. Ninety per cent, maybe ninety-five per cent of South Africans are as friendly as hell to us and as loyal or more loyal to the war effort. But there's a minority group that hates our guts – the Boer War throws long shadows. Some of 'em join the Services to grab the prestige a uniform brings. They seldom volunteer to fight abroad, or take the Blue Oath as it's called, but if they work hard they can still win promotion inside the country.'

Saffron believed he understood. 'Like Kruger?'

Price scowled. 'Shut up about Kruger. I'm not talking about anyone in particular: these are just facts every newcomer ought to know. Another thing: there are nearly three-quarters of a million Coloureds in the Cape, half white and half black. Some of the women can be damned attractive but leave 'em alone. It's a serious civil offence for a European to lay 'em. Got it?'

Saffron's nod was dubious as he tried to find the link between the hairy Kruger and sloe-eyed coloured girls. 'I hope so.'

'Good.' Price assumed a spurious cheerfulness. 'All you have to do, lad, is watch your step. Read DROs every day and everything should go fine. Now run along and make yourself comfortable. Sorry I can't give you a pass today

28

but station rules forbid new postings to go out on their first night. But I'll make it up to you tomorrow.'

Alarmed by all this consideration but realizing further questions were futile, Saffron enquired about Bickers. 'Is he on your staff, sir?'

'Bickers. Yes, he's got Course Nineteen in this block. You a friend of his?'

'We met on the draft coming over,' Saffron explained.

Taking Saffron by the arm, Price led him outside and pointed across the quadrangle. 'The fourth door down is the instructors' staff room. Wait in there and I'll send Bickers to you. It's break time in five minutes.'

CHAPTER 3

The staff room Saffron entered was empty of personnel. It contained two tables littered with dirty ashtrays, and rows of wooden lockers. Half a dozen chairs were scattered about the linoleum-covered floor and technical posters lined the walls. The windows were open but a strong smell of stale tobacco lingered in the room.

Saffron positioned himself at the window overlooking the quadrangle. Across it a row of classroom windows faced him. In the far corner was a counter with racks of equipment behind it. A youth wearing khaki overalls, the working dress of South African air mechanics, emerged from a lecture room carrying a .303 Browning. Walking the length of the quadrangle he handed it to a corporal who appeared behind the storeroom counter. Saffron tried to see if Bickers was lecturing in the classrooms opposite but the glare of sunlight was too strong.

The South African trainee returned to his classroom. The door had barely closed before an electric bell rang. Seconds later all hell broke loose. Doors were hurled open and the quadrangle turned into a sea of laughing, cursing men. Ignoring the despairing shouts of NCOs, they surged towards the doors at the far end. As Saffron gazed in astonishment, a huge trainee with the physique of a heavyweight wrestler, was tripped and flung down to the lawn. His head struck a stone surround and Saffron had visions of a mortuary. Instead the man sat up, shook his bleeding head, and with a yell that turned the blood cold, vaulted back and dived into a group of men like a Springbok forward going for the line. Saffron could feel the crunch of bone as the entire party were flung into the mass of men already jammed in front of the doors.

'Christ,' he muttered, awed by the mayhem.

The heaving mob began to thin and the din to subside. As Saffron turned away the door was flung open and Bickers appeared. 'Saffron! You've made it, you old bastard.'

Laughing their pleasure, the two men shook hands. 'I'd have met you in,' Bickers said. 'But we've a couple of instructors off sick today.'

Saffron glanced through the window at the disappearing mob. 'What happened to them? Were they clobbered or knifed?'

Bickers grinned. 'You think that's rough? Wait until payday.'

Saffron offered his cigarettes to the Londoner who shook his head and pulled out his pipe. 'Do you teach 'em all day long?'

'No, we get a few hours on conversion courses. But we're with them eighty per cent of the time.'

'How do you handle them? With a Sten?'

Bickers' long face broke into another grin. 'No, I manage with a Smith and Wesson these days. But what are you worried about. As an SAI you'll be on aircrew.'

'Wrong. I have to report here in the morning.'

Bickers let out a mocking guffaw. 'You! On bush apes? Price must be slipping.'

'Why?' Saffron demanded.

'Why? You're too bloody posh, mate. The bush-apes need men of the earth. Men who talk their language.'

'Your sort, I suppose. Up the Revolution and all that crap.' Saffron eyed Bickers suspiciously. 'You're not trying to indoctrinate them, are you?'

Bickers was packing tobacco into his pipe. 'I might drop in the odd word now and then.'

'Out here? With all those millions of blacks waiting in the wings?'

'It's fertile ground, mate.'

'It's fulminate of mercury,' Saffron told him, horrified.

30

'You'd better keep that big mouth shut or they'll hang, draw, and quarter you.' He nodded at the window again. 'Why the big rush outside?'

'Char time. There's a canteen alongside the parade ground.'

'Don't you want a cup?'

Bickers glanced at his watch. 'I'm a bit short on time now. I've only one more lecture and then I'm finished. You got a billet yet?'

'I'm in 27.'

'Mine's 35. I'll drop in to see you when the lecture's over. Around 5.30. I suppose you couldn't get a pass for tonight?' As Saffron shook his head: 'Pity. I'd have shown you the bright lights.'

'What's it like here for passes?' Saffron asked.

Bickers, who had been cheerful for longer than Saffron could remember, became his old lugubrious self as he struck a match. 'Bad, mate. Price is all right but the bloke in charge of the entire instructional set-up is a weirdie called Sedgley-Jones. We're supposed to put our passes through his admin stooge before they go to Price. And he's a bastard through and through. Hates the RAF like the devil hates holy water.'

Saffron thought he already knew the worst. 'Is he a warrant officer called Kruger?'

Bickers looked surprised. 'You've heard about him already?'

'You can say that again.'

The intrigued Bickers had forgotten the match that was burning down to his fingers. 'What's that mean?'

Saffron explained. There was a sudden, startled yelp from Bickers as he dropped the match. 'Christ!' Nursing his fingers he stared at Saffron. 'I don't believe it. What did he do to you?'

'He didn't do anything. Just said he'd remember me, that's all.'

'And by the centre he will, mate. Do you know who he is?'

'You've just told me. The CFI's admin-stooge.'

Bickers made an impatient gesture. 'No, I don't mean that.'

'Then what do you mean?'

'It's bad, mate,' Bickers muttered. 'Really bad.'

In spite of himself Saffron's voice began to rise. 'Will

you get on with it and tell me what all this is about?'

'There's no need to shout,' Bickers complained.

'You'd make anybody shout. Why the hell can't you get to the point?'

Bickers gazed at the angry Saffron, then gave a malicious shrug. 'All right. You want it, you've got it. He's the CFI's boyfriend.'

It went clean over Saffron's head. 'Boyfriend?'

'One thing's for sure,' Bickers grinned. 'You never went to a public school. He and Sedgley-Jones are a couple of fairies. Got it now?'

'That hairy bastard?' Saffron looked aghast. 'The CFI's boyfriend? I don't believe it.'

'You will, mate, believe me. Ask any of our instructors.'

'It's impossible. I mean, you've only to look at him. He's bloody horrible.'

'Love's a wonderful thing, mate. Even for hairy fairies.'

Saffron dropped weakly into a chair. For a moment Bickers showed sympathy. 'Don't take it too hard. You can't be certain they'll gang up on you.' Bickers tried to hold back the quip but it escaped him. 'You never know – Sedgley-Jones might take a fancy to you.'

He grinned shamefacedly at the look Saffron gave him. 'One thing's clear, mate – we know why Price is trying to keep you on armourers. He wants to keep you away from them.'

Remembering Price's vague warnings, Saffron suffered a wave of apprehension. 'You're a bloody ray of sunshine, aren't you?'

'It's best to be prepared, mate. You know how touchy some fairies can be. One thing's certain. It's going to be tough getting passes.'

Self-pity brought a groan from Saffron. 'Why? I'd only been in the camp half an hour.'

'It's you, mate. You always did draw trouble.'

A South African corporal entered the room. Wearing overalls, he was hefty, with a wide humorous face topped by a shock of fair hair. His polished boots clumped on the linoleum as he approached the table. He glanced at Saffron, nodded, then turned to Bickers.

'You haven't seen the AP on the 20mm Hispano, have you? I thought I left it on the table.'

'Maybe Morris took it,' Bickers suggested. 'He's taking that new conversion course this afternoon.' He motioned at the seated Saffron. 'Meet a fellow sacrifice. He starts with us tomorrow morning. Corporal Saffron, an SAI. Corporal MacFarlane.'

The hefty corporal gave a broad smile as he shook Saffron's hand. 'Hija! Glad to be here?'

'He's very glad,' Bickers said. 'He's just had a fight with Kruger.'

MacFarlane whistled. 'Already? What happened?'

Bickers told him. Saffron did not like the glance the two men exchanged or the sympathetic way MacFarlane clapped him on the shoulder. 'Cheer up, man. It's not you personally. He hates all your mob.'

'What have we done to him?'

MacFarlane gave a broad, infectious grin. 'Maybe one of you stood him up sometime.'

'He's having trouble believing Kruger's a fairy,' Bickers said. 'He thinks he's too hairy and horrible.'

The grinning MacFarlane went to the door. 'They come all shapes and sizes. Didn't you know that? Keep your chin up, Saffron. We're all on your side.'

The bell sounded as he passed the window. Bickers grimaced at the gloomy Saffron. 'Once more unto the breach.'

Trainees began returning to the quadrangle, their dejected behaviour in ludicrous contrast to the scene fifteen minutes earlier. 'They hate lectures,' Bickers said, going to a locker and taking out a notebook. 'Half an hour and they're ready to explode.'

Saffron tried to rally. 'What are you taking now?'

'Pyrotechnics. Imagine this shower on a squadron with rockets, flame floats and a couple of signal cannon. They'd blow the bloody place apart. Coming?'

Saffron followed him outside. Everywhere disconsolate trainees were filing into classrooms. Bickers pointed to a doorway at the far end of the quadrangle. 'That's mine. Happy Corner.'

A shout drew their attention. Price was at his door, waving at them. 'I want you to change billets, Saffron. I like my NCOs to billet with their own men. You're in Number 33 now.'

'You mean this'll be the course I'll be taking, sir?'

'Right. Course 21. You can get to know them this evening.'

'Does this mean Saffron will be staying on armourers, sir?' Bickers asked.

Price turned on him testily. 'It means only what it says, Bickers – that Saffron starts lectures on Course 21 in the morning. After that I'm not God, I can't prophecy the future.'

Bickers looked shaken as the tiny Flight Lieutenant withdrew into his office. 'It looks bad, mate. Something's happened already.'

Saffron glanced back apprehensively. 'You think so?'

'Sure of it. Price isn't usually as snappy as that.'

'You know, you're in the wrong business,' Saffron gritted. 'You should be an undertaker or gravedigger.'

Bickers looked hurt. 'I can't help the set-up here, can I?' His face brightened. 'I'll tell you what. I'll stay in tonight and we'll have a drink in the Mess. OK?'

'You mean you'll stay in and cheer me up?'

'Right. We'll talk about it later. Around 5.30.'

They halted outside a lecture room. From the sounds that reached them a football match was being played inside. Squaring his shoulders, Bickers nodded at Saffron and disappeared. His yell rang out a couple of seconds later. 'I'll do you lot – I mean it! Get back to your seats and shut up!'

Grinning ruefully Saffron crossed the parade ground and transferred his kit to his new billet. In spite of the heat outside, the cubicle was relatively cool, and seeing there were fifty minutes before Bickers' arrival, he lay back on the bed and closed his eyes. He had slept badly on the train the previous night and in spite of his apprehensions about Kruger he soon dozed off.

He awoke forty minutes later under the impression someone had lit a fire on his belly. Snatching up his shirt he discovered a cluster of red lumps surrounding his navel. All his worst misgivings about the sand were realized. 'Fleas,' he muttered in horror.

Saffron belonged to that small but luckless minority to whom a flea bite represented an inch-wide swelling that would itch and torture for a week. As he remembered Kruger and then gazed at his stricken belly, the Puritan in Saffron began wondering if he were being punished at last for his lotus life in Training Command. Dropping his shorts and underpants, he dabbed calamine lotion on his wounds. Then, trying desperately not to scratch the tormented area, he began searching for his attacker. He had cleared his underpants and was starting on his shorts when there was the pound of footsteps and the hut door crashed open. It was the signal for the silence to explode in a blood-chilling riot of shouts and yells.

His white buttocks straining with the effort, Saffron discovered that on tip-toe his eyes just cleared the three-quarter door that partitioned off his cubicle. They widened at the scene before him. A yelling mob of air mechanics were thundering past. The entire hut rocked to its foundations beneath their booted feet. As Saffron's eyes followed them in horrified fascination, a bed crashed over as two men rolled across the wooden floor in seemingly mortal combat. The yell that cheered them on sounded like the Kop during a Liverpool–Everton derby.

Saffron fell back in dismay. He caught sight of his naked nether regions, with the calamine drying whitely around his navel, and the thought of death or injury in such ludicrous circumstances made him snatch at his clothes and draw them on. Feeling braver, he rose on his toes again.

The fight seemed over and the entire gang of men were grouped around a bed towards the far end of the hut. Saffron pushed open the door and stepped cautiously out. When nothing fell on him he continued down the length of the hut. The men's attention was held by something in the centre of the group and Saffron was not noticed until he was twelve feet away. Then someone hissed a warning and as men swung round Saffron caught sight of a huge air mechanic thrusting something beneath the mattress of the bed.

Saffron drew closer. 'What are you all up to?'

He now saw the man who had hidden the object was the giant who had tumbled and struck his head in the quadrangle. At close quarters he looked even more formidable. Built like a heavyweight wrestler, he had one ear that looked as if at some time it had been torn off in a rugby scrum and stuck back without reference to the other. His nose had been broken and his eyes were deep set beneath jutting brows. Yet by some miracle the total effect was not displeasing and the bashful grin he gave Saffron contained no hostility.

'I'm Corporal Saffron. I'm the NCO in charge of this billet and I'll be taking you for lectures tomorrow. So we'd better start on the right foot. What are you hiding under that bed?'

A loud murmur of dismay sounded. The giant grinned uneasily at the trainees, then at Saffron.

'You can speak English?' Saffron asked sarcastically.

There was a titter. 'Yes, Corporal.' The sound was like nails being shaken in a rusty can.

'Then talk it. What's your name?'

'Van der Merve, Corporal.'

'All right, Van der Merve. Tell me what you're hiding.'

'Nothing, Corporal.'

Saffron pushed forward. 'If it's nothing you won't mind my seeing it, will you?'

The men fell reluctantly back as Saffron caught hold of the mattress and heaved. A long club, resembling an old-fashioned night stick, lay on the planks beneath. Breathing hard, Saffron dragged it out. 'What's this for? Me?'

There was an outburst of uneasy laughter. 'Then who?' Saffron demanded.

A slim young trainee with mischievous eyes pushed forward. 'It's for baseball, Corporal.'

This time the laughter had a tone of relief. 'What's your name?' Saffron asked.

'Moulang, Corporal.'

'You the joker of this outfit?'

'I beg your pardon.'

'Never mind. Just don't take me on, Moulang, or your feet won't touch.' Saffron scowled again at the heavy club. 'What's this for?'

'I've just told you, Corporal. It's the only bat we could get for baseball.'

'Then why hide it?'

Moulang's face was almost babylike in its innocence. 'If we leave it lying around someone from one of the other huts might steal it.'

The low titter that came was followed almost immediately by a murmur of assent. Glaring at Moulang, Saffron shouldered the club. 'All right, if that's the situation, the safest

36

place for it is in my cubicle. When you arrange a game you can come and ask for it. Happy now?'

The giant Van der Merve opened his mouth to protest but closed it at a sign from Moulang. Feeling that if he had not scored a knock-out at least he had won on points, Saffron retreated to his cubicle with his prize. Closing the door he listened. The sounds that reached him were querulous and disappointed. Saffron wished he knew why.

CHAPTER 4

Bickers, lowering his seventh pint to the small table, stretched himself expansively. 'You know something? I've got tomorrow afternoon off.'

Saffron's glance was full of envy. 'On a Thursday, a weekday?'

'Yes. My lot are down for the range tomorrow. Live bomb fusing. Only SAIs can take 'em on that. A job you'll get,' Bickers pointed out uncharitably.

'I can't wait.'

Bickers grinned. 'No one's blown the place up yet, although there've been some close calls. It's the bush apes, you see. They're a bit ham-fisted with detonators.'

'That I can believe.'

Saffron's jaundiced eyes roved over the Corporals' Mess. A wooden hut, it boasted a bar, two threadbare carpets, and a miscellaneous selection of hard chairs and tables. Although it was claustrophobic and cheerless, from the number of NCOs present it clearly compensated many men by the duty-free beer it dispensed. Saffron, who put a much higher price on his freedom, turned moodily back to Bickers.

'Do you have a date tomorrow?'

Bickers gave a lecherous wink. 'The best, mate. Ready for it day or night. Pity you can't join me. She's got a friend.'

'Well, I can't, can I?' Saffron said irascibly.

'Maybe you could meet us in the evening. If you get a pass, that is.'

'Why the hell shouldn't I get a pass? Price promised me one.'

'Don't bite me,' Bickers grumbled, displaying the touchiness of the half-drunk. 'It's not my fault you've had a fight with Kruger.'

'Who's biting you? Only must you be a Jeremiah all the time?'

'The trouble with you, Saffron, is you don't like facing the facts.'

'Oh, shut up.'

Bickers rose with exaggerated dignity. 'I'm going to fetch two more beers. By the time I get back your manners might have improved.'

'I don't want another beer. I'm going to turn in.'

Bickers looked shocked. 'At 9.30! You're not still worrying about that club you found? How could it be meant for you? They haven't had time yet to get to know you.'

'Thanks,' Saffron said sarcastically.

Beneath the counter a small dog was lapping beer from a saucer. 'Hang on,' Saffron said, his curiosity awakened. 'Do you know anything about a Great Dane called Nuisance?'

Bickers turned back unsteadily. 'Everybody here knows Nuisance.'

'What do you know?'

'He's the bloody Navy's dog. Able Seaman or something. Picks up drunks in Cape Town and takes 'em to the Soldiers' Club. Used only to help sailors but they say he helps the RAF now.' Bickers gave a hiccup. 'Won't look at soldiers though. Must be the colour of the uniforms.'

'You're taking me on,' Saffron said resentfully.

'No, I'm not. The bloody dog's human. He comes here sometimes when there's a big parade or a passing out ceremony. Catches the train to Dryberg and then hitch-hikes.' Bickers gave a glassy grin. 'The boys say he wants to take the salute but the CO's too mean to stand down.'

At the rude word Saffron called him, Bickers turned towards the bar. 'Hey, MacFarlane. Come and tell Saffron about Nuisance. The sod won't believe me.'

The hefty MacFarlane, surrounded by a drunken group of NCOs, did not hear his shout. As Bickers, muttering to himself, lurched forward, Saffron rose quietly and escaped outside.

After the thick smoke of the Mess the air was fresh and he took deep breaths of it as he made his way between the lighted huts. He found his own hut door open and the lights

on. Only four men were present. Van der Merve and Moulang were seated on a bed at the far end and two other
trainees were stretched out on their respective beds opposite.
A radio alongside Van der Merve's bed was going full blast.
As he started down the hut, Saffron saw the slim youth
nudge the giant's arm. His lips moved but Saffron could
hear nothing for the radio.

'Turn that bloody thing down,' he shouted.

Moulang reached out and the din subsided. The youth's
eyes were bright with mischievous lights. 'Good evening,
Corporal. How do you like the camp?'

'I'll tell you that when I've seen more of it. Where is
everybody?'

'A few are out on pass. The rest are in the canteen.'

'Why aren't you in the canteen?' Saffron asked suspiciously.

Moulang shrugged and turned to the giant alongside him.
'We've no money. Have we, Piet?'

The giant grinned. 'Maybe the Corporal would like to lend
us some. Only until Friday.'

'That'll be the day. How long has your course been here?'

'Just over a week,' Moulang told him.

'So you've had some instruction already?'

'Yes. Since Friday. Are you taking us tomorrow, Corporal?'

'That seems to be the general idea.'

Saffron did not like the glance the youth gave his grinning
companion. 'Are we the first South African course you've
taken, Corporal?'

Saffron wondered how he could know that. 'Yes.'

'Then let's hope we don't cause you too much trouble.'

'You won't,' Saffron promised grimly.

A voice across the hut made him turn. One of the trainees
was pointing at his brevet. 'Is that an air-gunner's brevet,
Corporal?'

'Yes. What's your name?'

'Bekker, Corporal. Did you get it in England?'

'Yes. Why?'

The trainee, a stocky youth with freckles, swung his legs
eagerly over the side of his bed. 'What's it like over there?
Were you in the Battle of Britain?'

'I'm hardly a bloody fighter pilot, am I?'

'But you must have taken some part in it.'

'I did,' Saffron grinned. 'I battled it out with the local wenches. Some put up as good a fight as the Germans.'

The roar of laughter was interrupted by Moulang's sly voice. 'Why haven't they put you on observers, Corporal? They say you're an SAI.'

Christ, they know already, Saffron thought. 'You're a real gen man, aren't you, Moulang? You share the office with the CO or something?'

The trainee's eyes shone mischievously again. 'You know how it is, Corporal. News gets around.'

'It certainly does,' Saffron grunted. 'Like tracer bullets. What time's lights-out here?'

'10.30.'

'Who puts 'em out?'

'The Duty Sergeant.'

'Good. Then I can get some shut-eye.' Saffron waved a hand at the radio. 'And keep that thing down. I don't want any complaints. All right.'

Moulang's smile was innocence itself. 'Of course, Corporal. Sleep well.'

Eyeing him warily, Saffron retreated to his cubicle and closed the door. That was the one, he thought as he undressed. As bright as a polished button and itching for mischief. And using the good-natured but dumb giant as his stooge. Slipping between the blankets, Saffron went to sleep promising himself he wouldn't give the little sod an inch of rope.

Saffron awoke just before eleven. Accustomed to service conditions he had not been disturbed by the return of the trainees from the canteen: their very noisiness had reassured his subconscious. The sounds that awoke him were of a different order, a low whisper and soft footsteps outside his cubicle.

Slipping from his bed he listened. He heard another whisper and then a torch clicked on outside his door. Expecting the door to open any minute, Saffron braced himself but the light faded as the intruders moved down the sleeping hut. Hastily slipping on his shorts, Saffron returned to the door. Opening it a few inches he saw the torchlight playing on the floor at the far end of the hut. The shadows of two men showed against it. Saffron edged towards the light switches and suddenly jerked them down.

'All right. What's going on?'

His voice faded at the scene before him. A tall, gangling sergeant with a Hitler-type moustache was holding the torch. The man beside him was Kruger. Without preamble the barrel-like figure of the Warrant Officer began marching towards Saffron while startled faces rose from beds on both sides of the hut.

'Corporal Saffron! You're on a charge.'

Saffron gaped. 'I am? What for?'

Kruger swung round on the sergeant. 'Tell him, Sergeant Fourie.'

The man pointed at the bare floorboards. 'Your hut's in a filthy condition, Corporal.'

'Filthy condition?'

Kruger took over. 'Have you bad eyesight?'

'No; I've good eyesight. And I can't see anything wrong with it.'

Kruger swung a polished boot and dragged a cigarette stub towards him. The sergeant reached beneath the bed and pulled out two more. As Kruger moved nearer to him, Saffron saw the jubilation in the man's small eyes. 'You haven't read Station Orders, have you, Corporal?'

'I haven't had much time, have I – sir?'

'Station Orders should be read within three hours of arrival. They say that all billets shall be clean and tidy before lights out.' Kruger pointed to an empty cigarette packet that the sergeant was displaying. 'You call this shambles tidy?'

'That's bloody silly,' Saffron said recklessly. 'Who cares as long as the place is clean for morning inspection?'

'Don't you bloody silly me, Corporal. Station Orders are Station Orders and don't think that because you're in the RAF or wear a brevet that you can break them. Sergeant, make a report and see he's in my office at 10.30 tomorrow morning.'

'Very good, sir.'

Kruger walked past Saffron and at the door faced the twin rows of awakened trainees. 'The rest of you get your heads down or I'll have the lot of you on a charge for being so filthy. Put the lights out, Sergeant.'

41

With a last glance at Saffron, Kruger motioned the duty sergeant to follow him outside. The lights clicked off and the door closed a second later.

Saffron, who wanted to kill someone at that moment, found himself halfway down the hut. 'Couldn't any of you have warned me about this?'

In the darkness he recognized Moulang's voice. 'It's never happened before, Corporal. At least not since we've been here.'

Saffron realized he was almost certainly telling the truth. 'Maybe not, but you've dropped me into it, haven't you? By the centre, you'll pull your fingers out tomorrow.'

There were sympathetic sounds as he walked back to his cubicle and even murmured apologies here and there. As he dropped dejectedly on his bed, there was a light tap on the door. The slim figure who slipped inside could have belonged to only one trainee. Moulang closed the door carefully before coming forward.

'What the hell do you want?' Saffron growled.

The trainee's voice sounded almost in his ear. 'You made a mistake this afternoon, Corporal.'

'I did, didn't I?' Saffron said savagely. 'I ought to have had the lot of you crawling about the floor picking up your damned dog ends.'

Moulang hushed him. 'I didn't mean that. You shouldn't have taken the club from Van der Merve.'

Without knowing why, Saffron lowered his own voice. 'I shouldn't? Why?'

'Kruger's got a bad name among the trainees. He's already put Van der Merve on two charges. So we thought it was time he was given a lesson.'

Saffron gaped. 'You don't mean do him in?'

'No, Corporal. Just teach him a lesson.'

Saffron decided his entire posting was a surrealist nightmare. Homosexual officers, dogs that hitch-hiked, and now this. 'You said you didn't know he was coming round tonight.'

'We didn't know. But we heard he was going to the bomb dump. And it's deserted after 18.00 hours. And dark too.'

Saffron's eyes were huge and his voice hoarse. 'Who was going to do him?'

'Only me and Piet. That's why we needed the club.'

'You're pulling my leg, Moulang. You have to be.'

'No, Corporal. You've seen the club yourself.'

'Then for Christ's sake why are you telling me? By rights I ought to march you straight off to the Guard Room.'

'There wouldn't be much point in that, would there, Corporal?'

No point at all, Saffron decided. The hoarse question he heard shocked him. 'When does he go to the bomb dump again?'

'Perhaps not for months. That's the trouble. But we might get a chance somewhere else. Can we have the club back, Corporal?'

The result was never in doubt although Saffron's better nature put up a token fight before he drew the club from beneath his bed. 'You do realize that as far as I'm concerned this is only for baseball?'

From the way Moulang's eyes glowed in the darkness Saffron wondered if he were a jinnie or hobgoblin. 'Of course, Corporal.'

'And for God's sake tell Van der Merve to be careful. He looks strong enough to knock the top off Table Mountain.'

'Don't worry about anything, Corporal. Good night.'

The door closed triumphantly. Tearing off his shorts Saffron sank into bed with a groan. He closed his eyes but sleep would not come. At first he attributed it to Puritan remorse: if everyone took the law into his own hands, how could the Services function and the war be won? Then the self-honesty that was Saffron's cross asserted itself. Remorse be damned. His alter ego was putting the boot into him for his initial blunder.

With that clash of conscience resolved, Saffron hoped for sleep. But with the blankets nicely warmed up the fleas were having the feast of their lives and his body was bathed in liquid fire. Scratching and cursing, longing for the dawn that seemed centuries away, Saffron ruminated bitterly on the fate of good intentions.

CHAPTER 5

Saffron emerged from the huts, reached the edge of the parade ground, and halted. 'I don't believe it!'

Bickers, red-eyed from the previous evening in the Mess, attempted a grin and failed. 'Toy soldiers, mate. That's what we are. Bloody toy soldiers.'

The early morning sun had only just cleared a distant hangar and rectangles of shadow lay over the parade ground. Men were straggling across it like sleepwalkers and coalescing into squads. In striking contrast to the human scene, a record-player built on a movable trolley was standing erect in the centre of the tarmac square and howling out martial music. NCOs, looking as comatose as their pupils, were trying hoarsely to make themselves heard over the din.

'What am I supposed to do?' Saffron asked in some panic.

'You drill your squad, mate, that's what you do. Up the hill and down the hill, like the Duke of York.'

'But I've never drilled a squad in my life.'

'Then now's your chance to learn,' Bickers grunted unsympathetically.

Saffron, one of those unfortunates whose eyes never open properly before 10 am, only now recognized the figure standing alongside the absurd record-player. Kruger, wearing immaculately-pressed tunic and slacks, appeared to be staring straight at him.

'You're not telling me that bastard's in charge!'

'Who else?' Bickers asked. He started forward with a groan. 'I'll have to go. Find your squad and try to follow the rest of us.'

Conscious of Kruger's eye on him, Saffron stared desperately around for his squad. The giant Van der Merve aided recognition and Saffron hurried forward. In his hypochondriacal state his squad seemed to possess more alert and mischievous faces than the rest of the school put together, and the cheerful 'Good morning, Corporal' that Moulang offered him did nothing to dispel his apprehension.

'All right. Get into threes,' he muttered.

The trainees began dressing up. Next to Saffron the burly

MacFarlane already had his squad to attention and Saffron struggled to eavesdrop over the din.

'Squad – right *turn*! Squad, by the left – quick *march*!'

Hoping he had got it, Saffron faced Course 21. But no one is quicker than the serviceman to spot uncertainty and Saffron's squad had him taped before his first nervous order.

'Squad, attention!'

His emphasis was premature and the thud of boots sounded like the rattle of musketry.

'Squad – right turn!'

All but two of the men obeyed. Moulang and Van der Merve turned left. 'I said *right* turn!' Saffron hissed.

Moulang gave him a cheerful smile. 'Sorry, Corporal.' He nudged his grinning companion. 'The Corporal said right turn, Piet.'

The giant looked surprised. 'Did he?' The two men turned in opposite directions to join their tittering companions. His face turning red, Saffron braced himself.

'Squad, by the left – quick march.'

Once again he wrongly accentuated the command. Half the squad started forward on the 'quick', the rest on the 'march'. The result was catastrophic. Legs collided and the squad collapsed like a punctured concertina. Sweating profusely in spite of the morning chill, Saffron ran after them. 'Halt! Halt!'

The men disentangled themselves. Van der Merve was bellowing with laughter. 'Shut up!' Saffron snarled, not daring to look Kruger's way. 'Attention! By the left – quick march!'

This time he got the squad off on the same foot. To the distorted howl of Colonel Bogey, arms swinging briskly, Course 21 swung in a solid phalanx across the parade ground.

For a moment Saffron felt he could relax. The bastards were under way and from the look of them they'd done their fair share of square-bashing. He even felt able to glance round. Fifty yards away Bickers was doing a sleep-walking act alongside his marching squad. More relaxed, Saffron turned back. And immediately froze.

The phalanx that was Course 21 was marching straight at the record-player and the ominously motionless Kruger. Sprinting forward, Saffron opened his mouth, only to choke

45

as he discovered he had forgotten the command of 'about face'.

In a flash panic had him and he could remember only one word of command. Halt. It would mean the entire squad confronting Kruger eyeball to eyeball but anything was better than a collision. Saffron opened his mouth again and this time knew pure horror. Panic had frozen his larynx.

The squad of men turned into a juggernaut as it bore down on Kruger. Thirty yards, twenty yards, the vector was shrinking by the second. Hot and cold, Saffron prayed. Oh, God, help me, because if you don't the bastards are going to trample him down. . . . Cheeks a bright scarlet, eyes popping, he made his last effort.

'Squad . . . Halt . . .' For the effort Saffron expended, the croak he managed was that of an elephant bringing forth a mouse. Yet someone must have shown him mercy for with a stamp of boots Course 21 halted less than ten yards from the glowering Kruger.

Bathed in sweat, Saffron sank back on his heels. With a glance at Course 21 that took the grin even off the face of Van der Merve, Kruger walked stiff-legged towards Saffron and halted no more than two feet away. His expression was a mixture of dislike and gratification.

'You're really asking for it, aren't you, Corporal?'

Saffron gave a dismayed croak. 'You can't believe that was deliberate.'

'Are you pretending it wasn't?'

'Of course it wasn't.' With his voice still u.s., Saffron decided ill fortune must be made to pay for itself. 'My voice went and I couldn't stop them. Listen to it.'

'I'm listening, Corporal. And I'll say this. You're a good actor as well as a liar.'

Before the indignant Saffron could reply, Colonel Bogey expired in a series of rhythmical clicks that resounded around the parade ground. As the NCOs barked commands and marching squads halted, Kruger moved back to the record-player. His shout made a distant figure stiffen.

'Corporal Van Zyl! Come over here and drill this squad.' As the echo of the shout died away, Kruger's swagger stick swung round and pointed at Saffron. 'And you remember to be in my office at 10.30. Sharp.'

* * *

46

Price sat back in his chair with a start. 'Already?'

Saffron, whose voice had not yet recovered from his parade-ground ordeal, nodded gloomily. 'They found an empty cigarette packet and a few butts and matchsticks on the floor. At 23.00 hours.'

'He's really after you, isn't he, lad?' Price sounded curious as well as sympathetic. 'Are you sure you didn't kick him in the crutch as well?'

Seeing Saffron's face light up, Price hastily dismissed the thought. 'Technically he's got you. Station Orders say that all billets must be tidied up before lights out. They also say all NCOs must be conversant with the rules within three hours of their arrival here.'

'But, sir, that's bloody silly. In the RAF it doesn't matter what conditions the billets are in as long as they're tidied up for morning inspection.'

Price, whose sharp face resembled a pointer sniffing for scent, nodded. 'And that, lad, is your defence. At 10.30 you'll be marched in to see the CFI, who'll ask if you are willing to accept his punishment. You'll say no. Nothing else. Just no. That means he'll have to refer you to the CO. When he asks for your defence, you'll give him that bit about the RAF. All right?'

Saffron was doing his best to listen. The exercise and ordeal had inflamed his flea bites and he was on fire from neck to ankles. 'Yes, sir.'

'The CO's a nice old boy and it's my bet you'll get off. Particularly as I intend having a quiet word with him first. I feel I let you down in forgetting to warn you to read orders.' Price leaned forward as Saffron furtively rubbed one leg against the other. 'Is anything wrong, Saffron?'

'Wrong, sir?'

'Yes. Why are you squirming about like that?'

Saffron, who was now trying to rub an elbow against his burning stomach, paused guiltily. 'Squirming, sir?'

'For God's sake stop repeating everything I say. Have you got the itch or do you want to pee?'

Provoked, Saffron suddenly jerked up his shirt. 'I'd a hell of a night, sir. Look. It must be the sand this place is built on.'

Price's eyes opened wide at the sight of Saffron's red-noduled belly. 'Good God. What were they? Tarantulas?'

47

'Fleas, sir. I'm allergic to them.'

Price sank back into his chair sympathetically. 'It's all happening, isn't it, lad?'

'I'm afraid it is, sir,' Saffron said, tucking back his shirt.

'Did they get your voice too?'

'No. That happened this morning. On the parade ground.' As Saffron went on to explain, Price gazed at him wonderingly. 'Someone's got the Indian sign on you, lad. Right on your kop. So you've provoked Kruger again?'

'Not deliberately, sir. I hadn't drilled a squad of men before and I forgot the orders.'

Price blinked hard. 'You hadn't drilled a squad of men before?'

'No, sir. Nobody does any drilling in aircrew. You know that.'

'That's true.' Price tried to sound casual. 'Did you tell me the date of your birthday?'

'April, sir. April 4th.'

'You don't know the exact time?'

'No. But I think it was sometime in the morning.'

'In the morning,' Price repeated, then pulled himself together. 'You are sure you know what to do? Not a word except what I've told you. When it's over, come and see me.'

'Shall I start a lecture, sir?'

'No, you're free until 10.30. It'll give your voice a rest.' Price's reflective eyes followed Saffron to the door. 'But if I were you, I think I'd wait in the staff room. You never know, do you?'

Saffron looked puzzled. 'Know what, sir?'

Price shook his head as if to clear it. 'Never mind. Good luck, Saffron.'

CHAPTER 6

Kruger pushed open the office door and began barking. 'Left right, left right, left right – halt! Left turn!'

Cap tucked beneath his left arm, Saffron stared stiffly ahead. Seated at a desk in front of him was an officer in his middle thirties. Fair-skinned, he was of medium height and

48

build. His hair, receding slightly at the temples, was blond and wavy. There was an arrogant upper class look about him that was aggravated by pale blue eyes and a somewhat petulant mouth. Saffron, who until now had assumed Sedgley-Jones was a South African, noticed with surprise the three blue bands on his shirt epaulette.

The man's pale eyes moved over him like a botanist examining a beetle. 'You are Corporal Saffron?'

The question, put in an expensively-acquired drawl, made one thing certain. If Saffron had not entered the office with prejudice, he had prejudice now. His yeoman ancestors had found no cause to love the class Sedgley-Jones represented and his youthful years had given him no chance to expurgate a vague inherited hostility.

'Yes, sir.'

The Squadron Leader indicated a report sheet spread on the desk before him. 'You haven't started very well at Breconfield, have you, Corporal?'

With Price's instructions well in the forefront of his mind, Saffron did not answer. A snarling bark from behind made him jump. 'Answer the Squadron Leader!'

'I've been put on a charge, sir,' was the safest thing Saffron could think to say.

'What does that mean, Corporal? That you feel innocent of the charge?'

'I didn't say that, sir.'

'But surely you inferred it?'

'I didn't infer anything, sir.'

'Then you plead guilty?'

'No, sir.'

Sedgley-Jones glanced down at the report sheet. 'The Duty Sergeant reports that at 22.47 hours last night he visited your billet and found it in an untidy condition. Is that true?'

'I'm not saying anything, sir.'

The pale eyes seemed to glow as the officer leaned forward. 'Are you being impertinent, Corporal?'

'No, sir.'

'You are either guilty or not guilty. If your billet was untidy you are guilty. Do you deny the sergeant and Warrant Officer Kruger found pieces of paper, cigarette ends and other rubbish on the floor?'

Sweat was making Saffron itch again. 'I'm not saying anything, sir.'

Sedgley-Jones's eyes lifted to a point over Saffron's shoulder and held there a split-second. He then leaned back in his chair.

'You do understand that if you do not defend yourself I shall have to assume you guilty?'

When Saffron remained silent, the man raised a quizzical eyebrow. 'I'm beginning to wonder if you realize what is happening to you, Corporal. Do you?'

It was one question Saffron could not resist. 'I assure you I understand very well, sir.'

The sudden whitening of the man's cheeks and the glance he gave Kruger told Saffron he had made an alarming mistake. 'You won't gain anything by this impertinence, Corporal. If you refuse to defend yourself, it only leaves me to pass sentence. I take it you are prepared to accept my punishment?'

At last, Saffron thought. 'No, sir.'

He heard a sharp grunt behind him. The stare he received from Sedgley-Jones was unnerving. 'Who put you up to this, Corporal?'

Saffron gazed straight ahead. 'No one, sir.'

'Then you'll be well advised to think again. The CO is a very busy man. If you bother him with a case like this, he's likely to punish you far more severely than I am.'

'Just the same I'd rather see him, sir.'

'But this is a petty offence, Corporal. Don't you realize that?'

Satisfaction allowed Saffron the luxury of a comment. 'It hasn't sounded that way so far, sir. I prefer to see the CO.'

Behind him Kruger drew a deep breath. Sedgley-Jones was erect in his chair. 'Very well, Corporal. I shall pass the details of your charge over to Wing Commander Mottram.' He gave Kruger a tight nod. 'Take him away, Warrant Officer.'

Saffron hardly remembered being marched out. His next vivid memory was confronting Kruger face to face outside the Flight Administration Offices. 'Price put you up to this, didn't he?'

'No one put me up,' Saffron lied.

'It's not going to help you, Saffron. You know that, don't you?'

About to answer back, Saffron saw the malevolence in the man's small eyes and decided against it. 'What do you want me to do now?'

'You go to the Education Block and wait there until I call you. And by the Lord Harry you'd better be there.'

Swishing his cane like a sword of vengeance, Kruger marched off across the parade ground. Saffron crossed to the quadrangle and gloomily entered Price's office. Price, who was thumbing files in a cabinet, turned curiously. 'Well, how did it go?'

'I'm seeing the CO, sir. I have to wait here until he calls for me.'

For a moment Price resembled a rebellious prefect who had just pulled a fast one on his form-master. 'How did the CFI take it?'

Reaction made Saffron momentarily forget the rules of the game. 'Those two fairies are thicker than thieves, sir. From the way Sedgley-Jones acted you'd have thought it was his head I'd threatened to knock off.'

Price's wicked grin was instantly suppressed. 'Saffron, you're talking about an officer in His Majesty's Armed Forces. Another crack like that and I'll jump on you with both feet. Understand?'

'Yes, sir.'

Price fished in the pocket of his bush-jacket. 'Cigarette?'

'Thank you, sir.'

Price accepted Saffron's light and blew smoke at the ceiling. 'I've had a word with the CO and you should be all right. But no barrack-room lawyer stuff. Just keep to the facts.'

'Shall I give a lecture now?'

'You feel in the mood to take on Course 21?'

'No, sir,' Saffron said promptly.

Price gave his impish grin. 'You're causing me a lot of trouble, Saffron, but there are one or two things I like about you. Go back to the staff room. I'll tip you off when you're wanted.'

Saffron was marched into the CO's office at 12.30 hours. The man he faced this time was in his late forties with huge bushy eyebrows and a round, ruddy face. His expression as he watched the two men enter made Saffron think of a military Mr Pickwick. With his RAF tropical tunic tight round his ample stomach, he was enough of an avuncular figure to give Saffron hope, although his eyes suggested he had been tippling a few pre-lunch gins. His voice, as distinct from Sedgley-Jones, had a fruity flavour with an accent Saffron could not place.

'You're Corporal Saffron?'

'Yes, sir.'

'You arrived yesterday and today you're on a charge. It's a bit bloody quick, isn't it, lad?'

Finding no adequate answer, Saffron decided to pass. As he expected, there was a parade ground yell from Kruger. 'Answer the Wing Commander!'

Mottram glanced at the Warrant Officer benignly. 'What's he expected to say, Mr Kruger? Yes?'

I love you as a father already, Saffron thought, as he heard Kruger's discomforted mutter. Mottram pushed the report sheet forward. 'You know the details of the charge, Corporal?'

'Yes, sir.'

'Then you know you're not being charged with murder?'

'Murder, sir?'

'Yes, lad. I'm trying to find out why you've refused the CFI's punishment and stopped me going to lunch.'

Saffron took a deep breath. 'I didn't think it called for punishment, sir.'

One huge eyebrow lifted. 'Does that mean you're denying the Duty Sergeant's charge?'

'I'm not denying anything, sir. But this is the first station I've been on that operates under South African jurisdiction. In the RAF, as you know, an NCO is only responsible for the state of his hut at morning inspection. I thought the same rules applied here.'

For the briefest moment Saffron thought he discerned a twinkle in the Pickwickian eyes. 'You sound like a lawyer, lad. Are you a lawyer?'

'No, sir.'

'Then perhaps you don't know that ignorance of the law is no excuse for breaking it.'

'I'd only been in the camp eight hours, sir.'

Mottram turned his bluff face towards Kruger who was standing at attention alongside Saffron. 'Not very long, is it, Mr Kruger?'

The muscles of Kruger's face were as tight as the muscles of his clenched buttocks. 'Station Orders are supposed to be read within three hours of an NCO's arrival, sir.'

'But how's a new arrival to know that, Mr Kruger?' Mottram was scanning the contents of a file he had drawn towards him. 'You've a good record here, Saffron. Bloody good, in fact. I'm going to dismiss this charge. But get those orders read.'

In his imagination Saffron could feel the heat of Kruger's frustration singeing the right sleeve of his tunic. 'I read them this morning, sir.'

'You did. Good. Then put your cap on, lad, and off you go.'

Saffron donned his cap with something of a flourish. Kruger's bark had a choked sound. 'Left turn! Quick march!'

Saffron didn't move. 'Might I ask a question, sir?'

'I don't see why not, lad.'

'Can I apply for a transfer to active service?'

Kruger gave a violent start and exploded. 'Sir! All applications must be made through the laid-down channels. Through myself and Squadron Leader Sedgley-Jones. As an NCO, Corporal Saffron must know that.'

'Quite, Mr Kruger, quite. But as the Corporal is already here, it'll save time if we stretch a point.' Glancing down at Saffron's file, Mottram's Pickwickian face showed astonishment. 'One, two, three. . . . From these records you must have applied every week since you've been over here!'

'I have, sir,' Saffron confirmed.

'But why, lad? Aren't you happy in this country?'

The note of concern threw Saffron off balance. 'I suppose so, in a way. But. . . .'

'Then there you are,' Mottram beamed. 'You mustn't think it's obligatory to volunteer for danger. After all, these records show you have been in action. Are your parents alive?'

'Yes, sir.'

'Then you must think of them, lad. After all the worry you've given them when you were flying, think how relieved

53

they must be to know you're safe and sound. You don't want to make them old before their time, do you?'

'Of course not, sir. But. . . .'

'There are no buts about it, lad. You aren't itching to go and kill people, are you? You aren't a trigger-happy paranoic?'

By this time Saffron was having the gravest doubts about himself. 'No, sir. It's just that. . . .'

'I know, lad. One gets these ideas when one's young but you'll soon grow out of 'em. Remember we need instructors like you. Can't get enough of 'em. Now off you go and settle down. Thank you, Mr Kruger.'

Bewitched and bewildered, Saffron threw up a salute. Alongside him there was the vicious stamp of Kruger's boots and Saffron was certain of only one thing as he marched out. That a fused bomb was right on his heels.

Saffron was sitting in Bickers' cubicle when the Londoner returned from lectures.

'How'd it go?' Bickers asked. 'Firing squad after morning parade?'

The still dazed Saffron shook his head. 'I got off.' He gave Bickers a précis of the story, finishing: 'Where did they get the old man from? Surely he can't be a regular?'

Bickers' reply surprised him. 'He is. They say he's a South African who joined the RAF between the wars. When they started the Commonwealth Training Scheme I suppose he was a natural to come back here. Nice old sod, isn't he? Got a few weird ideas, like the early morning parades, but his heart's in the right place.'

'Weird ideas?' Saffron said. 'He thinks anyone who wants to go on active service is paranoic.'

Bickers, unbuttoning his shirt, paused. 'Well, aren't they?'

Saffron gave him a look. 'What the hell does he think this school's training men for? The Salvation Army?'

Bickers drew off his sweat-soaked shirt. 'It gets you that way in time. You teach guns and bombs until it's like teaching history or mathematics. You forget what the bloody things do to people.'

'You mean the school becomes a thing in its own right?'

'Something like that. How did Kruger take it?'

Saffron's expression changed at the memory. 'He followed

me outside and said a few choice words. Like if I thought I'd got away with it, to think again.'

'He's really got it in for you, mate, hasn't he? It couldn't be love-hate, could it? Rejection symptoms?' At Saffron's reaction, Bickers grinned. 'What did Price say?'

'He chuckled his head off. I think he dislikes the two of 'em more than I do.'

'He probably does. He's worked with them longer.' Bickers picked up a towel. 'What lectures have you got this afternoon?'

'None. Price says I'm to sit in with MacFarlane this afternoon to get the feel of things and give my voice a chance to recover. I'm to start first thing in the morning.'

'Hope your insurance is paid up,' Bickers said. When Saffron made no response, the Londoner slapped him across the shoulders. 'I don't see what you're looking so gloomy about. You're the guy who's supposed to like action. Isn't that what you're getting?'

CHAPTER 7

The following morning as the lecture rooms were filling Price called Saffron into his office.

'How's your voice, lad? Better?' As Saffron nodded, Price moved towards the window with his nervous, sparrow-like strides and gazed out.

'I'd a visitor yesterday afternoon. Squadron Leader Sedgley-Jones dropped in to have a word about you.'

Saffron's start was not lost on Price who nevertheless appeared to be following the antics of two trainees who were leap-frogging down the quadrangle. 'He said he'd taken a look at your record and with all those qualifications it seemed a waste you weren't in his section.'

The irony of his present wish to remain in the armament section was not lost on Saffron. 'You haven't transferred me, have you, sir?'

Always edgy when the interests of his men were threatened, Price turned and scowled. 'Of course I haven't transferred you. I pointed out that he'd promised me the next instructor posted here and I held him to it. But there's something you must appreciate. As a senior armament instructor you're under-employed lecturing armourers, and as soon as a junior AI gets posted here, you'll have to move over. You do see that?'

Saffron was showing relief. 'Yes, sir.'

Price turned back to the window. 'There were a couple of things I couldn't prevent, however.'

Saffron tightened again. 'What, sir?'

'I had to promise that if they ever need an SAI urgently because of sickness or whatever, I'd loan you over. And you have to take a short gunnery course right away?'

'Gunnery course?'

Price's way of answering one question with another was characteristic. 'Have you seen the Hawker Hinds we have here?'

Saffron had seen his first Hind the previous day, rising unexpectedly into the late afternoon sky. A tiny, graceful two-seater biplane, it had brought nostalgic childhood memories of oil-stained men in goggles, breeches and sheepskin jackets by compliment of Biggles and American pulp magazines.

'Yes, sir. What do you use them for?'

Price's eyes twinkled. 'Gunnery, lad.' He grinned at Saffron's expression. 'The observers do their ab initio course on them.'

'Gunnery! But they're as obsolete as SE5s or Bristol Fighters.'

'The point, lad, is that we've nothing else. All the modern stuff with power turrets either stays in the UK or goes to the Middle East.'

'But the whole technique in power turrets is different!'

Price gave a malicious grin. 'Don't be so bloody toffee-nosed just because you've got an air-gunners' brevet! You're forgetting that all the combat kites the Americans supply to the South Africans don't have power turrets either. So this course isn't as bad a grounding as you think. In any case, it's on the agenda and every SAI has to complete a course before he can instruct.'

Saffron was displaying all the indignation of a professional told to re-learn his trade. 'So although I'm a qualified air gunner I now have to learn how to use a bow and arrow. That's what it adds up to.'

56

'When you teach archery, lad, you have to be an archer. So don't argue – just get on with it. Kruger's going to fit the flying in between your lectures. You'll get a timetable later. Now off you go to your bush apes.'

As Saffron opened the door, Price's impish voice checked him. 'You're starting with the Smith and Wesson .45, aren't you?'

'Yes, sir.'

'Then you'd better be careful – the Old Man hates burial services. If you have to shoot any of 'em, wing 'em in the arm or leg.'

Saffron slammed the butt of the revolver against the table. 'Moulang! Shut up!'

The glance he received from the youthful trainee was full of hurt innocence. 'I wasn't talking, Corporal.'

'Yes, you were. To Van der Merve.'

'I think you're mistaken, Corporal. I never talk in class.'

There were cat-calls and laughs. Saffron glared down the rows of grinning faces. 'Don't act the funny man with me, Moulang.'

'No, Corporal. Anything you say, Corporal.'

Breathing hard, Saffron held up the revolver. 'All right, we'll start again. I want the stripping sequence. You – Van der Merve. What comes off first?'

Like a mischievous bird whispering in the ear of its hippopotamus host, Moulang leaned towards Van der Merve, who sat at the desk alongside him. The huge Afrikander grinned his appreciation. 'I always begin with the dress, Corporal. And then make for the bra.'

A yell of delight rocked the classroom. Saffron's grip tightened on the revolver. 'You asking for jankers, Van der Merve?'

The giant gave him a bashful grin. Moulang answered for him. 'He doesn't mind, Corporal.'

'What do you mean – he doesn't mind?'

'He prefers drilling on the parade ground to lectures.' Moulang threw a glance round the tittering trainees. 'Most of them do.'

With a sinking heart Saffron realized the slim Afrikander was probably right. He had already noticed the enthusiasm the trainees showed at morning parade. Blanking off his

57

imagination at what it signified in terms of discipline, Saffron pulled himself together.

'I'm going through it once more. Then one of you will repeat it with your back to the blackboard. If you make more than one mistake, you'll write the sequel out fifty times. So you'd better listen.'

For a moment the chuckles died away. 'One,' Saffron said, hammering his points with a piece of chalk against the blackboard. 'Remove the side plates. Two, take out the cylinder assembly. Three, remove the side stocks. Four, take out the main spring. Five, remove the safety slide. Six, take off the hammer. Seven. . . .'

A sibilant hiss made him spin round. All the faces in the room were turned to the quadrangle window where a willowy young WAAF could be seen passing by. Before Saffron could react, there was a cheer and the full establishment of thirty men leapt up and hurled themselves at the window for a better look. Saffron, thrown back by the onrush, sagged in defeat against the blackboard.

'They probably intend to kill me,' Saffron said gloomily.

Bickers gave a guffaw and lifted his lunchtime mug of tea. 'Who? The armourers or Sedgley-Jones?'

'It's not funny,' Saffron said indignantly. 'Have you had a look at those old crates? They're only held together with glue and bits of string.'

Bickers cast a malicious glance at Saffron's brevet. 'I thought you were the intrepid airman afraid of nothing. When's your first trip?'

'Three this afternoon. Low level gunnery at Eerste Rivier, wherever that is.'

'It's a bombing and gunnery range in the Cape Flats. Right alongside the sea. It's better than being cooped up in a classroom full of apes, isn't it?'

Saffron, whose appetite had been damaged by his confrontation with Course 21 that morning, pushed away his plate with a shudder. 'If it's any worse, God help me.'

CHAPTER 8

Harness tight beneath his crutch and juggling with a parachute and two ammunition drums, Saffron walked stiff-
legged across the tarmac. Bickers, carrying two more
ammunition drums, was alongside him. A free period that
afternoon had put the Londoner in an unusually cheerful
frame of mind and with his hands thrust through the leather
straps of the drums, he was clapping them together like cym-
bals. His friskiness earned a glare from Saffron. 'Don't you
know those VGO pans are delicate? I've enough troubles
without you causing me a stoppage as well.'

Ahead of them was a Hind with its engine ticking over.
One mechanic was giving it a final check from the pilot's
seat and a second mechanic, suffering from acne, was climbing down from the gunner's cockpit. The pilot, a South
African with a pencil-thin moustache, was in close conversation with a burly figure all too familiar to Saffron. As Kruger
spoke to the pimply-faced mechanic before the man moved
away, Bickers dug an elbow into Saffron's ribs.

'What's the pilot's name?'

'Mostert.'

'You think he could be another fairy?'

Saffron gazed at him bitterly. 'Is that why you came
along? To cheer me up?'

Bickers grinned. 'Just the same, Laughing Boy's probably
telling him to give you a good going over. I'd see I was well
strapped in if I were you.'

Saffron eyed the open-cockpit biplane with some trepidation. 'How the hell do you strap yourself in?'

'No idea, mate. But there must be straps or string or
something.'

The Hind's elevators lifted, its Kestrel engine began to
roar throatily, and it strained against its wheel chocks. As
the warrant officer and the pilot ducked out of the slipstream,
Kruger noticed the approaching men and passed some comment to Mostert. He then turned to Saffron, shouting above
the roar of the engine.

'You've taken your time, haven't you? I said 3.30 prompt!'

'One of the ammo drums I drew from stores was faulty,' Saffron shouted back. 'I had to go back for another.'

'If you'd started getting ready ten minutes earlier, it wouldn't have mattered, would it?' When Saffron made no reply, Kruger turned his aggression on Bickers.

'You! Why aren't you at lectures?'

The sudden attack took Bickers by surprise. 'I've a free period this afternoon, sir.'

'And so you came to hold his hand. Is that it?'

Bickers looked undecided whether to grin or look contrite. 'I was helping him to carry his ammo, sir.'

Kruger snatched the two drums from him. 'He's a big boy now. He can carry his own equipment. Get back to the staff room. A free period doesn't mean you're entitled to wander all over the airfield.'

Giving Saffron a look of dismay, Bickers walked off. Kruger's expression as he watched him go gave Saffron a pang of remorse. It would be hard on Bickers if Kruger's dislike rubbed off on him now that the Afrikander had discovered Saffron and the Londoner were friends.

In the Hind the mechanic throttled back the engine. Climbing out on the wing root and jumping down, he nodded at the pilot. 'She's OK, sir.'

The pilot motioned Saffron towards him. His unfriendliness told Saffron that Kruger had already spread his poison. 'Anything you want to know before we take off?'

Before Saffron could ask one of a dozen questions, Kruger pushed forward. 'Sir, you've only got forty minutes before Youngsfield take over the range. Corporal Saffron's been given his instructions and in any case he's supposed to be a qualified air gunner.'

Bastard, Saffron thought. He asked the one question he felt justified. 'Have we got RT?'

'No. You'll have to manage with my hand signals. I shall do alternate figure-8 run-ins. Target on the port side, then on the starboard. All right?'

With at least half a dozen other questions bugging him, Saffron tossed his parachute into the rear cockpit and climbed in. A Scarf ring containing one VGO encircled him. A pair of goggles and a helmet lay on the seat. Reaching for the ammunition drums the pilot handed up to him, Saffron noticed four spigots protruding from the side of the cockpit. Tentatively trying a drum on one, he relaxed as it clicked home. Storing away the remaining drums he began searching for a seat belt as the pilot donned goggles and helmet and climbed into the front cockpit. With his seat little more than a canvas-covered stool, Saffron could see nothing that remotely resembled a safety belt. Fumbling beneath the stool he found only a short chain with a clip at the free end. As the chocks were pulled away and the Kestrel took on a louder note, Saffron lifted his red face and hammered on the headrest behind the pilot. The man throttled back and turned his head impatiently.

'What's wrong?'

'How do I keep in this thing?' Saffron yelled.

The pilot stood up and indicated the seat of his parachute harness. As he dropped back Saffron heard the word 'monkeychain' through the slap-slap of the propeller. Fumbling at the seat of his harness he discovered a small metal ring and his face lightened. Groping for the chain he snapped the clip in place. The pilot stared round again. 'All right?'

Avoiding looking at Kruger, Saffron nodded. Engine revving, the Hind quivered and began rolling forward. Crouched behind the tiny triplex windshield to protect himself from the blast of air, Saffron felt a judder as the plane rolled from the tarmac to the grass. Although a windsock showed they were heading into the slight breeze, he expected a lengthy taxi to the nearest runway. Instead the engine note turned into thunder and before he knew what was happening the small biplane, with its low wing loading, went up like a lift.

Gaping down, Saffron watched the airfield fall away and then turn like some slow-moving top as the Hind headed for the Cape Flats. Kruger was still visible, now a tiny figure crossing the tarmac towards the Administration Block. Aware the gunnery range was only minutes away, Saffron tried to accustom himself to his new surroundings. Deafened by the uninsulated roar of the engine and the piercing scream of wires he peered into the cockpit. The tray before him was clearly a receptacle for his parachute and he lowered it inside and secured the quick-release straps. With more room

61

to manoeuvre, he then wriggled round to take a look at the Scarf mounting and machine-gun.

He noticed the VGO was equipped with a Norman Vane and ring sight instead of the modern reflector sight. Deciding to create a good impression by being ready for action as soon as they were over the range, he removed an ammunition drum from a spigot and wriggled round. With both hands gripping the drum he then rose and reached out for the machine-gun.

He let out a yell of dismay a second later as his head and shoulders rose above the windshield. The 150 mph slipstream, striking him like a sledgehammer, hurled him against the locked machine-gun, whose butt drove into his stomach. The drum, torn from his grasp, struck the Hind's tail fin with a frightening clatter and went spinning earthwards. Shaken and winded Saffron collapsed into his bucket seat. The pilot, who had felt the impact on the Hind's fin, threw back an alarmed glance. As Saffron weakly displayed an ammunition drum he showed both relief and irritation. His gestures made it clear there was to be no further attempt to load without his permission.

The Hind was flying at little more than a thousand feet. The mountains that stood behind Cape Town and its suburbs were falling behind and the land below turning into a flat stretch of scrub and sand. Ahead was the bright blue mirror of the sea. The scrubland appeared deserted but as the Hind swooped lower Saffron caught sight of a hut nestling among sand dunes. A red flag was flying from it. As the Hind swept past, a green Very light soared up. It was a signal for the pilot to jab a finger at Saffron's machine-gun.

Gingerly, Saffron removed a second drum from its anchorage. Ahead of him the pilot was making gestures that were meaningless to him. Gripping the drum as if his life depended on it, Saffron hunched round in the cockpit and braced himself. This time, prepared for the blast outside, he was partially able to withstand it although it tore at his helmet and goggles like some screeching wildcat. Edging himself forward, his elbows on the cockpit rim, Saffron managed to get the drum as far as the gun breech and was about to guide it on to the spigot when the slipstream got a claw behind his goggles and lifted them. With eyes streaming, his instinctive reaction was to clap a hand to his face.

Immediately, with a howl of triumph, the demon wind tore the drum away and hurled it into space.

Two gone and two to go, Saffron thought, dropping back once more. As he sat there numbly, the Hind's engine gave a snarl and the nose lifted. At two thousand feet it levelled out and to Saffron's consternation the irate pilot rose from his seat.

His first reaction was panic. Mostert must have had enough and was going to jump! Snatching for his own parachute, Saffron paused as the pilot bent one arm into a semi-circle and thrust the other arm through it. As his goggled face glared back at Saffron, the Hind, controlled only by his knees, wobbled all over the sky. Saffron's panic abated. Rude signs were better than abandonment.... As he grinned apologetically back, Mostert yelled something, jabbed a finger at the remaining ammunition drums and then at the gun. Praying for guidance, Saffron reached for one of the drums. As he stared at it the Hind dropped a wing, forcing Mostert to sit down and grab the controls. It was the moment Saffron found enlightenment. Thrusting an arm through the leather strap on the top of the drum, he thumped Mostert's head-rest. Glancing back, the pilot nodded vigorously, then closed his eyes in thanksgiving.

Heartened, Saffron took a firm grip of the edge of the drum and rose for the third time. The slipstream took his arm round like a discus thrower but this time the strap prevented the drum being torn away and once Saffron was facing the rear-pointing gun he discovered the wind pressure actually assisted him to clamp the drum onto its spigot. Yanking back triumphantly on the VGO's cocking handle, he thumped Mostert's headrest.

The Hind went immediately into a dive. Wires screaming, it levelled off only a hundred feet above the sea of scrub. Mostert was pointing forward and Saffron braved the slipstream to peer through the interplane struts. Four hundred yards ahead a white panel was suspended upright on a metal frame. Before Saffron could take a good look the panel flashed past their port wing and disappeared among the sand dunes.

Engine howling, the Hind went into a climbing turn. Remembering Mostert's preflight instructions Saffron unlocked the VGO and swung it to starboard. The act meant turning the gun into the full fury of the slipstream. Tugging and panting, Saffron moved it two feet and then it stuck. A second to recover his breath and he heaved again. This time he could move the mounting no more than six inches and Saffron decided that either the assister gear on the ring was faulty or he was the feeblest gunner in the RAF. Tugging with all his strength he managed to bring the gun to a thirty-degree starboard bearing and no more. For any further lateral movement he would have to rely on the gun swivel itself.

The Hind had completed a 180 degree turn and was now heading back towards the target. As Mostert jabbed a finger forward, Saffron crouched behind the VGO. His un-accustomed exposure to the elements was making him feel he was doing a thousand miles an hour rather than 150. The slipstream was bringing mucus down his nose and tugging grotesquely at his mouth. Because of his inability to turn the gun mounting to its full beam position, he had one leg jammed agonizingly behind the bucket seat. In the few seconds left to him he was trying to remember what little he had been told about old-fashioned ring and bead sights. The ring sight gave the deflection for enemy speed. The swivelling Norman Vane foresight allowed for own speed. This one was fully extended. Then wasn't the answer to line the bead in the centre of the ring and blast away.

Don't be a moron, Saffron. Own speed was a variant and so was target distance. So what – you can estimate them, can't you? I might if my leg wasn't broken and this bloody snot wasn't choking me! How did those old-timers cope, up at 15,000 feet in the cold of Northern France? Saffron de-cided they must have been supermen.

The slipstream lifted his goggles again and he brushed away tears. It was his undoing. The white flash that appeared at the Hind's wing tips had darted behind the tailplane be-fore he had time to curse. The violent waggle of the Hind's wings hinted Mostert suffered no such inhibitions.

The Hind snarled up into another climbing turn. Bracing himself, Saffron swung the gun mounting towards the port side. It went easily at first and then jammed at precisely the same angle of turn. Squirm and wriggle behind the gun as he did, Saffron could not line it remotely on the target until it was almost halfway between wingtip and tail. As the total sighting time at best was three seconds, he could do no more than fire a short, desperate burst in the general direction before it again vanished tantalizingly behind the tailplane.

With the Hind doing figures of eight round the target area, the farce continued. Twigs flew off bushes, sand dunes were peppered as though by hailstones, but the target looked as virginal as ever. As Mostert pointed at his watch and signalled he was making his last run, Saffron threw caution to the winds. Jamming the VGO stock into his shoulder he waited until the mocking white panel entered his limited arc of fire, then squeezed the trigger and held it. Hosing the stream of bullets, intent on redemption, he did not even notice the tailplane behind which the target had taken refuge. His first intimation was a loud ping and the sight of a rudder stay flailing frantically in the slipstream.

'God,' Saffron muttered, ceasing firing.

Mostert, who had felt the impact of the bullets, took a startled glance back and immediately put the Hind into a shallow climb. Saffron, deflated and horror-stricken, sat facing aft, unable to take his eyes off the flailing stay. When the Hind was high enough for both men to use their parachutes if the need came, Mostert put it through a few gentle manoeuvres. When everything held together he headed back for Breconfield. His landing resembled a cat feeling its way down a roof with loose tiles. As the Hind ceased rolling he turned and gave Saffron an expressive look. Revving the engine again, he taxied to the tarmac and switched off. As two mechanics came running out he turned again to Saffron. His mouth moved but post-flight deafness was afflicting Saffron.

'I can't hear you,' he yelled.

Mostert tore off his goggles. His hoarse shout seeped through the blanket of silence that surrounded Saffron.

'I said that's the last time! Even if they threaten to shoot me. Where the hell did they find you? In a Nazi saboteur school?'

Saffron's legs felt rubbery as he jumped out. He hardly noticed the pimply-faced mechanic whom he had seen earlier climb up into the rear cockpit. He gazed somewhat plaintively at Mostert who followed him to the ground a moment later.

'My gun mounting had only restricted movement. That's why I couldn't line up on the target.'

Mostert was still yelling as if his deafness were permanent. 'Is that why you lost two ammo drums before we even reached it?' Tearing open Saffron's overalls he jabbed a derogatory finger at his brevet. 'What's this supposed to be? A flying arse-hole?'

Indignation added to reaction made Saffron reckless. 'How was I to know the right way to load an ammo drum on the bloody kite? I was taught to fly against Nazis and 109s, not Von Richofen and his flying circus.'

Mostert's anger turned to disbelief. 'Are you telling me you got no instruction before I took you up?'

'Not a thing. All I got from Kruger was some crack that he'd no instructors to waste teaching RAF air gunners their job.'

Mostert looked horrified. 'I don't believe it. Christ, I might have been killed.'

Fully aware that to exacerbate the pilot's anger might provoke a situation already delicate enough, Saffron had a sudden rush of blood to the head. 'I wasn't even warned the VGO had no interrupter gear. Crazy, isn't it?'

'Jesus Christ, you could have shot the tail right off,' Mostert muttered. Recovering, he snatched Saffron's arm and yanked him grimly across the tarmac. 'Come on. You and me are going to have a word with Kruger.'

Bickers took a reflective sip of beer. 'You're sure you're not getting persecution mania?'

'I'm telling you it was that pimply-faced mechanic,' Saffron snarled. 'It didn't occur to me at the time but when I went back later to check the mounting it was working perfectly. He'd fixed it in some way before I took off.'

'Did you go and see him?'

'Too true I did. The little sod denied everything, of course.'

Bickers stroked his long face. 'Kruger's all kinds of a bastard but I can't see him doing a thing like that. I mean, what's the point?'

'That's easy enough. To discredit me.'

'Who to?'

'Price, Sedgley-Jones. The CO for all I know. He knows

66

I've a decent record. But it'll only take a few things like this to wreck it.'

Bickers was still showing scepticism. 'He's taking chances though, isn't he? What if Mostert had taken his complaints higher?'

'Who could he have gone to? Only Sedgley-Jones. And for all I know he might be in it too.'

'You see,' Bickers announced. 'Persecution mania.'

'If Kruger wasn't behind it, why didn't he see I was given some instruction before I took off?' Saffron demanded.

Bickers nodded maliciously at Saffron's brevet. 'Maybe he thought a big gen man like you would be insulted by advice.'

'Whose side are you on?' Saffron asked bitterly.

Bickers grinned. 'How did he take Mostert's complaint?'

'How does a bear take a smack on the snout? If looks could kill they'd be laying me out.'

'Wait until he hears what you said to the pimply-faced mechanic. Then you'll be really popular. When's your next trip?'

'Next Monday morning.'

'You'll check your equipment this time, won't you?' At the look Saffron gave him, Bickers gave a somewhat abashed grin and picked up Saffron's glass from the table. 'Have another drink, mate. For someone who likes action, you're taking all this hard.'

CHAPTER 9

Shading his eyes from the sun, Saffron stretched his legs and gazed around him luxuriously. The small beach on which he was lying was flanked by two narrow promontories of granite rocks. Although the day was hot and calm, the South Atlantic had a swell and was breaking against the rocks in a series of white explosions. The shallow cliff behind the beach was dotted with gaily-painted bungalows and was lush with bushes. A backdrop was provided by twelve mountain peaks that seemed to rise sheer from the sea.

Saffron, wearing a pair of swimming trunks, dropped back onto the sand with a sigh of contentment. Two weeks had passed since his arrival at Breconfield and Price had given him his first halfday. With Bickers on duty, Saffron had sought his advice where to spend it and the Londoner's advice had been Clifton on the far side of Cape Town. Although the journey had taken him over ninety minutes by train and bus, Saffron had already decided the trouble was justified.

All things considered, Saffron would have described the last week as uneventful. He had flown twice more on his gunnery course, with two different pilots, and all had gone well. Course 21 still made every lecture an ordeal and the fleas gave him a trial by fire every night, but with the stoicism of the serviceman, Saffron had already accepted these as crosses that must be borne. The animosity of Kruger and Sedgley-Jones, a cross of a very different kind, appeared, if only for the moment, to have fallen from his back. Bickers' explanation was that he had exaggerated their animosity in the first place and life was now back to normal. While agreeing it was possible, Saffron was more inclined to give credit to a sea target being built off the coast of Eerste Rivier. A brain child of Sedgley-Jones's, it was nearing completion and with both the SCI and Kruger supervising the work, vendetta time was at a premium. In his more pessimistic moments Saffron believed that when the target was finished his troubles would return.

Today, however, with a golden haze hanging over the surf and the sun warm on his body, Saffron was ruled by optimism. No man unless he was crazy – and Kruger was never that – could maintain malice indefinitely over such a trivial encounter. He had vented his spleen a couple of times and now, providing he, Saffron, kept out of trouble, the affair was over. Humming 'Over the Hill' beneath his breath, Saffron beamed contentedly round the deserted beach.

A shrill barking drew his attention and he saw a small Sealyham terrier dive from a flight of steps at the far end of the beach and race towards a cluster of seagulls. As the indignant gulls scattered, a girl appeared on the steps. She was wearing sunglasses, the briefest of tailored shorts, and carrying an expensive-looking beach bag. Her long, shapely legs and the Nordic richness of her massed blonde hair made Saffron's eyes glow like a pointer spying a quail. Reaching the sand, she threw a casual glance in his direction and then disappeared behind a large boulder.

Saffron released his breath. Paradise had lacked one thing and here it was. He watched the dog with both envy and impatience as, after chasing a squawking gull, it ran behind the boulder and joined the girl. The two emerged a minute later, the girl now wearing a two-piece swim suit. Perfectly proportioned, with limbs that might have been dusted with gold, she walked to the centre of the beach and sank on to the sand. She was wearing a thin golden chain around her throat and a slim watch on her right wrist. As she smiled at the antics of the barking dog, Saffron caught a glimpse of glossy lips and white, even teeth.

Until that moment he had been like a greyhound in the slips. Now, with the girl a mere fifteen yards away, he had a change of mood. There had to be a catch somewhere. Any moment now a rich, hulking husband or boyfriend would stomp across the beach and wreck the dream. He watched the girl draw a gold case from her beach bag and light a cigarette. Expensive too, he thought pessimistically. She probably spent more on having her hair set than the RAF paid him in a week. The more you thought about it, the bigger waste of time it was.

Then his inner pendulum, reaching the limit of its oscillation, swung the other way. A chance like this and he'd let it go begging? Didn't he ever want to sleep again? As the Sealyham caught his eye and gave a bark, Saffron snapped his fingers encouragingly. Eyes bright beneath their bushy brows, the dog ran a few paces towards him and stopped. This time Saffron tried a low whistle. Wagging his stumpy tail, the dog sank on his belly and edged another couple of feet forward. As Saffron made encouraging sounds, he was rewarded by an amused laugh.

'If you want to make friends with Caesar, why don't you come over here and I'll introduce you?'

Low and throaty, the girl's voice had an accent that sent shivers down Saffron's spine. Heart thudding with excitement, he tried to look casual as he picked up his clothes and sidekit and dropped on the sand beside her. 'Thanks. I'd like that.'

She removed her sunglasses. Her green-grey eyes were cool and totally devoid of embarrassment as she ran them over Saffron and then called the dog towards her. 'Come here, Caesar, and be introduced.'

The dog wagged his tail dubiously. When the girl ordered him to sit, he rocked back and raised his two front paws. 'There,' the girl announced. 'This is Caesar. And you are?'

'I'm Saffron. Alan Saffron.'

She glanced at his folded bush-shirt and blue cap. 'Of the RAF?'

'That's right.'

'Then shake hands with Caesar and perhaps he will introduce me.'

The girl's command of the situation made Saffron think she must be older than himself although no trace of it showed in her smooth limbs and unblemished face. Wishing he could match her poise, he took one of the dog's sandy paws. 'He doesn't seem too keen to talk. So perhaps you'd better tell me yourself.'

'My name is Synevva. Synevva Helgman.' The hand she offered him was slim and sun-tanned. 'Are you on leave?'

'No. I'm stationed here. I arrived two weeks ago.'

'At what camp?'

'Breconfield.'

'I know it. I have friends there.'

'Anyone I know?'

She dismissed the question as if it were irrelevant. 'Do you fly?'

'Sometimes. I'm an instructor. Do you live in Cape Town?'

'Yes. I have a flat in Tamboers Kloof.'

All Saffron's earlier excitement was back. He tried to see if she were wearing a ring but her left hand was half-buried in the sand. As he turned to pat the dog that was now fussing around him, he heard her cool, amused voice. 'Would you like a cigarette?'

She was offering him the case with her left hand and Saffron saw she was wearing neither wedding nor engagement ring. He began wondering if fate were making amends in one superlative gesture.

'Thanks.'

As she snapped on a lighter and he leaned towards her, he caught the scent of expensive perfume. 'Do you come here often?'

She glanced at the sunlit, deserted beach. 'Yes. It is my

70

favourite place. But not at the weekends. Then it is too crowded.'

It was a remark that evoked a dozen questions but Saffron felt too inhibited to ask any of them. The girl nodded at the dog who had put a paw on his leg.

'Caesar likes you. That is a good sign.'

'It is?' Saffron's pat on the dog's shaggy head was a benediction.

'Very. Caesar is an excellent judge of people.'

Saffron's old confidence was oozing back. 'Do you take notice of him?'

Her eyes met his with quizzical innocence. 'Of course. And particularly where men are concerned.'

'Remind me to buy him some chocolate,' Saffron said.

The girl laughed. As she turned to bury her cigarette, one of her legs brushed against Saffron and he felt goose-pimples down his back. 'Do you like swimming?'

'Yes. Very much.'

'What do you do when you're not swimming?' he ventured.

'I paint. And sometimes I teach.'

'Teach what?'

'Painting. I am an artist.'

It's a bloody film script, Saffron thought, surreptitiously pinching the back of his thigh. Any minute now the violins will start up, she'll turn misty-eyed, and then the lights will come on and it'll be time to go out into the rain.

'You do it for a living?'

'I sell my work, if that is what you mean.'

'Then you must be good.'

She gave an amused shrug. 'There are some people who think so.'

'Can I see your work sometime?'

Her eyes moved speculatively over his lean, muscular body. 'Perhaps.'

'When?'

She reached forward and put a finger over his lips. 'Don't be so eager.' Drawing back, she rose and took off her watch and sandals. 'I'm going in for a swim now. Are you coming?'

Before he could answer she ran down to the water's edge. Her movements had all the grace of a young girl. For a moment he sat watching as she splashed water over her arms and legs. Then, throwing aside his cigarette, he ran forward and plunged headlong into the waves. He emerged a moment later glassy-eyed and gasping. 'God!'

Her laugh followed him as he staggered back to the beach. 'Didn't you know the water was cold at Clifton?'

His body felt as if it had been dipped in frozen fire. 'Cold!' he muttered, towelling himself furiously. 'It's lethal.'

She returned five minutes later when Saffron's heart had recovered its normal rhythm. Although her slim body was glistening with water, by some feminine miracle she had kept her thick blonde hair dry. 'If you don't like cold water you should swim at Muizenberg or Fish Hoek,' she told him, picking up her towel. 'It is the Indian Ocean at the other side of the peninsula and much warmer.'

She began to towel her legs and arms. Lying watching her, the infatuated Saffron decided he had never seen anyone so graceful. Showing no embarrassment beneath his gaze, she dried her neck and shoulders and then held out the towel.

'Will you dry my back, please?'

Saffron obeyed as if he had been invited to handle the Crown Jewels. As he stroked the smooth, unblemished skin above and below her brassiere strap, his face came within three inches of her perfumed hair and his heart skipped alarmingly.

Thanking him, she sank back on the sand and closed her eyes. Afraid to move in case she drew away, Saffron lay motionless. A tendril of hair, a twig of gold, was curled over one smooth cheek. As his eyes took in greater detail he saw a pulse beating in her throat and the blonde down on her legs glowing golden in the sunlight. The Adam in Saffron had never been as alive as this. Invisible waves seemed to be radiating from the girl and bringing a feverish excitation to every atom of his body. With such extraordinary kinematics going on it seemed unbelievable the girl was unaffected by them and yet she appeared to have gone to sleep. Saffron decided to try will power. Closing his eyes he concentrated. Come on, Synevva. Give him a break. He's out of practice. Give him a green light, touch his arm or his shoulder, and he'll take it from there.

He opened one eye. The girl hadn't moved a muscle. Saffron tried again, concentrating this time until he felt his head would burst. He sat up hopefully as the girl stirred, only to slump back at her words.

'I shall have to be going in a few minutes. I have a dinner date tonight. Can I drop you off anywhere?'

Although it had been his intention to stay the afternoon on the beach, Saffron walked with her to the road where her car, an open-topped convertible, was parked. Throwing her beach bag into the back, she motioned him in alongside her. A moment later the car went off like a released rocket.

'How long do you expect to be at Breconfield?' she asked as they took the twisting contour road towards Sea Point.

Saffron was finding difficulty in sharing his eyes between the long, tanned legs only inches from his own and the incensed motorists they were recklessly passing.

'I don't know. It might be months. Even a year.'

'Couldn't it even be for the rest of the war?' When he did not answer, she threw him a glance. 'What is it? Wouldn't you like that?'

Saffron almost told the truth, then, seeing a lorry looming ahead, decided it was not the time for gravity. 'I would sometimes, like today.'

It still proved almost fatal. In giving him a smile she missed seeing the oncoming car and they passed between it and the lorry with inches to spare. Her unperturbed voice sounded through the scream of a horn.

'You pay nice compliments. Do you know that?'

'I do?' Saffron's eyes were on the next obstacle, a bus about to pull out from the kerb. She swerved round it, made a pedestrian leap for his life, and carried on without missing a beat.

'Yes. You have a gift for making a woman feel like a woman.'

She must be talking about the way I look at her legs, Saffron thought. Around them the traffic was growing denser as they neared the centre of the city. Amber lights shone at an intersection ahead, the signal for her to accelerate. Seeing the lights change to red, Saffron decided it was more restful to keep his eyes closed. Thirty seconds later she turned to him. 'Where would you like me to drop you?'

Saffron was torn between the desire to remain with her and apprehension of the hazards ahead. Self-preservation won the day. 'This will do fine.'

She drew into the kerb with a squeal of tyres. Jumping

out, he reached for his sidekit. 'Where are you going now?'

'To my flat. To change.' At his expression she gave an amused laugh. 'No, you can't come. I told you; I have a date tonight.'

Saffron had no difficulty in looking crestfallen. 'I am going to see you again, aren't I?'

A smile played about her lips. 'Perhaps.' As he was about to argue, she checked him. 'Wait. What are you doing next Friday evening?'

'Nothing. Are you free?'

'I am going to a dance at the Town Hall with some friends. Perhaps you would care to come with us?'

'Haven't you a free evening? I don't want to share you with a crowd of people.'

Behind her dark glasses her eyes were enigmatic. 'I am afraid you will have to if you want to see me.'

Saffron, who knew that he would cross the Indian Ocean in a barrel if she asked him, gave a sigh. 'All right. Where do I meet you?'

'We'll pick you up in the lounge of the George Hotel at eight o'clock. Will you be able to get a late pass for the evening?'

'That's no problem,' Saffron heard himself say.

'Good. Then I will see you next Friday.' Before Saffron could find further words to delay her the car shot away. His last glimpse of her was a slim arm waving as the low-slung car zipped past a line of traffic and disappeared down a side street.

CHAPTER 10

Face thunder-black, Saffron pushed his way into the staff room. Bickers, chatting to MacFarlane and Prentice, another instructor, turned as he dragged out a chair and slumped down.

'Wouldn't he play?'

Lighting a cigarette, Saffron ground the match savagely into an ashtray. 'No.'

'You can't be that surprised,' Bickers ventured.

When Saffron made no reply Prentice broke in. 'What's the problem, Alan?'

'He met a Scandinavian girl yesterday who says she's an artist,' Bickers said. 'He claims she's the greatest thing since Eve. She's invited him to a dance on Friday but Kruger won't recommend a late pass.'

Prentice exchanged a glance with MacFarlane. A few years older than his fellow-instructors, Prentice was liked and respected by them. In the early days of the war he had served with the South African forces in Abyssinia and Somaliland and although an armourer by trade, in the confused conditions that had existed at that time, he had often flown as an air gunner against the Italians. A married man, he now lived out with his wife in Cape Town. He and Saffron had a mutual respect for one another, and although Prentice's marriage procluded a closer association with them, both Saffron and Bickers had visited his home on a couple of occasions and met his wife.

MacFarlane had caught Prentice's glance. 'What's her name?'

'Synevva Helgman,' Saffron muttered.

MacFarlane gave a loud guffaw. 'Who are you kidding?'

Saffron stared at him. 'What's that supposed to mean?'

'You've been reading the social columns of the *Argus* one time too many. Synevva Helgman doesn't go out with NCOs. She's got half the officers in the Cape chasing her fanny.'

Saffron, who had just remembered that MacFarlane and Prentice were local men, began showing interest. 'Then you've heard of her?'

'Man, you can't pick up a paper without seeing her name. She's one of the Cape's socialites. So who are you kidding?'

Saffron gave Bickers a bitter-sweet glance. 'You believe me now?'

Showing reluctant respect, Bickers tried to redress the balance. 'She must be one of those society bints who get a kick from going out with plebs. Gets turned on with rude words and bristles down her cleavage.'

'Eff off,' Saffron said irritably.

'What are you going to do now?' MacFarlane asked.

'How the hell do I know?'

'If I'd a date with Synevva Helgman I wouldn't let a late pass stop me. Live now, pay later.' MacFarlane turned to Prentice. 'I saw her at a charity concert a couple of months ago. Nobody looked at the stage – they couldn't keep their eyes off her. Man, she's really something.'

'After only two weeks here he gets a date with Synevva Helgman,' Prentice said with amused envy. 'How lucky can you get?'

Saffron, who was gloomily toying with a copy of *Tee Emm*, the RAF news bulletin, gave him a look of disgust. Grinning, Prentice went to the door. 'I'm off to lunch. Anybody coming?'

MacFarlane went outside with him. As Bickers moved to follow them, Saffron gave a sudden start of excitement. 'Hang on a minute.'

He pushed a copy of *Tee Emm* towards the curious Londoner. 'You know these characters?'

Bickers glanced down at the open page. 'Who doesn't?'

'The South Africans don't,' Saffron told him triumphantly. As Bickers stared at him, Saffron lowered his voice. 'What's your opinion of the CO? You think he's got a good sense of humour?'

'The CO? What's he got to do with it?'

'I'll explain in a minute. Has he got a good sense of humour or not?'

'I'd say he has.'

'That's all we want. Now listen.'

Bickers was looking shocked when Saffron finished. 'You must be out of your blockers. No one's going to fall for a crazy scheme like that.'

'You're wrong. Those MPs at the gate aren't the same type as MacFarlane and the other South African instructors. They're like the lads on my course. Mostly farmhands who sometimes have difficulty in speaking English, never mind reading it. What's more, I'll lay odds they don't know half the names of the RAF officers and NCOs on a camp of this size.'

'You know what'll happen if you get caught. Kruger and Sedgley-Jones will use you for target practice on the range.'

Saffron beamed. 'That's the beauty of it. We wouldn't take Sedgley-Jones's punishment. And when the CO realized what we'd done, he'd split a stitch. Anyone with a sense of humour would.'

'So he'd split a stitch. You'd still see the inside of the glasshouse.'

'Never. He'd appreciate the joke so much he'd lessen the punishment. Perhaps even let us off with a caution. After all, we're not forging real names. And it shows initiative, doesn't it?'

Bickers drew back sharply as if he had just seen a snake under the copy of *Tee Emm*. 'Now wait a minute. What's all this *we* stuff? It's you who wants the pass.'

'You'll have to help me by signing one name. We can't keep on changing the signatures or they will smell a rat.' When Bickers let out a cry of protest, Saffron used cunning. 'Don't you see – this isn't just for Friday. It's a long term project. Whenever you want a late pass, I do the same for you.'

Bickers began to nibble the bait with caution. 'Let's get it straight. You want to try it out next Friday. What happens if you're caught?'

Saffron seldom had difficulty in following Bickers' line of thought. 'To you, nothing. I'd say I forged both signatures.'

Bickers began to relax. 'On the other hand, if it does work, we go on forging the same signatures on future passes?'

'Right. All we'll need are a few pass forms from Price's office with the CGI stamp on them. That's no problem. He leaves the stamp on his desk.'

There was a long silence before the cautious Bickers nodded his head. 'All right. Let's give it a try. What names do you suggest?'

Saffron drew the *Tee Emm* towards him again. 'How about PO Prune and Sergeant Binder?'

Bickers frowned. 'Binder's a dog. Prune's dog.'

'We can promote him to sergeant, can't we?'

'What's the point?'

'It makes it funnier, doesn't it?'

Bickers was beginning to look suspicious again. 'Who are you supposed to be?'

Saffron put his suggestion casually. 'I suppose the one who counter-signs is likely to get into the worst trouble. So I'll be Prune if you like.'

There was an immediate egalitarian reaction from Bickers. 'Why the hell should I be Binder?'

'Sergeant Binder,' Saffron reminded him. His grin spread. 'You have to admit the name fits.'

'You've a bloody nerve, Saffron. I'm Prune and you're Binder or the whole thing's off.'

Saffron's eyes twinkled wickedly. 'I'd settle for Binder if I were you. Think what your comrades might do to you if you take a commission and the Revolution comes!'

With a squeal of brakes, the two 25cwts stopped a hundred yards from the fusing area. Saffron jumped down from the cab of the leading Bedford and gave a yell. 'All right. Everybody out!'

The tailboards fell with a clatter and Course 21, caged up for the last twenty minutes, burst out like a flock of oversized puppies. Someone hurled a ball high into the air and half a dozen trainees went after it with a howl of glee. Van der Merve grabbed Moulang and another man and, punching them playfully, rolled over and over in the sand. Startled birds clattered from the surrounding bushes and terrified animals went to earth.

Saffron's bawl of anger followed them. 'Belt up and come back here! Van der Merve! What the hell do you think you're doing?'

The grinning men straggled back and formed a semi-circle before him. Saffron glared at them bitterly. 'You've forgotten every bloody thing I've said, haven't you? Don't ask me why you have to spend an afternoon fusing live bombs. If I'd my way I wouldn't bring you within ten miles of one – what you do on operations later is someone else's worry. But as it's part of the syllabus, you'd better behave. I don't intend ending up a hole in the ground because you cretins can't learn that live bombs are dangerous.'

The high-spirited chatter momentarily died away. Ahead the macadamized lane forked left and right, the left lane leading through the scrub towards a distant, turf-covered mound.

'That's the bomb store,' Saffron said. 'Note it's well away from the fusing area in case of accidents. For the same reason you never fuse bombs on an airfield less than seventy-five yards from buildings, stores or aircraft. All right. Let's get started.'

He led them down the right fork towards a sandbagged, brick hut. Near it was a tractor with two bomb trolleys strung out behind it. As the party approached the hut, a corporal and two men in overalls emerged. The corporal spoke to Saffron and then walked over to two bombs that lay in a patch of soft sand forty yards away. Lying as if in quarantine from their fellows, the bombs possessed a menacing quality that quietened the chatter of the trainees as they noticed them.

The men in overalls, two resident armourers, followed the party to the bomb trolleys. Saffron pointed at the miscellaneous selection of bombs displayed on them. 'Here you are. The real things. By that I mean they're filled with amatol and only need exploders and detonators to make them lethal.' He pointed to a swollen monster on the rearmost trolley that had green, red and white bands painted round its nose. 'What's that, Van der Merve?'

'A bomb, Corporal,' came the cheery reply.

By this time Saffron had learned a certain embittered patience. 'That's very good, Van der Merve. What sort of bomb?'

There was a doubtful pause as the laughs died away. 'A 2,000 lb, Corporal?'

'Now think! What are 2,000 lb bombs used for?'

'Ships, Corporal?'

'Warships, Van der Merve. Warships with deck armour. So what do bombs used against them need to do?'

Another pause. As the men began tittering, Moulang, standing alongside the giant, muttered something that made Van der Merve beam. 'They must go down fast, Corporal.'

Saffron threw a scowl at Moulang. 'You mean they need a high terminal velocity. So what shape have they to be?'

'Long and streamlined, Corporal,' Van der Merve said as Moulang's lips moved again.

Saffron slapped the bomb's rounded belly with a sarcastic hand. 'Does this look streamlined to you?'

He received a bashful grin. 'No, Corporal.'

'Then it isn't a bloody 2,000 lb bomb, is it?'

'No, Corporal.' As Moulang covered his mouth with his hand, the giant's face brightened. 'I know, Corporal. It's an anti-submarine bomb.'

Saffron glared at Moulang again and then stared round the arc of grinning faces. 'Does anyone know?'

No more than six hands rose. Saffron picked the nearest. 'Yes, Du Plessis.'

'It's a 250 lb Light Case, Corporal.'

Saffron muttered an obscenity and pointed at Moulang. 'All right, Clever Trevor. Tell them.'

The small Afrikander's bright eyes mocked him. 'I think it's a 4 lb incendiary, Corporal!'

At the back of the party the two resident armourers were exchanging grins. Saffron's breath hissed through his teeth. 'You're picking the wrong day for it, Moulang. Any more and I'll put a detonator up your arse.' His voice rose. 'That goes for the rest of you. You'd better pay attention because tomorrow morning you're getting a test and anyone getting less than 60 per cent won't see the outside of the camp for a week.'

With the horseplay momentarily under control, Saffron led them along the trolleys, identifying each bomb in turn. When he had finished he gave the two armourers a signal and a minute later, headed by the tractor, the trolley train was trundled back towards the bomb store.

Course 21 was led to the two bombs in quarantine. The resident corporal, an Irishman, was sitting straddle-legged across one bomb and smoking a cigarette when Saffron approached him. Short, balding, with bad teeth and breath, the man gave him a grin. 'You've got a right bunch of Charlies there, haven't you?'

'You haven't seen anything yet,' Saffron said, feeling bloody-minded. 'Wait until they start bashing the dets in with their fists.'

The man left the bomb as if it had suddenly turned red-hot. 'I've an indent to get in before 5 o'clock. You can manage without me, can't you?'

'No, I can't,' Saffron said maliciously. 'For all I know there could be a saboteur among this lot, just waiting his chance. You stay here and if you see one of 'em sneaking a detonator, shoot the bastard in his tracks.'

Leaving the corporal gaping after him, Saffron crossed over to a wooden box lying in the sand. Satisfied that it contained the correct components, he called the squad of men towards him, eyeing with relish the trepidation some were showing.

'All right. This is the crunch. Any tomfoolery now and we could all go up in pieces of dogmeat.'

With even Moulang looking thoughtful, Saffron had a

sense of revenge as he motioned the squad round the box of components. 'You've everything in here you need. Pistols, detonators, keys, measuring rods, washers, the lot. As you take each component out, check it, particularly the pistols. Then you bring the bits and pieces over here.'

Faces sober, the trainees gathered round the two menacing bombs. Saffron kicked each in turn with his foot. 'These are two 250 lb GPs, probably the commonest bomb you'll meet. Note they're lying on soft ground. At the moment they're inert. That means you could drop 'em from the back of a lorry on to cement and they wouldn't explode. The amatol they're filled with is like coal – to ignite it you need a match, paper, and wood. In the case of a bomb, that means a pistol, a detonator and an exploder. The detonator's the sensitive component. Handle it roughly or drop it and you could be in trouble. Got that?'

There was a murmur and an anxious nodding of heads. Eyes gleaming, feeling for the first time he had Course 21 where he wanted it, Saffron kicked the bombs again.

'So you can have practice on both types we've given you a Mk III with a central tube and a Mk IV with exploder pockets. To save time only the first man will measure the tubes and fit in the correct number of washers. After that each of you in turn will do the tricky bit, inserting the detonator and screwing in the pistol. To ring the changes, you'll each be given a different delay, which means you'll have to chose the correct coloured detonator. Remember you take nothing for granted. Any sand or dirt in the tube could set the detonator off. So you put your finger in before your banger. Got it?'

There was a nervous titter. Motioning them back, Saffron nodded at Moulang. 'You're the one with plenty to say. Get the Mk III ready for fusing.'

As he expected, the small Afrikander, although showing some nervousness, knew how to measure and pack in the exploders, and in five minutes both bombs were ready. Kneeling beside the wooden box Saffron removed the lid of a tin container. Inside, slotted into holes to prevent movement during transit, the detonators resembled a cluster of huge, coloured nails. Saffron drew one out and held it up with exaggerated care.

'Here they are. 3.52″ of ASA mixture. If they won't slide

in easily, don't try to use force. Check the tube and if it's OK, try another.' He returned the detonator to its container and glanced at Moulang. 'So far so good. Now give the Mk IV an eleven second delay.'

Moulang's hand hesitated a moment over the container, then drew out a blue detonator. Pushing the other trainees back, Saffron followed him to the second of the two bombs. The resident corporal, who had been watching the proceedings anxiously, began backing away. Kneeling alongside the bomb, Saffron watched Moulang check the tube was clean before sliding the detonator inside. As he glanced at him questioningly, Saffron saw there was sweat on the young trainee's face.

'Do you want me to put the pistol in too, Corporal?'

'Yes. Finish the job. What number do you want?'

'A Number 30, Corporal.'

Secretly Saffron had to concede the little sod had done his homework. 'Get on with it then.'

Moulang fetched the pistol and gingerly screwed it home. As he rose somewhat unsteadily, a murmur of congratulations came from the ring of trainees. From the way things were going Saffron decided he too could afford a gesture of recognition. 'Not bad at all, Moulang. Now take the stuff out and we'll try someone else. You, Bekker. I want the Mk III to explode on impact. That means you want an instantaneous detonator.'

One by one, with varying degrees of success, the trainees identified their correct components and the delicate work continued. To save time Saffron used the bombs alternately. All went well until Du Plessis, perhaps the most nervous trainee in the squad, approached the bombs with a Number 49 detonator. As he moved towards the tail of the Mk IV, the detonator slipped from his trembling hand, struck the bomb casing with a clatter, and fell into the sand.

For a moment the hush was like an explosion. Then, finding they were still alive, the squad released its corporate breath in a series of coughs and curses. The resident corporal was crossing himself fervently. About to unleash the invective all instructors reserve for such occasions, Saffron caught a glimpse of Du Plessis's terrified face and relented. 'Go and have a cigarette. You can have another try later.'

As the grateful trainee backed away, murmurs, laughter

and then horse-play began breaking out among the ring of men. Thinking the accident would increase their tension, Saffron felt surprise until he realized the high-spirited trainees had taken the failure of the detonator to explode as evidence that he, Saffron, had exaggerated the afternoon's perils. Freeing themselves from the hook, with half an hour of pent-up tension to release, Course 21 were out to take revenge. Already six of them were packing down into a scrum with a ball at their feet. With a howl another four men piled into the ruck. The Irish corporal took one look and then fled for the shelter of his hut. Saffron's yell rose over the tumult as he snatched up the detonator from the sand.

'Pack it in, you crazy bastards. Do you want to get us all killed?'

He had to stuff the detonator into his pocket and fight his way into the scrum before it broke up. 'I'll do you lot,' he said hoarsely. 'I mean it. Get back to those bombs. On the double!'

The grinning men drifted back. No one noticed Van der Merve poking about curiously in the box of components. Standing over the bombs again, the sweating Saffron tried to regain his former ascendancy. 'Don't you morons realize how lucky we are? If that det had exploded, we could all be shovelling coal for Uncle Nick. I'm not bulling you. It's true. You, Du Toit. Fetch me the detonator and pistol for a six hour delay.'

As the ring of men parted, Saffron noticed Van der Merve for the first time. The grinning giant had the box of detonators in his hand and as Du Toit walked towards him his arm came back. 'Here,' he called. 'Catch!'

A second later the horrified Saffron saw the tin sailing through the air towards Du Toit. Like a photoflash, his mind recorded the sight of cursing men scattering in all directions. His action as he hurled himself forward was pure reflex. His shoulder caught the paralysed Du Toit and sent him sprawling. Only a desperate thrust of Saffron's legs enabled him to regain his balance and fling himself again with arms outstretched at the falling tin. He caught it like a diving cricketer a couple of feet above the ground and clutching it to his chest rolled over and over in the sand. Awareness that he was still alive came when he tasted grit in his mouth and felt the terrified hammering of his heart.

His first conscious thought was strangely devoid of anger. That does it, Saffron. CO or no CO, you put in for a transfer tomorrow while you're still alive. Then, as if a tourniquet were released, fury came gushing down Saffron's every artery. Trainees scattered as he leapt to his feet.

'Where's Van der Merve?'

Someone pointed. Grinning uncertainly, the giant was still standing alongside the components box. Brandishing the detonators like a grenade, Saffron started forward. His first steps were wobbly but he gained momentum with every stride.

'I'm going to kill the bastard,' he yelled.

Behind him Moulang shouted for the giant to run. Watching Saffron coming, Van der Merve's expression changed from uncertainty to alarm. He took a couple of backward steps, took another glance at Saffron, then turned and bolted. A moment later, as trainees flung themselves to the ground in their convulsions, pursued and pursuer vanished into the trees.

CHAPTER 11

The tap on the classroom door made Saffron turn. Lieutenant Davidson was framed in the rectangle of sunlight. 'May I have a word with you for a moment, Corporal?'

As Saffron started forward Course 21 stirred in anticipation. 'Shut up and don't move,' Saffron snarled. 'Not even your eyelashes.'

The tall, pleasant-faced South African was smiling as Saffron followed him outside. 'They tell me you've some hard boys on your course.'

'Hard boys? I've got Genghis Khan and his hatchet men. What do you want?'

'You've heard about Sedgley-Jones's pride and joy?'

'Which one?' Saffron grinned.

'The sea target. With coloured lights, a Christmas tree, and a choir of angels.'

'It's finished, isn't it?'

'Yes. They're staffing the quadrant huts this afternoon. Sedgley-Jones is as eager as a kid to try it out, so I'm to take an Oxford over this afternoon. Like to come?'

Saffron looked surprised. 'Don't say he recommended me?'

'No. I'm to pick my own crew. And Price said you were top in bomb-aiming on your SAI course. All Breconfield, and for all I know Wingfield and Youngsfield as well, will be looking on so I don't want bombs dropping all over the sea.'

'What time are you going?'

'16.00 hours. Don't worry about your course. Price said he'd arrange a replacement instructor.'

Saffron needed to hear no more. 'Great. Is anyone else coming?'

'We're supposed to simulate a normal exercise. So we'd better take a third man. Is there anyone you'd like with you?'

Saffron had a kind thought. 'Can I take Bickers?'

'I don't see why not. I'll arrange it with Price.' Davidson showed both humour and a nice historical perspective as a crash and a deafening roar of laughter came from Saffron's classroom. 'Better get back before the hordes invade Constantinople.'

Saffron tapped Bickers' shoulder. Following his finger, Bickers saw a hut 6,000 feet below nestling among sand dunes. A second hut lay half a mile to the west.

Bickers, looking hot and voluminous in an oversize pair of overalls, put his lips to Saffron's ear. 'You'd better live up to that report of yours, mate. Because Big Brother is sure to be watching you.'

Saffron gave him a look of dislike at the reminder. Loving flying as he did he had accepted Davidson's offer without hesitation, particularly as it meant escaping Course 21 for an hour. Now doubts were creeping in. With so many ungovernable factors, bombing was always a chancy business and Kruger would be certain to pounce on any errors with glee.

He drew reassurance from the feather-bed steadiness of the Oxford's flight. And the sea on their port beam looked like blue glass. Perfect conditions for bombing, he told himself as he checked the settings on his CSBS computer. Ten

85

seconds later Davidson glanced round and nodded. Saffron saw Bickers' lips move and could only guess what he said as he crawled into the nose.

The bombsight before him was a Mk 9c. Plugging in his intercom, Saffron set on the bombsight the Oxford's height, airspeed, and the readings on the computer. Checking the TV setting was 955, he lifted his mask.

'OK, Dave. I'm ready to take a wind reading.'

There was a crackle, then Davidson's pleasant voice. 'OK, Alan. I'm holding her now.'

The Oxford droned on straight and steady as Saffron squinted down the drift wires, fiddled with the knob, and drew a grease pencil line across the compass bowl. At his signal Davidson changed course 120 degrees and Saffron repeated the procedure. A third bearing and he had his triangle on the compass bowl. Clamping it down, he gave the reading to the pilot.

'It's only five mph from 180, Dave. Almost the same as at ground level.'

'Good. Sounds like a piece of cake. Tell me when you're ready.'

Too good, Saffron thought. Nothing to blame if I mess it up. 'I'm ready now. But let's have a look at the target first.'

The sun that was warm on the back of Saffron's head swung away as the Oxford banked seaward. When it returned it was on his forehead. Gazing down he watched the narrow beach with its line of surf fall behind and give way to the blue-grained sea. Half a minute later a round ring with a dot in its centre appeared. Although the sea target was only a tiny bulls-eye at 6,000 feet, in reality it was a fifteen-foot floating platform surrounded by a ring of pontoons with a hundred foot radius. Gazing down curiously, Saffron heard Bickers' dry voice over the intercom. 'You know what MacFarlane calls it? Sedgley-Jones's ring!'

Davidson's cough suggested he was suppressing laughter. 'It's bloody small,' Saffron complained.

'It cost the earth just the same,' Davidson said. 'It's festooned with bulbs and think of the length of cable they've had to sink.'

The target was dead below Saffron now. 'All right, they light it up at night. But how do the quadrant huts pick up the bombs?'

'They've devised some scheme of mixing incendiary powder in with the smoke filling. I've never seen the bombs burst, but they say they give a red stain in the dark.'

Pushing forward, Saffron watched the target slide out of sight below the fuselage. 'I still think they'd get better results with their old camera obscura.'

The shimmering horizon ahead began to tilt. 'We'd better get cracking,' Davidson said. 'Are you ready?'

Saffron said yes and the compass swung as the Oxford turned on a new bearing. Snapping on the main and selector switches, he settled behind the bombsight. 'Left, left,' he called.

Obediently the Oxford swung a couple of degrees to port. The target was now visible, only a few inches from the drift wires. Calling corrections, Saffron brought it carefully into line. With his thumb poised over the bomb release, he squinted down the sights.

'Right . . . right. Steady!'

Undisturbed by turbulence, the bulls-eye slid smoothly down the drift wires. Saffron's hand tightened on the bomb tit. 'Steady . . . steady . . . bomb gone!'

Glancing down he watched the small grey $11\frac{1}{2}$ lb practice bomb fall away. Athough diminishing in size, it remained beneath the Oxford for a few seconds until air resistance caused it to fall back. Straining forward Saffron could still see it, a tiny dart that seemed to leap forward as it neared the sea. For a moment it vanished altogether. Then there was a puff of smoke and a yell from Saffron. 'How's that?'

The Oxford banked steeply as Davidson tried to take a look. 'How close?'

'Inside the pontoons!'

'You're sure?'

'Certain.'

'Then you like the conditions?'

'Like them? They're bloody nearly perfect.'

'Great. Then let's try again.'

With Davidson varying his compass approach, Saffron dropped another ten bombs. His estimate was that all fell within forty yards of the target, excellent bombing even allowing for the near perfect conditions. With all nervousness gone, hoping now that Sedgley-Jones and Kruger were in touch with the exercise, Saffron came in on his twelfth run.

His compass and drift wires, pointing dead ahead, told him that this time the Oxford was running with the light wind. If anything the aircraft was more rock steady than ever; the drift wires were not deviating by a degree. Without the need to call corrections, Saffron was able to devote his entire concentration on to the dot sliding towards his sights. Squinting, holding his breath, he tightened his grip on the bomb release and then squeezed. 'Bomb gone!'

He knew it was good the moment the bomb fell away. Pushing forward he watched its progress. A tiny dart against the immensity of sea, it plunged down, dropped back, leapt forward, vanished a moment. Then, as a puff of smoke appeared, Saffron gave a gasp of disbelief.

'I've hit the bloody thing! Right on the button.'

He heard Davidson's startled laugh. 'You mean it's another one inside the pontoons?'

'No. It hit the target.'

The Oxford banked violently. Davidson sounded amused, incredulous and worried all at the same time. 'I can't see anything.'

'Of course you can't. The smoke's blown away.'

'That's probably it. It drifts and gives a false reading.'

Before Saffron could reply, Bickers came in with a guffaw. 'Stop bulling us, Saffron. Nobody hits the target. Even I know that.'

'For Christ's sake. . . . I tell you I put one right on the button. Go back and I'll do it again.'

Davidson sounded thoughtful. 'How many bombs have you left?'

Saffron checked with his 3073. The Oxford's light-series carriers carried sixteen and he had dropped twelve. 'Four.'

'I think that's enough, don't you? How about letting Bickers have a go?'

Bickers, whose duties as a junior armament instructor did not embrace bombing, came in enthusiastically. 'Can I?'

Saffron, who by this time had the bit in his teeth, growled an objection. 'He hasn't a clue. All he'll do is mess up my grouping.'

'No, I won't,' Bickers said indignantly. 'I've used a bomb-sight dozens of times.'

'On what?' Saffron jeered. 'The simulator.'

'There's not that much difference.'

Davidson's humorous voice broke up the argument. 'Let him have a go, Alan. If he makes a mess of it, I'll see you're not debited with his bombs.'

Left with no choice, Saffron backed out and dropped disgruntedly into the co-pilot's seat. Grinning maliciously, Bickers squeezed past him and crawled into the hatch. Davidson waited until they had settled and then banked towards the target. As the Oxford steadied, the coast lay dead ahead.

The gleeful Bickers plugged in his intercom and waggled a foot. 'Where's the bomb tit?'

'Where it always is,' Saffron said. 'In the bracket over your left shoulder.'

Bickers grunted something and settled down. Fifteen seconds later his enthusiastic instructions began. 'Left ... left.... No, that's too much. Right ... right. Still more ... Steady. No: we're off again. Left, left. ...'

Swinging its nose like a bewildered snake, the Oxford droned over the target. Saffron was waiting for the bomb gone sign from Bickers but the Londoner was still squinting down the sights. Unable to see the position of the target from their seats, Davidson and Saffron exchanged puzzled glances. The coast was closing fast when Saffron, certain they had overshot, reached down and jerked Bickers' leg.

'What the hell are you doing?'

There was a startled grunt from Bickers. 'What did you do that for?'

'Do what?'

'Jerk my leg.'

'I did it to wake you up.'

'I wasn't asleep,' Bickers said indignantly. 'I'd overshot and was waiting for another run-in.'

'So what does it matter?'

'It made me jump. I pressed the bomb tit.'

Davidson stiffened. Following his glance Saffron saw why. With the coast so close, a falling bomb would almost certainly reach it. About to tilt the wings, Davidson changed his mind. 'Can you see the bomb?'

'Yes.'

'Then watch it closely and see where it lands.'

As he sat back and waited, Saffron saw the pilot was looking anxious. In front of him, Bickers was pushing himself
forward with his toes as he followed the bomb down. Four
seconds later the intercom crackled as if it had a malfunction. Davidson lifted his mask.

'Has it struck yet?'

Bickers' voice sounded far away. 'Yes.'

'Where did it land?'

There was no reply. Davidson's voice rose impatiently.
'Bickers, this is serious. Where did it land?'

Bickers sounded plaintive, a man to whom fate has been
unkind. 'I could be wrong. You said yourself how the smoke
drifts and gives a false reading.'

The grit of Davidson's teeth sounded loud over the intercom. 'Bickers! For the last time, where did the bloody
thing land?'

There was a profound sigh. 'Right on top of a quadrant
hut,' Bickers muttered.

CHAPTER 12

The two beefy MPs were at the door of the Oxford almost
before its wheels stopped rolling. As its three occupants
jumped out, one man stepped in front of the two corporals
while the other approached Davidson.

'Squadron Leader Sedgley-Jones wants to see you and
your crew, sir. At once, please.'

Davidson glanced tightly at Saffron and Bickers, slammed
the buckle of his parachute harness, and threw the webbing
back into the Oxford. As the two corporals copied him he
nodded at the MP. 'All right. Let's go.'

Sedgley-Jones, Kruger and Price were waiting for them
in the SCI's office. Sedgley-Jones, pale and incensed, was
seated at his desk. Kruger, resembling a piece of teak carved
by an expert in the macabre, was standing erect at his right
side. Price, looking more like a miscast gnome than ever
with his thin legs and baggy shorts, was standing at the far
side of the room. It was his expression that brought home
to Saffron the seriousness of the incident.

Although Davidson led them into the office, Saffron

noticed with trepidation that he was the one who drew the first glance from Kruger and Sedgley-Jones. Then, as the MPs withdrew outside, the SCI's pale-blue eyes moved to the pilot.

'I take it you know why you're here, Lieutenant?'

Although Davidson was looking pale, he was clearly ready to put up a fight. 'No, sir.'

'Don't prevaricate, Lieutenant.'

'I'm not prevaricating, sir. I would like to know why those MPs were sent to bring us here. Are we under arrest?'

Sedgley-Jones leaned forward. 'Does this mean you are pleading innocence to all that's happened?'

'All what's happened, sir?'

From the breath he took, Sedgley-Jones was not finding it easy to keep his temper. 'I asked you to take a bomb-aimer over the new target and to test out the quadrant huts. I didn't ask you to put two bombs right on the target and destroy six weeks' work.'

Erect alongside the South African pilot, Saffron felt a glow of professional pride through his apprehension. Two bombs. Better than he had thought. His glow was doused as Sedgley-Jones, his control slipping, turned on him.

'You meant to do this, didn't you, Corporal?'

Kruger stirred uneasily. Saffron gazed straight ahead. 'Lieutenant Davidson asked me to go on a bombing exercise with him, sir. I took sixteen practice bombs and dropped them to the best of my ability. Which I thought I was expected to do.'

Two red spots suddenly glowed in Sedgley-Jones's pale cheeks. 'You thought I wanted a brand new target smashed to pieces?'

This time Kruger cleared his throat loudly. Conscious that while the target remained the subject of contention, the officer could only make a fool of himself, Saffron answered with some aplomb. 'I bombed the target, sir. I understood that was what it was for.'

Across the room Price gave Saffron a fierce scowl. Sedgley-Jones's lips went pale but by this time Kruger's message had reached him and although his eyes remained hostile, his tone changed.

'You appear to be a very good bomb-aimer, Corporal.'

'Thank you, sir.'

'So good you can hit a fifteen-foot target twice in one exercise.' Sedgley-Jones glanced down at a piece of paper on his desk. 'Using only thirteen bombs. I would say it is almost a unique feat.'

'The conditions were very good,' Saffron said modestly, trying not to see the frantic gestures Price was now making. 'And we must have got the wind speed and direction just right.'

'I agree. Then the conditions allowed no possibility of error? What I mean is that a bomb aimer of your skill couldn't possibly have missed the target by a couple of miles or more?'

Knowing what was coming, Saffron knew as certainly there was no way of avoiding it. 'No, sir.'

Sedgley-Jones leaned forward. 'Then, Corporal Saffron, how did it happen that you planted a bomb right on the roof of the northern quadrant hut? At this very moment two WAAFs are having treatment for shock. Do you deny wilfully aiming a bomb at that hut?'

Saffron was acutely conscious of Kruger's triumphant expression. 'Yes, sir. I do.'

'You deny it, even though you have proved you are an expert bomb-aimer and admit that conditions were almost perfect. Are you saying the bomb didn't drop from your plane? Before you answer that, remember both quadrant huts had binoculars on you from the moment you commenced bombing.'

'I'm not denying it, sir.'

'Then what's your explanation?'

Saffron was wondering apprehensively if Davidson was going to let him down. He relaxed as the pilot broke in.

'I can answer that, sir.'

Sedgley-Jones transferred his eyes sharply. 'How?'

'It happened when we were making our thirteenth run-in. There must have been a hang-up on the carrier because the bomb didn't drop off until we were almost over the coast. By sheer bad luck it seemed to fall near the quadrant hut.'

The red dots returned to Sedgley-Jones's cheeks. 'Not near, Lieutenant. On. Are you saying a hang-up caused a direct hit?'

'I know it's a million to one, sir, but that's what happened.'

'But if you had a hang-up why didn't you turn out to sea and try to dislodge it. It was criminal to keep on flying towards the coast.'

Saffron held his breath as he watched Davidson defend the one weak link in their concocted story. 'At that time I didn't know there was a hang-up, sir. I . . .'

'You mean Corporal Saffron never told you?' Sedgley-Jones said quickly.

'No, it wasn't that. It was a temporary malfunction in my earphones. And not hearing him I kept steady on the bearing so he could plot the bomb's fall. That's why we were so near the coast when it fell off.'

Sedgley-Jones's expression made Saffron feel hysterical. 'If you didn't hear Saffron report he had a hang-up, how can you be so sure he did report it?'

'Because Corporal Bickers heard him and naturally assumed I'd heard him too.'

Sensing he might be going to lose his victim when a moment ago all the odds had seemed to favour him, Sedgley-Jones turned all his venom on the unfortunate Bickers who until this moment had not said a word.

'What were you doing in the plane?'

'Just making up weight, sir,' Bickers offered nervously.

'Who said you could go?'

'Lieutenant Davidson wanted a third man, sir. So Corporal Saffron mentioned me and Flight Lieutenant Price gave me permission.'

Looking as if the entire world were conspiring against him, Sedgley-Jones glanced at Price. As the tiny officer nodded, he turned his spite back on Bickers.

'Did you drop any bombs?'

Bickers looked shocked. 'Me, sir? JAIs aren't allowed to.'

'I'm not asking if you're allowed to. I'm asking if you did.'

'No, sir. Definitely not.'

Sedgley-Jones sat back in his chair. 'You are a friend of Corporal Saffron's, aren't you?'

Bickers gave Saffron a doubtful look before answering. 'I suppose so, sir.'

Sedgley-Jones's voice had a chilling hoarseness. 'I know you are, Corporal.'

There was a long silence as the officer's pale eyes moved from man to man, to end on Saffron. He doesn't believe a word we've said, Saffron thought, but he knows there's nothing he can do about it. Saffron did not know whether to feel gratified or apprehensive as Sedgley-Jones suddenly threw a pencil down on his desk and turned to Kruger. The frustration in his voice made the warrant officer jump.

'Don't just stand there, Mr Kruger! You've heard the evidence – a hung-up bomb falls six thousand feet without human guidance to fall slap on a quadrant hut. A million to one fluke if you discount the dozen or so gremlins it must have taken to guide it down and tamper with the radio at the same time. Dismiss those MPs and get these three out of here! Thanks to them, you and me have weeks of work to catch up.'

Bickers flung down his cap and dropped on his bed. 'Three direct hits in one afternoon. And you tell me you're not a Jonah.'

Saffron lit a cigarette and exhaled resentfully. 'Don't exaggerate.'

'Exaggerate? All over the Union and probably in Australia and Canada too, thousands of guys are trying to hit targets every day and nobody ever does. Yet you invite me up and then smash Sedgley-Jones's pride and joy twice. Jonah would have been jealous of you, mate.'

Saffron eyed him maliciously. 'You didn't do so badly yourself, did you? One bomb and bang – two WAAFs having babies.'

Bickers nodded bitterly. 'That's what I mean. If you hadn't made me jump I'd never have pressed the bomb tit. And then think of all the factors that had to be just right – wind, approach, airspeed, altitude, temperature – Christ, it makes one sweat to think about it. They ought to discharge you, mate. You're a menace to the war effort.'

Saffron, who had the uneasy feeling there might be something in Bickers' contention, covered with a scowl. 'Stop talking balls.' Pulling a piece of paper from his bush-jacket, he glanced round the cubicle. 'Got a pen?'

Bickers snatched the paper from him and gave a grunt of protest. 'Oh, no. Not after this afternoon.'

'Why not? Nothing's changed.'

'Nothing's changed? You see the look Sedgley-Jones gave me? Before it was just you, Tweedledum. Now it's Tweedledum and Tweedledee. You think I'm going to get myself in any deeper?'

'This is just the time to fight back. Don't you know that? In for a penny, in for a pound!'

'So you can get Synevva Helgman into bed? You think my name's Joe?'

Saffron tried blandishments. 'What about when your turn comes? How often have you moaned to me about the chances you've missed by having to be back in camp by midnight. If this works you'll be laughing. A warm bed all night and she'll bring you breakfast before you start back. You can't pass it up.'

For the briefest moment Bickers faltered. Then he rallied indignantly. 'You could fake both signatures if you wanted to. You just want me to share the blame if you're caught.'

'That's ridiculous. I want you to share the benefits.'

'Some benefits if Kruger gets on to us.'

'You've just said you're in it as deeply as I am now. So strike out and take chances. Be hung for a sheep instead of a lamb.'

Bickers gave a grunt of disgust. ' "In for a penny" – "hung for a sheep". You sound like a bloody dictionary of proverbs.'

'Proverbs have a way of being right, haven't they? What's that other one – "to accumulate, one has to speculate". Now that you're in trouble with Kruger, life's going to be hell unless you take a few chances.'

Bickers suffered a bout of self-pity. 'Why had you to be on my draft? Who hates me up there?' Snatching a pen from his shirt, he scrawled vindictively on the pass. 'I hope they catch you, Saffron. It's worth the risk just to get you off my back.'

CHAPTER 13

As Mostert leaned unsteadily across the table his arm knocked over a glass of gin. Ignoring it he breathed whisky into Saffron's face. 'It still makes no sense to me, Corporal. No sense at all. . . .'

The girl alongside him, a fluffy blonde, giggled nervously. 'Stop it, Bob. Let's have a dance.'

The pilot pushed her back. 'I don't wanna dance.' His drunken eyes focused on Saffron again. 'You haven't answered me, Corporal. I want to know why Synevva invited you tonight. You a Wing Commander in disguise or something?'

If I were I'd soon bounce you, Saffron thought truculently. Before he could answer the music stopped and both men's eyes turned to the dance floor. Packed with couples in evening dress, it began to thin out as the dancers returned to their tables. At the far side Saffron caught sight of Synevva. A somewhat frail South African major was steering her back to the table. Looking incredibly elegant in a low-cut, lime-green evening gown, she was drawing admiring glances from all quarters as she chatted to the major.

For Saffron the evening had started auspiciously enough when the two Afrikander MPs in the Guard Room had not given his pass a second glance and he had made his way gleefully into town. His first hint that he must not expect too much of fate came when he entered the George Hotel and discovered a crowd of eager young officers surrounding the glamorous Synevva. One pilot in particular had caught his eye – Mostert of the thin moustache and caustic tongue. As Saffron, cursing his luck, had made for the bar, the girl had spotted him and pushed out of her circle of admirers.

'Alan! So you've made it. How nice. Come and meet my friends.'

There had been enigmatic lights in the girl's eyes as she made the introductions. In Saffron's hypersensitive mood all the officers, British and South African alike, had closed ranks on seeing his two stripes. As expected, Mostert had made the most of the moment.

'You've some odd friends, Synevva. This chap nearly shot me down over Earste Rivier a few weeks ago.'

The girl had lifted an eyebrow. 'Then he must be a good shot.'

Mostert had grinned round the circle of officers. 'There's only one snag to that. He was the gunner in my plane!'

There had been a roar of laughter from the half-tipsy officers. Before the embarrassed Saffron could react the girl had led him towards the door. 'I think it's time we started off, don't you? Will you fetch my coat, Bob, please?'

Neglected girlfriends had appeared as if by magic and the entire party had driven to the Town Hall where a large table was reserved for them. Here Saffron had been initially mollified to find his seat was next to Synevva's but as officer after officer had claimed her for dances and Saffron had been left with the choice of sitting alone or dancing with sulky girlfriends, he had taken to alcohol for solace. It had proved a fatal step. Normally a temperate drinker, Saffron discovered that his grievances, real and imaginary, had grown rather than diminished and Mostert's attack had come as the last straw. Taking it as evidence of what the other officers were thinking, Saffron made his decision as the major helped the girl into her seat. Noting his expression, she turned towards him.

'What's the matter? Has something upset you?'

'Yes, those toffee-nosed friends of yours,' Saffron growled. 'They hate my guts and I hate theirs. I'm getting back to camp.'

She made an immediate protest. 'You can't do that. The dance doesn't end until one o'clock.' A scented shoulder pressed against him. 'Are you sulking because I'm not giving you more attention?'

Saffron was never one to dance attendance on women, which is probably why he was successful with them. 'Give your attention to who you like. I'm leaving.'

She gave a delighted laugh. 'You are cross, aren't you? All right, I will. Corporal Saffron, may I have the next dance?' When Saffron scowled, she ran a teasing finger down his cheek. 'Stop looking so grumpy. It doesn't suit you.'

Across the table, dark with drink and jealousy, Mostert could take no more. 'You think this kind of thing's funny, don't you?'

The girl's glance was innocent. 'What kind of thing?'

'Bringing a corporal with you and embarrassing us all.'

Her stare was both cold and quizzical. 'Now why should that cause you embarrassment?'

'Are you pretending you don't know?'

'Darling, I'm not in the Army. I make friends with whom I please.'

Cursing thickly, Mostert turned his attention back to

Saffron. 'You had a bloody nerve to come here tonight. Can't you see when you're not wanted?'

There was aggression in Saffron's somewhat complex make-up but it usually took a bully to bring it out. He felt he was being bullied now. 'I've had enough of you. Why don't you shut up and disappear?'

The man's cheeks paled. Lurching over the table he tried to grab Saffron's collar. For Saffron, alcohol did the rest. Catching the pilot's arm he jerked him half way across the table.

'That's it! There's an alley alongside this building. If you've any guts you'll come out there and take your tunic off.'

As the cursing Mostert straightened himself, Saffron glared aggressively round him. With the other members of the party already on the dance floor, the only witnesses were the major, who was looking horrified, the fluffy blonde who was looking hysterical, and Synevva who appeared to be enjoying herself. She caught Saffron's arm as he began stalking away.

'You're not really going to fight him, are you, darling?'

With his egalitarianism badly bruised, Saffron was in a self-destructive mood. 'No, I'm going to kiss the sod! Coming to watch?'

He never remembered how he found his way into the deserted alley or how the even drunker Mostert found him, although afterwards he was to wonder if Synevva had anything to do with it because he caught sight of her in a doorway. The South African major must have followed her because he ran forward and tried to reason with Mostert. When all he got was a curse and the swing of a fist, he turned in desperation to Saffron.

'You mustn't fight an officer, Corporal. It could mean a court martial for you.'

Drunk though he was, Saffron did grant the major a glance. It proved a painful mistake because at that moment Mostert swung a punch that caught him in the mouth. Incensed enough to take on the entire officer corps, Saffron pushed the major aside and went in like a runaway steam hammer. When the red mist rolled away he found himself standing over the prostrate Mostert with Synevva tugging him one way and the major the other. As he drew reluctantly back, the major bent over the dazed pilot. He sounded half-hysterical.

'You do realize I'll have to report this?'

'Rubbish,' the girl snapped. 'Absolute rubbish.'

'But officers and NCOs can't be allowed to brawl in the streets. It's a matter of discipline.'

'Who started it?' the girl demanded.

'That's hardly the point, is it?'

'It's the whole point. Bob's been picking on Alan all night and got what he deserved. If you report a word of this to anyone, I'll never speak to you again.'

The dismayed major glanced again at Mostert who was beginning to stir. 'I suppose he's not badly hurt,' he muttered.

'Of course he's not. The best thing for both of them is to forget the whole affair.'

Saffron, suffering from alcohol, fresh air, and the after-effects of the fight, was dabbing his mouth when the girl turned to him. Fishing in his tunic pocket, she pulled out a pink ticket and handed it to the major.

'I'm going to get him back to camp. Fetch his things from the cloakroom and meet me in the car park.'

The major glanced again at Mostert who was beginning to show an interest in his surroundings. The girl pushed him impatiently towards the side door. 'You can come back for him afterwards if he's still here. Hurry up before they start on one another again.'

Saffron stared gloomily through the window at the lights of Breconfield. 'Bickers is right. He has to be.'

The darkness inside the parked car hid Synevva's smile. 'What does Bickers say?'

'He says I'm a Jonah. And I am. You saw that tonight.'

'But that was Mostert's fault, not yours.'

'Who cares who's fault it was? It happens all the time. Kruger, Sedgley-Jones, Mostert – you'd think I was on the other side.' Saffron turned to the girl with inebriated concern. 'I don't look like a German or a Japanese, do I?'

She fought back her laughter. 'I don't think so.'

'I must do. Otherwise why is everyone fighting me?'

She put her lips to his ear. 'I can tell you why Mostert went for you.'

'Why?'

'He was jealous.'

'Jealous?'

'Yes. Perhaps he guessed what I intended saying to you after the dance.'

Saffron was showing distinct signs of recovery. 'What was that?'

'That if you are a good boy and go straight to bed tonight, you can have dinner with me next week.'

The car rocked to Saffron's start. His voice was as hoarse as a bullfrog's croak. 'At your flat?'

'Yes. If you are able to get another late pass.'

Waiting to hear no more, Saffron made a grab at her. She allowed him a peck on the cheek, then pushed him back with a laugh. 'I said only if you were a good boy tonight.' Leaning across him, she opened his door. 'Give me a ring at the weekend.'

Saffron climbed reluctantly out and drew himself erect. She watched him with some concern. 'Can you manage on your own?'

' 'Course I can,' Saffron said stiffly.

'But aren't you supposed to wear your cap?'

Taking it from her he stuffed it on his dishevelled hair. Drawing him down she adjusted it, pushing him away when he tried to steal another kiss. 'Off you go. And for heaven's sake keep out of any more trouble with Bob Mostert.'

Swaying slightly on his feet, Saffron grinned at her. 'That mightn't be so easy.'

'Why not?'

'I'm flying with him in the morning on a gunnery exercise.'

She gave a gasp. 'You're not serious.'

'It's true. I saw it on orders today.'

'But Bob never mentioned it.'

'He probably hasn't read orders yet.'

Her laugh was full of disbelief. 'But if you knew this all the time, why did you have that fight with him?'

Saffron looked injured. 'What had flying tomorrow to do with it? Anyway, a minute ago you said it wasn't my fault.'

Her delighted laugh rippled out. 'You're quite crazy. Do you know that?'

He pushed his young, pleading face into the open car window. 'Give me another kiss.'

'No,' she smiled. 'Off you go and for heaven's sake watch how you behave in the morning.'

Grumbling, Saffron started off. After half a dozen steps he hesitated and turned. 'You know something? This time I think I'll do it.'

'Do what?'

'Shoot his bloody tail off!' Saffron muttered, resuming his unsteady progress towards the camp entrance.

CHAPTER 14

'Hey, Saffron! You'd better get a jildi on.'

Saffron, who was hastily pushing cartridges into a VGO magazine, glanced up from the loading bench. Bickers was standing in the sunlit doorway of the armoury. 'What's happening out there?'

Bickers approached him. 'Kruger stopped me as I came out of Number One hangar. He said you'd five minutes to get airborne.'

Muttering to himself Saffron grabbed another handful of cartridges and stuffed them feverishly into the magazine. A second magazine lay on the bench before him. Picking it up, Bickers discovered it was loaded. 'What's the exercise?'

'Under tail,' Saffron muttered.

Bickers, who had not seen Saffron since the dance, took a closer look at him and whistled. 'You look like a Highlander's jockstrap. What happened last night?'

With a headache and a queasy stomach, Saffron was distinctly unsociable that morning. As he grabbed for more ammunition the box overturned and spilled cartridges all over the floor. When Bickers made no move to pick them up, Saffron glared at him. 'If you can't help, piss off.'

Bickers grinned. 'If you think you're feeling rough, wait until you see your pilot.'

Saffron paused, half way between bench and floor. 'Where is he?'

'He was talking to Kruger when I came by. Someone must have clobbered him. He's got a black eye and a bloody great bruise on his cheek.' Bickers' grin was malicious. 'One way and another you two are going to have fun up there.'

'You don't know the half of it,' Saffron said, slinging his parachute over his shoulder and grabbing up the two filled drums. 'I'm the one who clobbered him.'

He was at the door before Bickers reacted. 'What's that supposed to be? A funny joke?'

Parachute bumping against his ribs, Saffron was already running across the tarmac. Ahead of him two mechanics were attending to the Hind, whose engine was ticking over. Kruger and the waiting pilot, Mostert, were in conversation by the Flight Office door. Saffron heard Bickers shouting after him but took no notice. As he reached the Hind, the pimply-faced mechanic jumped down from the rear cockpit. Feeling sick, his heart pounding from the sprint, Saffron let out a snarl. 'What've you done this time? Sawn through the cockpit floor?'

The man gave him a look of dislike and walked away. Across the tarmac Mostert had detached himself from Kruger and was making for the Hind. Slinging up his parachute and drums, Saffron was lowering himself into the cockpit when the pilot arrived. He gazed down with mixed feelings at the man's bruised and scowling face.

'Good morning,' he ventured.

Mostert said something but his words were lost as the engine fitter gunned the Kestrel. With a last hard look at Saffron, Mostert motioned the mechanic from the cockpit and jumped in. A moment later the chocks were dragged away and the Hind surged forward.

Trying to quell both his queasy stomach and his apprehension, Saffron hastily checked the gun mounting and cockpit for sabotage. Nothing appeared to be amiss and yet he felt a strong sense of unease as the Hind turned on the runway and began its take-off. At first he attributed it to the tension between himself and Mostert but the feeling persisted that it was something more urgent.

He began checking his equipment. His ammunition drums were on their spigots and he had brought a couple of Very light cartridges with him ... Centrifugal force, pressing his feet against the floorboards, momentarily distracted him and he paused to watch the airfield fall away. Engine thundering angrily, the Hind stood on a wingtip and made for the coast. As it levelled out, Saffron began his puzzled survey again.

He was wearing his helmet and goggles and his parachute was locked in its bin with the quick-release cord ... Parachute! His hands leapt to his chest and fumbled in dismay. Christ! He'd forgotten his harness! He stared down at himself in disbelief. The only thing comparable to an airman in 1942 forgetting his parachute harness was a City man forgetting his trousers. That's what Bickers must have been shouting after him ... Saffron's groan came from the heart. Mostert would have to cancel the exercise and the grist it would provide Kruger for mischief hardly bore thinking about.

Bathed in sweat as he crouched on his stool, Saffron wondered why he hadn't already alerted Mostert. The more time and petrol the Hind wasted, the greater his offence would be. And with a parachute harness as vital to keep a gunner in the cockpit as to allow him to escape from it, there appeared no way to cover his negligence. As one thought led to another, Saffron blanched. In his present mood Mostert was quite capable of indulging in aerobatics to test his passenger's stomach. In which case, unattached and minus parachute, Saffron would be flung from the cockpit like a stone from a sling.

The thought was more than enough. Clinging hard to the gun mounting, Saffron leaned forward in the icy slipstream to hammer on Mostert's head rest. Three seconds later he dropped back on his stool with a groan. He couldn't do it. His professional pride baulked at the vision of Mostert's scorn and Kruger's malice. The least he could do was to try to get through the exercise undetected. Bending down, he picked up the monkey chain and examined it. It was far too short to reach his shoulders or to tie round his waist. About to drop it and look for another means of survival, Saffron tentatively measured it against his legs. A second later he was wrapping it round his left ankle. There proved enough length for it to wrap round a couple of times before he tied it.

He tugged his foot experimentally. The steel links abrased his ankle through his khaki overalls but the loops held. Saffron decided that if the worst happened, there was now a chance he and the aircraft would not part company.

103

Not wishing to dwell on his reasoning in case he could find flaws in it, Saffron took a glance over the cockpit rim. The Hind was approaching the western perimeter of the range, with the sea three miles ahead. A rapid rocking of its wings made him glance at the pilot. Mostert was jabbing a hand and Saffron saw another Hind, towing a drogue, approaching them at two o'clock. Turning his goggled face, Mostert signalled him to load.

Saffron removed a magazine from its spigot and gingerly stood up. Accustomed by this time to the frenzied battering of the slipstream, he clamped the magazine on the VGO and pulled back the cocking handle. Below him the Hind was banking as Mostert brought it in at the correct angle of approach. Another waggle of the wings told Saffron to be ready.

The drogue aircraft was now sliding in at four o'clock. With no intention of testing his frail attachment by leaning over the side and raking the drogue as it passed below, Saffron knew his one hope of registering a decent score was to open fire at extreme range and he followed the drogue carefully in his sights.

The target Hind passed ahead and below but the drogue, nicely placed, came angling in at forty-five degrees. At a good three-fifty yards Saffron opened fire and in his mind's eye saw Mostert turn his head. With shells spewing from the VGO he held the trigger down in a long burst, his thinking being that the quicker he expended his ammunition the less time he would be in danger.

The drogue passed almost underneath him, an excellent target had Saffron dared to lean over and follow it but he was squatting on his stool when Mostert, glancing back irritably, put the Hind into a steep bank. A minute later the two machines were in position again, obliging the sweating Saffron to climb back on his feet.

Except that the drogue came in from the starboard quarter, the second approach was a repetition of the first, with Saffron again not daring to rake the drogue as it passed beneath him. This time Mostert swung round, thumped the fuselage with his fist, and gave a yell. Although the slipstream carried away his words, Saffron had no doubt as to their content.

Once more the planes swung apart, then closed. Saffron

whose reckless expenditure of ammunition had already exhausted one drum, hastily rearmed. This time the target aircraft was making a beam approach. Saffron, who knew the difficulties involved, paid grudging tribute to both pilots' skill as he lined up his sights. As the dot that was the other aircraft grew wings, a sudden turbulence made the Hind drop sharply. Saffron never knew whether it was his hangover or apprehension that brought on a fresh wave of nausea.

Fighting it back he waited for the drogue. At four hundred yards his finger tightened on the trigger, at three-fifty he commenced firing. Seeing his tracer flashing in and around the target, Saffron's professional instincts momentarily took over. It was only when he glimpsed the brown, out-of-focus backdrop of land behind the white drogue that the truth hit him like a sledgehammer. In his disgust that Saffron was not taking full advantage of the target, Mostert was rolling the Hind to make him follow it. With a yelp of dismay Saffron released the VGO and grabbed the gun mounting. The Very pistol clamped at the side of the cockpit bruised his side as his weight bore down on it. Lifting his tied foot he tried to establish the amount of slack on the chain; to his feverish imagination it seemed to contain yards.

In the front cockpit Mostert had decided to give his reluctant gunner a lesson. If the windy sod didn't stomach leaning over the side when he was the right way up, he could lean out the wrong way. Easing over the stick, Mostert prepared to roll the Hind very slowly on her back.

By this time Saffron was at panic stations. If the sadistic bastard rolled her beyond the vertical he'd fall out for sure. With all inhibitions forgotten, he tried to yell a warning but the howling slipstream mocked him. Fishing round desperately with his free leg he hooked it beneath the seat.

The horizon was now a hazy line directly above his head with the earth on one side and the sky on the other. As it tilted further over his shoulder Saffron knew the worst. Letting out a dry croak he closed his eyes. While one half of his brain went numb, the other snatched at and discarded thoughts at fantastic speed. Terminal velocity of the human body – about 120 mph. So no loss of consciousness as they used to believe – time to think all the way down. Legs driven into body or a fleshy sack full of splintered bones. All because he hadn't wanted Kruger or Mostert to know about his mistake. Pride? He'd walk round the camp in a hair shirt with a piss pot on his head if someone would get him out of this mess.

The horizon shifted again until the earth became the sky. All of Saffron's weight was now on his awkwardly twisted arms. With Mostert unconscious of the drama being enacted behind him, the inverted Hind flew on straight and true over the range. In a desperate attempt to ease the pain of his arms, Saffron tried to take more weight on his free leg. The attempt proved fatal, his foot losing its hold on the seat. As his body jack-knifed upwards, a flood of adrenalin gave Saffron another three seconds hold on the gun mounting. Then his grip tore away and with a croak of despair he slid from the cockpit.

In his terror he seemed to fall yards instead of inches before the wrench came that almost broke his ankle. With arms waving helplessly and his goggles steamed with sweat, Saffron dangled by his foot six thousand feet above the Cape Flats.

Mostert, who all this time had been humming maliciously, felt the jerk and glanced back. At the sight of the waving, dangling puppet that was Saffron, he raised a disbelieving arm and dragged it across his goggles. When Saffron did not disappear, he sank back and with the manner of a man certain he is having a nightmare but must placate it, he gingerly rolled the Hind back on an even keel. Able to grab hold of the gun mounting, Saffron collapsed on to his stool five seconds later and was promptly and violently sick.

Glancing back over his shoulder every few seconds in case Saffron should emerge again, Mostert flew straight back to Breconfield and landed. Before taxi-ing towards the hangars he throttled back the engine. His voice was hoarse with disbelief as he turned.

'Just what in hell were you doing up there?'

Covered in wind-frothed vomit, Saffron was too weak to offer resistance. 'I forgot my harness,' he muttered.

'You forgot your harness! And never said anything! When we were out on an under-tail exercise! You a bloody madman or something?'

Reaction allowed Saffron one flash of spirit. 'How the hell was I to know you'd fly the kite upside down?'

With the full implications coming home to roost, Mostert almost choked with resentment. 'If you'd fallen out they'd have thrown the book at me for not checking your equipment. Court-martial, the lot! You didn't give that a second thought, did you?'

Deciding in a mad world it was a reasonable enough criticism, Saffron gestured weakly at the hangars. 'Let's get back. I think I'm going to be sick again.'

The Hind taxied on to the tarmac while Saffron struggled to untie the monkey chain. As the two mechanics came out of the hangar, Mostert jumped to the ground. Up in the rear cockpit Saffron was testing his ankle. As he dropped back on the stool with a groan he received a glare from the pilot.

'Is it broken?'

'I don't think so. I'll try it again in a minute.'

'Not a thought of me,' Mostert muttered. 'I could be facing a court-martial this minute. Christ!'

Behind the approaching mechanics the dapper figure of Sedgley-Jones could be seen entering Kruger's office. As Saffron tested his ankle again, Mostert's tone changed. 'I suppose you'd like to keep this quiet?'

Any serviceman worth his salt has the instinct to sense when an adversary is contemplating withdrawal and few were better endowed with the instinct than Saffron. Nausea and pain notwithstanding, his ears pricked up. 'Who wouldn't?'

Mostert watched his painful efforts to climb down from the cockpit. 'On second thoughts you look to me as if you've had enough. If you can think of some excuse for that ankle, I'm prepared to forget the whole thing.'

Saffron swallowed his sarcasm. 'Thanks.'

'That's all right,' Mostert muttered. 'Want a hand?'

Lowering himself gingerly to the ground, Saffron discovered his ankle would support him. 'No, I'm all right.'

As the two mechanics came within earshot, Mostert lowered his voice. 'File your report as if nothing's happened. If it turns out you haven't got many hits, I'll say there was turbulence over the range. OK?'

Saffron nodded. As the pilot walked away Saffron saw the pimply-faced mechanic had noticed his vomit-stained suit and was gleefully nudging his companion's arm. Holding back until the man was almost alongside him, Saffron jerked a thumb at the rear cockpit. 'If you think this is bad, take a gander in there. You're going to need at least two buckets. I've filled it up to the stool.'

Grinning maliciously at the man's expression, deciding revenge could be sweet even when it was belated, Saffron limped away after Mostert.

CHAPTER 15

Holding the barrel of the gun like a pointer, Saffron tapped the breech block of the Browning that lay stripped on the table before him. 'What's this called?'

Thirty faces stared blankly back at him. Then a hand rose tentatively at the back of the classroom. 'Yes,' Saffron said hopefully.

'The locking piece, Corporal.'

The laugh that followed made Saffron grit his teeth. He stabbed the barrel at Moulang. 'You! What are you grinning at?'

Moulang's expression changed magically from hilarity to innocence. 'Me, Corporal?'

'Yes, you.' Saffron limped threateningly round the table. 'If you didn't know the name of that component, why did you laugh?'

'I can't think why, Corporal.'

'Then I'll bloody tell you.' It was only an hour since Saffron had been dangling head over tip above Eerste Rivier and his nerves were still on edge. 'You know the real name but you're trying to be funny. Right?'

No one could look as hurt as the imp-like Afrikander when the occasion demanded it. 'Funny, Corporal?'

'Yes, funny. And don't be. I'm not in the mood. Got it?'

'Of course, Corporal.'

Saffron's glare moved from face to face. 'We'll run through the names again. Then you'll come out individually and point them out. Repeat them after me. The barrel!'

A raucous shout followed. 'The barrel!'

'The breech block!'

'The breech block!' With his head splitting at every shout, Saffron went through the list of components. Seeing Moulang whispering to Van der Merve he pushed down the aisle towards them. 'You two got a special dispensation?'

Moulang glanced up innocently. 'Pardon, Corporal.'

'Why the hell are you whispering?'

'Whispering, Corporal?'

Saffron's voice dropped into a hiss of fury. 'If you repeat what I say just once more, Moulang, I'll gut you like a herring. Is that understood?'

'Yes, Corporal.'

Breathing hard, Saffron walked back to the platform. As he reached it a paper dart came floating past his ear. Gracefully banking over the platform it glided towards a window, nuzzled it gently, and fell to the floor.

Saffron spun round. Thirty men, holding back their hilarity with the utmost difficulty, stared back at him but his bloodshot eyes were on the grinning Van der Merve.

'That was you, wasn't it?'

'I don't know what you mean, Corporal.'

Beside himself with rage, Saffron made the fateful threat. 'I've had you, Van der Merve. Right up to here. One more move – just one more – and you'll be on jankers for the rest of this bloody war.'

Conscious he was deliberately picking on the weak, Saffron transferred his attention to Du Plessis. 'You! Come here and point out the rear sear.'

The timid Du Plessis rose and came obediently down the aisle. Grinning at Moulang, Van der Merve waited until he was opposite his desk, then stuck out a huge leg. The hapless Du Plessis stumbled forward and collided with the table. As it tilted back, components slid off, among them the casing of the Browning which dropped full on Saffron's lacerated foot.

With a howl of pain Saffron went straight into the air, then went berserk. Snatching up the gun barrel he hurled himself past the startled Du Plessis at Van der Merve. Before the giant could untangle himself from his desk, Saffron swung the gun barrel and caught him behind the left ear. Eyes glazing, the giant slumped sideways and lay unconscious in the aisle between the desks.

The roar of excitement from Course 21 died into a stunned silence. Horrified by his act, Saffron stood transfixed over the trainee's body. It took Moulang's voice, muted for once, to break the spell.

109

'Is he dead, Corporal?'

With a silent yelp of dismay, Saffron dropped and began fumbling for the giant's wrist. Unable to find a pulse he thrust a frantic hand into the man's overalls. The hairy mat his hand pressed on felt as if it were being thumped by a steam hammer.

Breathing a thanksgiving, Saffron was about to rise and call for medical aid when, in the time it takes lightning to strike, self-preservation assailed him with a host of feverish protests.

You can't do that, Saffron. If Kruger finds out he'll draw and quarter you. You must play it cool. Act as if it's a perfectly normal thing for an NCO to crack the skull of an air mechanic.

Saffron's panic counter-attacked immediately. You're getting feeble-minded. Do you really believe no one in a class of thirty is going to report you? Grow up, Saffron, and face it. Kruger's already sharpening his knives.

The battle swung back. All right, so you are playing for time. Why not? While there's life, there's hope too, isn't there? Maybe you can bribe the bastards. Give 'em an extra pass, promise 'em leave, anything. But go down fighting, Saffron. What have you got to lose?

With the threat of Kruger in the background, the issue was never in doubt. Lifting his sweating face, Saffron gave Moulang a contemptuous stare. 'You think his skull's made of paper? Of course he's not dead.'

Trying to hide the unsteadiness of his legs, he stood up. As Moulang moved towards the stricken giant, Saffron let out a snarl. 'You want the same? Sit down!'

Moulang dropped back into his seat as if he had been shot. A gleam of gratification entered Saffron's eyes. As he turned and limped towards the platform, a buzz of disbelief broke out and men rose from their seats to gain a view of Van der Merve. Saffron turned and the hush became almost palpable. In spite of the pit looming ahead of him, Saffron felt elation. The bastards were on the run at last! When the count was made, they wouldn't be able to claim them all as victories! He jabbed a hand at a gaping trainee. 'Bekker! Come out and show me the transporter.'

With the classroom like a church and man after man responding instantly to his orders, Saffron suffered a bout of

110

hysterical humour. Like the destroyer *Kelly* . . . Flags flying and guns firing just before the waves closed over her. When Van der Merve gave a groan and stirred, Saffron's bark rang across the classroom. 'No! Leave him.'

The trainees sank back. Returning to the dazed giant, Saffron noticed with secret alarm an egg-like swelling behind the Afrikander's ear.

'Had a good sleep?'

The syncophantic titters that echoed round the room encouraged Saffron to further excesses of masculinity. 'Get back to your desk. And remember – one more word out of turn and I'll clobber you again.'

The shaken giant dropped into his chair. As thirty apprehensive trainees obeyed him for the rest of the morning with an alacrity beyond his wildest dreams, Saffron experienced the heady wine of dictatorship. It was only when the hands of his watch approached 12.30 that sobriety raised its head again. All the sods were waiting for was the bell and then their feet wouldn't touch the ground to Price's office. The paths of glory, Saffron ruminated with elegiac gloom, led only to the glasshouse.

The lunch-bell sounded and Course 21 filed soberly out. It was only when the classroom was empty that Saffron saw Van der Merve had stayed behind and his apprehension grew when the giant rose from his desk and approached him. Perhaps he'd underestimated the extent of his woes. Perhaps the huge Afrikander intended to tear him apart before reporting him to Kruger. Grabbing hold of the gun barrel, Saffron tried to hide his alarm.

'What do you want?'

Van der Merve gave a bashful grin. 'I've come to say I'm sorry, Corporal.'

Saffron decided the strain of handling Course 21 had finally turned his mind. 'What?'

'I'm sorry for what happened, Corporal.'

Saffron's grip on the gun barrel slackened, only to tighten punitively. 'You being funny again?'

'No, Corporal. I mean it. Will you shake hands, please?'

The stupefied Saffron felt as if his hand were caught in a meat grinder. 'You're saying you didn't mind my clobbering you?'

'No, Corporal. It's what my father used to do. Only he used a knobkerrie.'

'A knobkerrie?'

The giant grinned. 'Yes, Corporal. Sometimes twice a week.'

All Saffron's resilience showed in the speed of his recovery. 'What about the rest of the course?'

'What about them, Corporal?'

'Aren't they likely to tell Mr Price or Mr Kruger? I wouldn't like you to get into any more trouble, Van der Merve,' Saffron added generously. 'As far as I'm concerned you've been punished enough.'

The giant's grin spread from ear to ear. 'They won't tell any tales, Corporal. I'll see to that.' He went to the door and turned. 'My guess is you won't have any more trouble with them, Corporal. But if you do, just let me know.'

A firm believer in ramming an advantage home, Saffron indicated the pieces of Browning gun lying on the table. 'This lot has to go back to the store. See to it, will you?'

'Yes, Corporal.'

With a mask of nonchalance hiding his incredulity, Saffron picked up his cap and went out into the quadrangle. As he passed the CGI's office, a shout greeted him. 'Saffron! Just a minute.'

Saffron entered the office. The birdlike Price, climbing into his tunic, indicated a slip of paper on his desk. 'Your gunnery score's just come in.'

As Saffron, prepared for the worst, picked up the slip he heard Price's chuckle. 'I'll say this for you, Saffron. You believe in rubbing it in.'

As Saffron stared blankly at the ink figure on the slip, Price's laugh, full of delicious malice, came again. '46%! That's bloody marvellous gunnery, Saffron. What did you imagine you were aiming at? Kruger's arse?'

Looking like a schoolboy threatened with a disaster, Saffron backed towards the door. 'May I leave the room, sir?'

Price eyed him with puzzled concern. 'You feeling all right, Saffron?'

Saffron turned and ran. Hurrying to his open window Price heard bouts of hysterical laughter echoing round the quadrangle before a door slammed shut.

CHAPTER 16

The vinegary-faced woman wearing hair-curlers and an apron went to the bedroom door and listened. 'It's my tele-prone. Don't touch anything while I'm gone. I'll only be a minute.'

Bickers gave a grunt as she clattered down the uncarpeted staircase. 'What's she think we'll do? Steal something?'

Saffron grinned. 'The licentious soldiery. Never mind that. Are you coming in or not?'

Bickers stared round the small room. It contained two single beds, a mahogany wardrobe, and a marble-topped washstand complete with jug and bowl. 'Ten bob a week's a hell of a lot of money!'

'Think what you get for it,' Saffron argued. 'Think of having a place to bring women to.'

For a second Bickers' eyes glinted. Then his long face turned lugubrious again. 'That old cow won't allow women in. They hate their own kind and no bloody wonder.'

'She goes out to work, so there'll be half days,' Saffron said. 'And she must go out some evenings. Anyway,' and he patted one of the beds, 'think how marvellous it'll be to come here at nights instead of tramping all the way back to camp.'

'It'll mean using faked passes,' Bickers grumbled.

'They've worked so far, haven't they? And the more times the guardroom see those signatures, the safer they'll get.'

'Like hell they will. They'll twig one of these days and we'll end up in a chain gang. I know why you want this place, Saffron. It's a place to bed down after you've banged that Synevva woman. And a chance to get away from the fleas.'

'What if it is? You get the same benefits, don't you?'

'Fleas don't bother me that much.'

Saffron could not resist the crack. 'We can't all have tough hides.'

'Funny, funny,' Bickers grunted, moving over to the win-dow. Opposite was a road junction with a small monument in the centre. As Bickers gazed out he saw a trolley bus run past the end of the road. 'I'll say this for it. It's well-situated.'

Saffron was quick to exploit his concession. 'Rondebosch. Couldn't be better. Half way to camp, half way to town. I tell you we'd be crazy to pass it up.'

'It's still five bob each. A whole quid a month. What's the use of a room if you've no money left for anything else?'

'You wouldn't be that short,' Saffron argued. Badly wanting the room, he adopted Machiavellian tactics. 'It would be one up on the officers, wouldn't it, to have better quarters than they have.'

Something stirred in Bickers' eyes even as he let out a loud jeer of disgust. 'You're pathetic, mate. Is that your only ambition – to live like *them*!'

Saffron had never looked so innocent. 'It's not so much to live like them, although we have the same rights to be comfortable, haven't we? I'd feel I was making a kind of protest against the system.'

Bickers' stare was black with suspicion. 'You're having me on, aren't you?'

'Why should you think that?'

'Because I bloody know you, Saffron, that's why?'

'Well, you're wrong. I admit I want to get away from the fleas but it's more than that. Don't forget all the things that have happened to me recently. Maybe I've changed, who knows? Anyway, I know I'd see it as an act of defiance.'

A last suspicious glance and Bickers turned back to the window. A few seconds later his mutter reached Saffron. 'I see there's a pub across the road.'

'Yes. A good one. Full of women in the evening. And the landlord likes the RAF.'

'How do you know that?'

'I tried it on Monday night when I heard this place was vacant. Got three free drinks and I was only in there half an hour.'

Bickers stirred uneasily. Sensing his man was almost down and hearing footsteps on the stairs outside, Saffron put the boot in. 'Don't feel you've got to take it for my sake. Morris is interested and so is Ainsworth. Naturally I'm giving you first option but one way or another we have to decide tonight or we might lose it to a civvie. What do you think?'

114

Bickers shuffled, scowled, and finally took the plunge. 'All right. But don't blame me when they find out and shoot us.'

The lift that Saffron entered on his arrival at Green Mansions, Tamboers Kloof, the following Thursday evening possessed all the good taste of its environment. On his way to the top floor its well-oiled machinery maintained a discreet silence. On his arrival its twin doors swept aside like the arms of flunkeys beckoning him to a royal assignment. Stepping out, Saffron saw two doors facing one another at the opposite sides of a polished teak landing. Pausing a moment to adjust his tie, Saffron started towards Number 14.

The bell he rang sounded like the chiming of an antique clock. He heard a dog bark and a moment later a coloured girl opened the door. Pert and pretty, she gave him an expectant smile. 'Good evening.'

Saffron cleared his throat. 'Good evening. My name's Saffron. I've a dinner engagement with Miss Helgman.'

The smiling girl stood aside. 'Come in, please.'

The small hall Saffron entered was full of flowers. A huge vase stood on an onyx table, two more vases on a bookcase. As the girl held out a hand for his cap, a glass-panelled door opened and the barking Caesar rushed out. As he leapt against Saffron's legs, Synevva appeared in the doorway. Her low laugh made Saffron glance up from the fussing dog.

'He really does like you, doesn't he?'

She was wearing a black, short-length frock that set off her blonde hair and tanned limbs to perfection. She stood there a moment as Saffron's eager eyes devoured her, then held out a slim arm. 'I'm so glad you could come.'

Conscious of the maid's curiosity, Saffron took her hand somewhat awkwardly. 'I'm not too early, am I?'

'Of course you're not. What have you got there?'

She was indicating the small bouquet of flowers in his other hand. As Saffron held them out he imagined Bickers viewing the scene and his murmur contained a touch of defiance. 'I got them from the flower-seller down the road. But they look a bit stupid beside all the flowers you've got in here.'

She lowered her face into the bouquet, then hugged his arm. 'Nonsense. They're lovely. It's very sweet of you.' She nodded at the maid as she led him towards the glass-panelled door. 'You can go now, Maggie. You won't forget to post my letters, will you?'

'No, madam.'

With a last glance at Saffron, the maid put on a hat and went out. Saffron's arm was lightly squeezed again. 'There. Now we're alone. Come and have a drink.'

To Saffron, conditioned to the austerity of barracks, the room he entered was like a scene from the Arabian Nights. Two crystal chandeliers, both alight, hung from a night-blue ceiling. The furniture was ultra modern and soft music was issuing from a record player. Exotic painting lined the walls. Crystal ornaments stood on tables or in window bays, imprisoning or reflecting the light from the chandeliers. Many were filled with flowers. But it was the floor that held Saffron's eyes. Covered by a sumptuous cream carpet, it had cushions almost large enough to be pieces of furniture scattered over it in unorthodox patterns. The effect was both artistic and sensual.

The girl was watching Saffron's face with some amusement. 'Well. Do you like my flat?'

'I've never seen anything like it before,' Saffron confessed.

She laughed and with a hiss of silk walked across to a cocktail cabinet. 'Now there's a non-committal statement! You'll find it'll grow on you after a few drinks. What would you like? Whisky?'

'Yes, please.'

She pressed a button and like a rabbit from a hat an illuminated host of bottles and glasses rose from the cocktail cabinet. 'Soda or water?' she asked over one tanned shoulder.

Saffron's fascinated eyes returned to her. 'Soda, please. Half and half.'

Thirty seconds later, a glass in either hand, she approached him. 'Why don't you relax and sit down?'

Saffron glanced round. 'Where?'

Handing him his glass, she sank gracefully down on one of the huge cushions. 'Try these. They're very comfortable.'

Hesitating, he chose one opposite her. With two feet still to descend he lost control and with a yelp of dismay tumbled backwards and spilt the whisky over himself and the cushion. The delighted Caesar bounded forward and smothered him

116

with licks. Red-faced, Saffron pushed the dog away and sat upright. 'I'm sorry.'

To his relief she was laughing. 'Everyone does that the first time they sit down with a glass in their hand. Keep still and I'll fetch a towel.'

He dried himself while she poured him another drink. As she bent down and handed it to him, his eyes were drawn to her deep décolletage where apple-white crescents swelled deliciously. Noticing his glance, she switched off the chandeliers and with a wall lantern providing the only light, sank down on the cushion beside him.

'That's better. As you comfortable now?'

Her nearness and perfume were turning Saffron's mouth dry. 'Yes. Very.'

Lighting two cigarettes, she placed one between his lips. 'You're tense,' she murmured. 'Try to relax.'

Awkwardly bunched up on the cushion, Saffron took a sip of whisky. 'I'm all right. Really.'

Sensing the direction of the wind, the girl drew back and tucked her shapely legs beneath her. 'You haven't told me yet what happened last Saturday morning when you flew with Bob Mostert. Was there any trouble?'

Relieved to have a topic of conversation, Saffron told her the full story. Her green eyes were huge when he finished. 'You might have been killed!'

'I nearly was,' Saffron grinned. 'With fright.'

'You say Bob didn't report you?'

Saffron was doing Mostert no favours. 'If he had, it would have meant admitting he hadn't done his job in checking my equipment.'

'So you both agreed to keep quiet?'

'That's right. Mind you, I doubt if he likes me any better.'

'He might like you even less if he knew where you are to-night,' Synevva murmured.

Saffron found distinct pleasure in the thought as she held out her empty glass to him. 'One more drink and then we'll have dinner. Will you pour them?'

With a second whisky inside him Saffron began feeling less like a barbarian in paradise. Putting out her cigarette, the girl rose. 'Are you hungry?'

'I think so.'

'You'd better be because I've done something special for

117

you. Do you know I'm a good cook?'

'I never thought of you cooking at all,' Saffron confessed.

She laughed. 'You're very frank, aren't you? Cooking is my hobby. Or at least one of them.' She pulled him to his feet. 'Come on. I don't want it to spoil.'

She led Saffron into a dining room that was all dark wood, silverware, and candlelight, and pointed to a bottle of champagne in a silver basket. 'If you'll open that, I'll go and see how the food's coming along.'

Clumsily snapping the seal, Saffron started with dismay as the cork shot across the room, followed by a cascade of champagne. The laughing girl put her head round the kitchen door. 'Don't worry. There's plenty more. Have a drink while you're waiting.'

Unnerved again and disgusted with himself, Saffron filled a glass and downed it. He had fallen straight into heaven and was acting like a clown. Glass in hand, he watched Synevva enter with a tray.

'What's the champagne like? Cold enough?'

'It's marvellous,' Saffron said, filling her glass.

They sat opposite one another as they ate, a lighted candelabrum between them. As the food and champagne relaxed him, Saffron's mood changed into fantasy. He was no longer a rough soldier blundering about in an alien environment. He was an intrepid explorer who had stolen into a forbidden cave and the girl opposite him, with the sheen of candlelight on her arms and golden hair, was Aphrodite herself.

Her amused question made him start. 'Why are you looking at me like that?'

He cleared his throat. 'You wouldn't ask that if you could see yourself.'

She gave a moue of pleasure. 'Thank you, sir. I think champagne must agree with you. Let's open another bottle.'

After that the evening began to run away with Saffron. Minutes or an hour later he found himself standing with her on the darkened balcony. The night was warm and still. With Tamboers Kloof high up on the mountainside, the velvet carpet studded with a million lights that was Cape Town lay below them. Her hand touched his arm.

'Do you like my view?'

The sky was alive with the calm stare of stars. The hushed

118

Saffron discovered his senses were abnormally acute. He could hear the rumble of the city, the cry of lonely ships, the hypnotic beat of crickets. The scent of wild thyme, aloes and her perfume filled his nostrils. He took a deep breath and the essence of all that was alive and exciting that night entered and charged his body. As the girl's hand burned his arm again Saffron knew that no matter what life might bring in the future, this would always be one of its magic moments.

CHAPTER 17

Saffron's mood changed as the girl led him from the balcony and drew the curtains. 'I haven't told you about my own flat, have I?'

'Your flat?'

He told her about the room in Rondebosch. 'Won't you get into trouble?' she asked.

'Not unless they find out.'

She reached out with her finger and playfully prodded his nose. 'What do you want it for? Girls? I'll have to come round sometime to check on you, won't I?'

'Will you?' he asked eagerly as she walked towards the record player.

'Perhaps. If you're a good boy and pour me another drink.'

She selected half a dozen records, switched on the player, and led him towards the huge cushions. As he dropped alongside her, she ran a hand down his cheek. 'Did you enjoy your dinner?'

He nodded enthusiastically. 'It was marvellous.'

'Good. You're feeling more relaxed now, aren't you?'

As he nodded again, she saw his eyes were fixed on a large nude painting that hung between two curtained windows. The subdued lighting threw a shadow over the face but the body, lying on a couch in an erotic posture, was fully exposed. She sounded amused.

'Haven't you noticed it before?'

His gaze pulled immediately away. 'No.'

'That's not much of a compliment.'

119

He frowned. 'I don't know what you mean.'

'Take another look.'

Feeling embarrassed he half-rose. His exclamation made her smile. 'You recognize it now?'

He dropped back. 'I thought you meant it was one of your paintings.'

'It is one of mine. All the paintings in here are mine.'

'You lay like that and painted yourself?'

His expression amused her. 'No. I painted it from a photograph a friend took of me. When I wanted details, all I had to do was look at myself. Do you like it?'

He gave a dubious nod. 'Yes. Very much.'

She gave an impatient exclamation and pulled him to his feet. 'How can you say that! Half of it's in shadow.' Switching on a wall light, she stood him before it. 'Now you can see it properly.'

The woman who gazed back at Saffron appeared to be welcoming a lover to her couch. Her lips were half-parted and her eyes heavy with desire. The same desire showed in the posture of her body with its out-thrust breasts and folded back legs. Saffron found the picture astonishingly erotic and wondered how much of this was due to its kinship with the woman alongside him.

'What do you think of it now?'

'It's beautiful,' he muttered.

'It or me?' she teased.

'Both.'

'That's sweet. I meant it to be a voluptuous study. I think it's come over, don't you.'

Saffron was having difficulty in taking his eyes off the provocative breasts and the long, slender legs. 'Yes. Very much.'

There was a few seconds of silence and then her low laugh. 'It's a funny feeling.'

'What?'

'You staring at my body like this.'

He walked back to the cushions and threw himself down. Switching off the light she followed him. As he reached out for his glass of whisky, she nipped his ear playfully.

'Well. Did you like what you saw?'

'What do you think?' he muttered.

Her lips moved to his ear. 'How would you like to see the original?'

Saffron discovered his heart was pounding painfully. Unable to answer, he nodded. Her whisper came again. 'Then come with me into the bedroom.'

He took another gulp of whisky, then followed her. The bedroom they entered was dark except for the subdued light that came through the open door. As he stood uncertainly beside the bed, her voice sounded behind him. 'Close your eyes and don't open them until I tell you.'

Swaying slightly, Saffron obeyed. He heard the hiss of discarded clothing, then the light patter of feet. The click of a light switch sounded a moment later and then her voice.

'You can look now.'

Saffron opened his eyes and gave a violent start. Heady with wine and excitement, his first thought was that somewhere between the lounge and the bedroom fantasy had taken over and his mind had returned to the oil painting. The naked girl spread out on the coverlet before him was lying in exactly the same provocative posture, with breasts raised and legs turned towards him. Even her parted lips, tumbled hair, and heavy eyes wore the same inviting expression. The erotic effect was further enhanced by a rose-tinted light that slanted low across the bed and framed her nakedness.

Her amused laugh broke the spell. 'Well, darling. Which me do you prefer?'

At this point Saffron lost control. Still fully-dressed he found himself on top of the girl, his mouth bearing down on her lips and his hand sliding punitively up between her legs. For a moment she responded fiercely. Then, laughing at his urgency, she pulled away. 'Not so fast, darling. Do you want it to be over before it has started? Let me help you take your clothes off.'

Saffron remembered little about undressing except that her probing, squeezing, throbbing fingers drove him to further heights of maddened desire. When he was naked she pushed him back on the bed and poised her slender body over him. Desire made her accent more pronounced than usual. 'I was not wrong about you. I like your body very much.'

He tried to roll on top of her. She pushed him back

angrily. 'You are in too much of a hurry! Love is an art, not a war. I have not kissed you yet.'

She slid down, lowered her head, and the sky exploded for Saffron. A minute later her wet lips rose to his mouth and osculated against it.

'Most men know only one way to make love,' she murmured. 'But there are many ways. Let me show them to you.'

As one delicious sensation followed another, Saffron was content enough to be a pupil. Her body was like india-rubber, shaping itself to every call she made on it. By 1.30 Saffron was still learning but by this time, although the spirit was willing, the flesh was growing weak. She sank down alongside him and switched off the light.

'Go to sleep now,' she whispered. 'We'll love again before the morning.'

She was asleep almost at once. Saffron took longer. With his sexual desires satisfied and alcohol producing its usual counteraction, puritanical elements in him were casting faint but irritating shadows. He had come hoping for sex but had he wanted sex as uninhibited as this? Although he had been a willing enough pupil, would he not have preferred to be the teacher himself?

Turning so as not to waken her, he gazed at the sleeping girl. The single sheet covering them had pulled down almost to her waist and her hair lay in tumbled coils over her shoulders and breast. As she sighed in her sleep Saffron damned his hypocrisy. He'd enjoyed every moment of a marvellous evening and now he was complaining because it had been too marvellous. No wonder things go wrong for you, Saffron. Even when you fall on your feet, all you do is look for faults. There isn't an officer at Breconfield or in the whole of Cape Town for that matter who wouldn't throw in his commission to change places with you. And this is only the beginning! The thought brought an expansive glow to Saffron. Nights with this enchantress – in place of Bickers, the Corporals' Mess and his flea-ridden bunk! The emotion he felt for the girl at that moment was akin to love.

With his puritanism effectively routed, Saffron was quickly asleep. It was the lift that awoke him. A light sleeper like many servicemen, he felt rather than heard its muted hum and his head was off the pillow when its doors slid open. As footsteps sounded on the landing and started towards the flat, his heart began to pound. Turning, he shook the sleeping girl.

'Synevva!'

Her head flopped on the pillow. He shook her harder. 'Synevva! Wake up.'

This time she stirred. Without knowing why, Saffron put his lips to her ear. 'Wake up! There's someone coming to the flat.'

She snuggled drowsily down. 'Not just yet, darling. Go to sleep.'

Saffron shook her feverishly as he heard the footsteps stop outside the flat door. 'Who the hell is it? Why don't you wake up?'

Her murmur came from the depths of sleep. 'It's probably my husband. He must have stayed in town tonight. It's nothing to worry about, darling.'

With a muted yelp Saffron sat upright, then leapt out of bed. His hiss of horror echoed round the bedroom. 'Don't just lie there! Get up! Put some clothes on!'

To his disbelief the girl had fallen asleep again. Dancing up and down in his panic, Saffron scrabbled about for his trousers, realized there was no time, yanked up his underpants and ran into the lounge. No escape there: only a hundred foot drop from the balcony. Trapped!

Wild-eyed, he ran towards the inner hall door as he heard the metallic sound of a key being inserted in the lock. At another time and place he would have noticed the uncertain fumbling before the latch was drawn and the outer door opened but his mind was digging wildly into a pile of panic-stricken thoughts and hurling them in all directions.

Her husband! An eyeball-to-eyeball confrontation! What do you say? Say good morning and nice-to-know-you? Introduce yourself and offer your hand? Or hit the bastard and run like hell? Only where? In your underpants. Oh, God! What have you got against me?

The outer door opened at last. Something crashed to the floor and a man cursed. Saffron froze. He's got a temper. Probably a gun too. A neighbour must have tipped him off. This is it, Saffron. A hell of a way to go.

Something moved behind the glass panel, then the inner door swung open. The shadowy figure that appeared looked enormous to Saffron. As the man stared at him, Saffron's mind screamed abuse. Don't just stand there, you fool. Do something. What? I don't know. Anything.

The man grunted something and advanced into the room. Saffron took a nerveless step backwards. No gun. Going to do it with his bare hands. What if I kill him, the wronged husband. Hissing crowds, black cap, swinging rope . . . Can't win, Saffron realized in horror.

'Who're you?'

To Saffron an outraged bear couldn't have sounded more formidable. In contrast his voice was like a mouse's squeak. 'Saffron. Alan Saffron.'

'Do I know you?'

It's the cat-and-mouse game, Saffron decided. 'No.'

'What're you standing there like that for? You all right?' Sadistic swine . . . 'Yes.'

'You don't look all right,' the man grunted. 'Where's Syn? Asleep?'

Saffron braced himself. 'Yes.'

'Congratulations. They don't all make it. I'm Lars Helgman, by the way. Syn's husband.'

Humming to himself, Helgman switched on a wall light and crossed over to the cocktail cabinet. The dazed Saffron saw he was a man in his early forties, thick-set with dark hair and a dark moustache. His eyes showed he had been drinking. Pouring himself a half-glass of whisky, he glanced round. 'Want one?'

Saffron was dying for a drink but kept his distance warily. 'No, thanks.'

The man lifted his glass. 'Skol.' Turning, he eyed Saffron critically. 'So you're the new boyfriend. She hasn't mentioned you. You in the Services?'

'The Air Force,' Saffron muttered.

'Pity.'

'Pity?'

'Pity she chose tonight. I was kept in town late and thought I'd use the flat.'

Struggling to understand, Saffron was only sinking deeper into confusion. 'You don't mind my being here?'

'Why the hell should I?'

'But don't you live here?'

'No. My place is over in Hout Bay. You should get Syn to

124

bring you out there sometime. Swimming pool, drinks, you'd like it.' The man downed his drink, then set his glass on the cabinet. 'Well, as things stand I'd better be on my way. Enjoy yourself.'

Saffron had long convinced himself the world he lived in was mad but there are limits even to madness and his impulsive suggestion almost touched off a bout of hysteria. 'Why don't you stay?'

He received an amicable slap across his bare back as the man made for the door. 'Decent of you to offer, old man, but it wouldn't be fair to Syn, would it? Don't worry about me. There's an hotel just round the corner.'

With his puritanism hammered to the floor and sobbing for help, Saffron's question was forced from him. 'Can I ask you something?'

The man popped his head back into the room. 'What, old man?'

'You won't take offence?'

'I don't know, do I? But shouldn't think so.'

'It's about you and Synevva. I mean, if the two of you live separate lives like this, what's the point in being married?'

The man's expression changed dramatically. 'That's a hell of a question, isn't it?'

'Is it?' Saffron asked in alarm.

'Yes, it damn well is. Syn's a great kid. What're you trying to do? Come between us?'

Saffron realized that somewhere he had made a horrible mistake. 'No. Not at all. I just can't. . . .'

'Just nothing! Listen, Saffron. If I woke Syn up and said I wanted to stay the night, you'd be out in the street. And so would any girlfriend of mine if Syn came round to my place. The kid and I have got our priorities right. Understand that?'

'Yes,' Saffron lied. 'I'm sorry. Only . . .'

He received a glare of dislike. 'Only nothing. I'd a feeling there was something odd about you, Saffron, the moment I walked in. Syn usually gets me to vet her boyfriends but you're one that's slipped through the net. I'm phoning her first thing in the morning. I don't like people who try to come between a man and his wife.'

The door slammed resentfully. Reeling down the room

Saffron gulped down half a glass of whisky before returning to the bedroom. He felt no surprise on seeing Synevva was still sleeping like a child. Slumping on the bed, he put his head between his hands.

The girl woke just before dawn. Turning, she reached out sleepily. 'Darling. Wake up.' A few seconds later she sat upright. 'Darling! Where are you?'

There was no reply. With his puritanism dealt a blow from which it might never recover, instinct had told Saffron it was wiser to go. One thought sustained him as he plodded sadly through the dark and empty streets back to Breconfield. For the rest of his life he would always remember his night in Aphrodite's cave.

CHAPTER 18

Saffron opened the door of the SCI's office cautiously. 'You want to see me, sir?'

Sedgley-Jones appeared to be reading a letter. He folded it, slipped it into a drawer, then turned his cold eyes on Saffron.

'Yes. Come in and close the door.'

Saffron obeyed and stood to attention. Drawing a pile of forms towards him, Sedgley-Jones kept him in that most ludicrous position for a full seven seconds before giving him a nod. 'Stand at ease, Corporal.'

Saffron made certain his right foot stamped down hard enough to rattle objects on the officer's desk. He earned a glance of disapproval. 'There's no need to drill a hole through the floorboards!'

'Of course not, sir. I'm sorry.'

Sedgley-Jones gave him another cold stare, then indicated the pile of forms. 'I've just received your weekly report on Observer Course 16.'

Saffron, who for the last two weeks had been giving bombing instruction to No 16 Observer Course while their regular instructor was on leave, decided a question was the safest reply until he knew what the score was.

'You have, sir?'

Sedgley-Jones lifted the top copy from the pile. 'This is

your report on Pupil Observer Villiers. You recommend that he is taken off aircrew training at once.' As Saffron nodded, the officer leaned forward. 'Your reason is "a permanent time-lag error". I'd like you to explain that expression to me, Corporal.'

Recognizing trouble when he saw it, Saffron proceeded cautiously. 'It means he has slow reactions, sir. It shows whenever he goes out on a bombing or gunnery exercise. He consistently overshoots the target.'

'Are you saying he has a physical defect?'

'Not physical in the general sense, sir. It's his nervous reflexes that are slow. Before he can react, the target's gone past his sights. It's a fault that can't be cured.'

Sedgley-Jones's pale eyes travelled from Saffron's expressionless face down to his polished shoes and back again before he spoke. 'I know you are a man of many parts, Corporal, so it's possible I still don't know all your qualifications. Are you by any chance a doctor too?'

Saffron gazed straight ahead. 'No, I'm not a doctor, sir.'

'Then will you please explain what God-given insight tells you a man has permanently slow reactions?'

'I know because I've had experience of it before, sir.'

'I see. So with your vast experience you recommend we ground a man who has had consistently high marks in every other subject?'

'A bomb-aimer's no good if he can't drop bombs or fight off enemy aircraft,' was Saffron's imprudent remark.

'Don't be impertinent, Corporal.'

'I wasn't being impertinent, sir. I'm giving you my reason why I'm recommending Villiers is remustered to ground staff.'

'Have you any idea how much money the Air Force has already spent on this man?'

'I think so, sir.'

'Then isn't it absurd to ground him at this stage? Probably all he needs is more practice. And even if it is his reflexes, he'll learn how to compensate for them.'

'He won't, sir,' Saffron said doggedly. 'There's no way of allowing for them. Not in combat, anyway.'

Sedgley-Jones's manicured hands tightened on the sheet of paper. 'I want you to withdraw this recommendation, Saffron, and to give this man more practice. You'll fly with him personally and do everything you can to help him. Do I make myself clear?'

In went Saffron's heels. 'I'll do all I can to help him, sir. But I can't withdraw my recommendation.'

Sedgley-Jones's cheeks went pale. 'What was that?'

'I can't withdraw my report, sir. It's what I believe and it's my duty to say it.'

'Your duty, Corporal Saffron, is to do as you're told. If I say you withdraw this report, you withdraw it.'

Breathing equally hard, Saffron glanced at the door. 'Then I shall want an officer to witness that order, sir. May I call in Flight Lieutenant Price?'

The paper in Sedgley-Jones's hand trembled as if in a high wind. 'Are you bent on self-destruction, Saffron?'

'I don't think so, sir.'

'You are,' Sedgley-Jones said hoarsely. 'Believe me, Saffron, you are.'

'If you say so, sir.'

Sedgley-Jones closed his eyes tightly. When he opened them he had regained a modicum of self-control. 'I'm going to ignore this recommendation. In the meantime you'll do everything in your power to help this pupil. I shall want another report in a week's time. Is that understood?'

'Yes, sir.'

'Then get out of my office.'

'Bastard,' Saffron said, dropping morosely into a chair.

MacFarlane, talking to Alec Prentice and another instructor at the far side of the staff room, turned and grinned. 'Again?'

'This time it's your own fault,' Bickers said, one buttock on the table. 'If he wants you to chuck out your report, why not? It's no skin off your nose.'

'But what I said is true. Villiers' reflexes are terrible.'

'So they're terrible. You think they'll lose us the war?'

'What about the poor sods who'll have to fly with him? How'd you like someone who can't hit a barn door at ten feet defending your back?'

The shrug of Bickers' shoulders gave his views of such hypotheses. 'That's their rough luck, isn't it?'

Saffron was genuinely shocked. 'That's a hell of a way to think.'

'Why? If we put the standards up as high as you'd like 'em, we wouldn't have an Air Force at all. You think the Jerries are any better trained?'

'But this bloke can't drop a bomb within a mile of the target.'

'So what? He can hit a bloody city, can't he? And that's what we're bombing these days. You want to get up to date, mate.'

'With instructors like you about, maybe that's why we're having to,' Saffron grunted with unkind intent. 'You're no Dead-Eye Dick yourself, are you?'

Struck below the belt, the indignant Bickers swung a low blow himself. 'You know why he's like this?' he asked the three instructors. 'It's that Synevva Helgman woman. She's thrown him over after only one night in bed. Must shake a man up, a thing like that.'

Saffron sat bolt upright. 'That's a bloody lie and you know it!'

'We've only got your word for it, mate,' Bickers said maliciously.

The good-natured Alec Prentice tried to check the sniping before it turned into full-scale warfare. 'Don't you know who this Villiers kid is?'

Saffron was still glaring at Bickers. 'No. Who?'

'His old man's a prominent politician in the Cape Provincial Government. Simon Villiers. You must have seen his name in the papers.'

Saffron was beginning to understand. 'The creep!'

Bickers gave a loud chortle. 'It's not so funny when the chickens come home to roost, is it?'

Saffron turned on him beligerently. 'And what's that supposed to mean?'

'Your system, mate. That's what it means.'

'You think it couldn't happen in Russia?'

'Never. It's not the old school tie that counts there: it's the sweat on your brow.'

'Then it's a bloody good job you're not there. You're about the laziest bastard on the station.'

Bickers gave a revengeful sniff. 'It's amazing what a bad night in bed can do to a man. What did she do – tell you it's too small?'

Saffron's chair clattered to the floor as he leapt up. 'You

129

make that crack once more – just once more – and I'll do you.'

The three hilarious South Africans moved forward to separate the two men but Bickers, a past master at avoiding danger, had snatched up his books and was already at the door. There he threw his last barb. 'There's no point in acting like a mad dog and biting all your friends. Your solution, mate, is to live within your capabilities and find a woman who's easier to please. Someone like a fifty-year-old widow.'

The three men grabbed Saffron as he launched himself forward. Eyes glinting maliciously, Bickers hurried out into the safety of the quadrangle. 'I'll have him for this,' Saffron said hoarsely. 'I will. You'll see.'

Yells of hysterical laughter sent an inquisitive cat running for its life. Saffron eyed the South Africans resentfully. 'It's not that funny. What if people believe him?'

Alec Prentice dried his eyes. 'Talk about a love-hate relationship. No wonder they call you Tweedledum and Tweedledee.'

'He's no more of a Commie than I am,' Saffron growled. 'It's just an excuse for easy-riding.'

A fourth instructor, an RAF corporal called Jones, entered the staff room. His eyes fixed immediately on Saffron. 'Why aren't you playing in the match tomorrow?'

Saffron gave a despondent shrug. 'I'm stuck with this bloody observer course. They've a ciné camera exercise in the morning.'

'So what? It's Saturday. You're still off in the afternoon, aren't you?'

'The match is down for the morning,' Saffron explained. 'Wingfield have a parade in the afternoon. Some big bug is visiting them.'

'But this is the important one. Price must be throwing a fit.'

'He is. But what can he do? Sedgley-Jones is behind it.'

'What about Mills or Johnstone? Can't either of them stand in for you?'

'Mills is already taking them. Johnstone's been given compassionate leave over the weekend. His father's had a heart attack or something.'

Alec Prentice, joining the discussion, was looking puzzled.

'But if they've got Mills already, why do they want you?'

'I'm supposed to go up in the target plane,' Saffron told him.

'In a Hind? But instructors never do that. What's the point?'

'It's a new idea the bastards have come up with. Their argument is that an instructor with combat experience can help to make the exercise more realistic.'

'But that's a load of bull. No pilot's going to take advice from the rear cockpit. Not even if they fit speaking tubes in.'

'Right,' Saffron said savagely. 'All I'll be able to do is sit on my arse while the pilot flies as he always flies. But it's a good way of getting at me and Price, isn't it?'

'I'll stand in if you like,' Prentice offered.

Saffron, who had forgotten Prentice's aircrew background, gave a start. Then he shook his head. 'You can't do that. You said you were going away for the weekend. What would Laura say?'

'She wouldn't mind putting it off. Not when she hears the reason. Only there's a chance they might turn me down. Remember I'm not an SAI.'

'They might try but Price wouldn't let 'em get away with it. It's combat experience they're supposed to want and you've got more than me.'

'Then it's settled. What kite are the observers using? Old Sally?'

Old Sally was an ageless Anson used for a multitude of purposes including camera gunnery. Saffron, whose gloom had perceptibly lightened, nodded. 'You know they've put a new starboard engine in her?'

'So I'm told. They say she flies in ever-decreasing circles now.'

'The sooner the better,' Saffron grinned. He followed Prentice to the door. 'Will you tell Price yourself? It'll look better.'

'Right after this lecture,' Prentice promised.

Saffron waited until the South African was a dozen yards away, then shouted after him. 'It's decent of you, Alec. Remind me to do the same for you sometime.'

Prentice glanced back. 'It's the least a man can do for someone with your problems.' His good-natured laugh fol-

131

lowed as Saffron bent down and pretended to throw a flower pot after him.

Saffron was lecturing to his armourers that morning and the break bell went when he was in the middle of a sentence. Traumatically conditioned, he paused and braced himself but although Course 21 shivered like an expectant puppy, it stayed obediently on its tail. Remembering his new status and determined to preserve it at all costs, Saffron finished his sentence and added two more before laying the chalk at the foot of the blackboard. His air as he faced the thirty tense trainees was that of a Roman centurion reviewing a clutch of slaves.

'All right. You've got ten minutes. Not a second longer. And I want none of that Rugby scrimmaging in the quadrangle. You'll walk out in twos. Van der Merve – take over.'

Respectful silence followed him as he swept out. Heady with power, he was making for the staff room when a yell from the other side of the quadrangle brought him down to earth. 'Saffron! Come over here on the double!'

The comical figure of Price was jigging excitedly up and down inside his shorts as Saffron approached. 'Alec's been to see me. Isn't it bloody marvellous?'

'Can you fix it with Kruger?' Saffron asked.

'They can't do much about it, can they? Not now Alec's volunteered.' The thought of beating Wingfield was making Price look like a wicked pixie as he rubbed his hands together. 'Now we can sort out that left wing of theirs. I don't want any nonsense, Saffron. I want him done in the first five minutes.'

The quadrangle had already emptied of the mass of armourer trainees. All that sounded now was the tramp, tramp of Course 21 as it headed for the swing doors. In his excitement Price failed to notice them.

'It could make all the difference. That little bastard's got the legs on all our other defenders.' Price rubbed his hands again in unholy anticipation. 'By the centre, we'll rub it in if we beat 'em, Saffron. We'll have a party in the Del Monico they'll talk about for twenty years.'

The vanguard of Course 21 had almost reached them. Price moved absent-mindedly aside, then gaped as the men, arms swinging, marched past in twos with the giant Van der Merve controlling them from the rear. 'That's your squad, isn't it?'

Savouring the moment, Saffron nodded. Price watched the trainees pass as if watching a vision. 'Is it a joke or something?'

'No, sir.'

'Then what the hell is it?'

'Nothing. I've just decided they need discipline.'

Price watched the last man vanish from the quadrangle, then swung round. 'All right, Saffron. How have you done it?'

'It's simple, sir. It's just a matter of impressing your personality on them.'

'Don't give me that bullshit, Saffron. What are you doing? Bribing 'em?'

Saffron hid his grin. 'Nothing like that, sir.'

'Don't lie. What is it – free booze?'

'No, sir.'

'Then you've got some women lined up for them?' When Saffron shook his head again, Price's bird-like eyes narrowed. 'Don't get the idea you're keeping this to yourself, Saffron.'

'I'm not keeping anything to myself, sir. I've told you. It's just a matter of personality and discipline.'

'You're a deep bastard, Saffron.' Price's scowl was ferocious. 'But the war effort's bigger than both of us. I'll get it out of you if I have to use thumbscrews. By the centre I will.'

CHAPTER 19

Football boots and sidekit slung over his shoulder, Saffron pushed into Bickers' cubicle. 'You ready?' Finding the newly-shaved Londoner combing back his hair, Saffron rounded his eyes mockingly. 'Beautiful. The Brylcreem Boy himself.'

'Girls go to these matches, don't they?' Bickers said, climbing into his tunic.

133

'They do when Breconfield play. Didn't you know we're the glamour team of the league?'

'The rest must be a pretty ropy lot,' Bickers grunted, slotting on his cap at just the right angle. 'The girls are the reason I'm coming, mate. While you're wasting your energy chasing a pig's bladder, I'll be playing the sidelines.'

Grinning, Saffron followed him out into the morning sunlight. 'Better than the classroom, isn't it? So don't let's hear any more about your losing out by being a friend of mine.'

His reminder that Price, in his delight that Saffron could play in the match, had given Bickers the morning off changed the Londoner's expression. 'The morning's still young, mate. I've still got plenty of time to break a couple of arms or legs.'

The words had barely left his mouth before a shout made both men turn. The gesticulating figure of Du Plessis was running from the quadrangle towards them. Panting, he drew to attention before Saffron.

'Flight Lieutenant Price wants to see you, Corporal. At once, please.'

'Where is he?'

'In his office.'

'Isn't he going to the match with us?'

'I think there's been an accident of some kind, Corporal. But I'm not sure what.'

Saffron began to run. Muttering his disbelief Bickers followed him. Price, looking pale and upset, met the two corporals at the door of his office. 'This is an emergency, Saffron. The match is off. Get fifteen men from your course and double' em over to the stores to collect a pick and shovel apiece. You'll also want a block and tackle. I've alerted the stores to have 'em ready. Then meet me at the transport we were using for the soccer team. Bickers had better come along too. Move, for Christ's sake.'

The bewildered Saffron paused. 'But what's happened, sir?'

'There's been a hell of a prang over the range,' Price muttered.

Saffron froze. 'Not the Hind?'

He was never to forget Price's expression as the tiny officer tried to look away. 'The Hind and the Anson. Straight in.'

134

'Oh, Jesus Christ!' Before Saffron could react, Price gave him a violent shove. 'Stop wasting time. We're needed out there.'

Price braked as the WAAF ran out of the quadrant hut. 'Which way, love?'

The white-faced girl pointed down a rutted track. 'About a mile down there, sir.'

'Has a crash wagon and two officers arrived yet?'

'Yes, sir. I showed them the way.'

Price's last question was asked gently. 'Are there any survivors, love?'

The girl was perilously close to tears. 'Nobody got out, sir. We saw it happen. It was horrible.'

Price nodded and revved the engine. Alongside him Bickers and Saffron sat in frozen silence. Rolling and bumping, its tyres throwing back sand, the 25cwt followed the track round the base of a large dune. As it crested a rise, Saffron pointed to a thin trail of smoke rising from behind another dune. Price swung the wheel over and a couple of minutes later drew up beside a crash wagon and Sedgley-Jones's estate car. Jumping out, Saffron ran to the rear of the transport and unhooked the tailgate. 'Come on. Everyone out.'

Slinging down their equipment, the subdued trainees jumped down into the sand. Telling Van der Merve to bring them as soon as they were ready, Saffron ran after Price and Bickers. As the shoulder of the dune fell away he saw another WAAF sitting on a grassy knoll and sobbing hysterically. Out of earshot of her, Sedgley-Jones and Kruger were talking to a distraught South African corporal. The uniforms of all three men were stained with soot and ash.

The group were on the perimeter of the crash area whose epicentre appeared to be another dune forty yards on, where the still-smoking fuselage of the Anson was protruding from its base. The crash had driven one wing and engine back into the fuselage and petrol from the ruptured tanks had completed the devastation. Foam had been sprayed on the wreck by the crash team Sedgley-Jones had brought and two men were currently spraying the second engine that lay a couple of hundred yards away. No civilian rescue teams were present – Saffron doubted if they had been alerted yet – and there was no sign of the Hind.

Price and Bickers had already reached Sedgley-Jones's party and as Saffron approached, the tiny officer drew him aside. 'It's going to be even nastier than we feared. I hope your men have strong stomachs.'

'Where's the Hind?' Saffron muttered.

Price nodded to the east. 'Over there. They've recovered one body and the other can't be found. So this job's more urgent. Let's go and see what has to be done.'

Saffron followed him into a shallow depression littered with scraps of metal. After a moment's hesitation, Bickers followed them. Among the smells that blanketed the hollow was one all too familiar to Saffron. A row of charred bushes hid the fuselage from sight until the three men pushed through them.

The foam-covered fuselage was now only forty feet away. Price, a few yards ahead of the other two, gave a low curse and stopped dead. Saffron followed his eyes and the blood drained from his face.

The corpse of a man was propped up by spars in the vicinity of the mid-upper turret. The fury of the fire had charred the left side of the body to ashes but by some freak of incineration the right side, although stripped of clothes, had been left almost intact. Like some grotesque harlequin, the black and white creature stared at the three horrified men through the skeleton fuselage. 'Oh, my God,' Bickers muttered.

Saffron felt a tap on his shoulder. Alongside him, Price was looking drawn and pale. 'It's bloody nasty, isn't it? But I think it's better you tackle this mess than the other one, don't you?'

It was a moment before Saffron understood why he was being given a choice. 'Whose body did they find, sir?'

Price looked away. 'The pilot's.'

'Then I'd rather take a party to the Hind, sir.'

Price scowled. 'I don't think you should.'

'Please, sir.'

The tiny officer hesitated a moment, then turned away with an exclamation. 'All right, I'll fix it with the SCI. Now let's go and make up the working parties.'

* * *

With Sedgley-Jones giving priority to the Anson and its gruesome cargo, no objection was raised to Saffron taking a salvage party to the Hind. The party, consisting of Saffron and five men from Course 21, were driven over to the crashed aircraft by the South African corporal who was in charge of the quadrant huts.

The Hind was nearly a mile away. The mid-air collision had torn the wings off and the fuselage, weighted by the engine, had plummeted down and buried itself in the sand. With no parachutes seen by the quadrant observers, it was assumed that Prentice was buried somewhere near the engine and Saffron's first task was to dig out his body.

Perhaps because of its high terminal speed and the deep sand, the fuselage of the Hind had not caught fire. It had driven into the sand at a slight angle and after estimating where the engine might be, Saffron started his men digging. An hour of back-breaking work brought little reward, the sand seeping back into the hole almost before their spades emerged. With the sun high overhead and all six men stripped to the waist and caked in sand, Saffron had to commence shift work, three men digging while three rested.

Van der Merve and Moulang were in his party. Unlike their comrades, none of the five high-spirited trainees had seen the Anson at close quarters and as their spades brought up only sand or fractured pieces of metal, the grisly purpose of the work began slipping from their minds. Horseplay had begun breaking out and Van der Merve, worth three men when he was digging, had asked Saffron if he might go for a swim.

Resting on his spade during his five minute break, Saffron gazed back. The haze of smoke over the distant dunes betrayed the site of the crashed Anson. Saffron wondered how Bickers was faring. So far the worst task had fallen on the other party although by this time they must surely have cut all the bodies out. Remembering Bickers' earlier designs, Saffron felt an alarming impulse to laugh. Football, girls, cheering crowds, and then, out of the blue, this. The treachery of life.

The clink of metal made him turn. Van der Merve drove down his spade again, then straightened his broad back and grinned up at Saffron.

'Something solid down here, Corporal.'

Saffron jumped down into the excavation. Men gathered round him as he scraped an oily, sand-covered mound that lay to one side of the crushed fuselage. 'It's the engine all right,' he said. Remembering the South African corporal had walked back to the south quadrant hut, he gazed round the circle of faces. 'Any of you drive?'

'I can, Corporal.' It was Moulang.

'I want you to take the transport over to the other party and ask if they've finished with the block and tackle. Bekker and Stein, go with him. Get a move on. We don't want to be here all day.'

Gazing down at the sand, Saffron had an afterthought. 'Moulang!'

'Yes, Corporal.'

'Better bring a couple of sacks with you as well.'

The transport arrived back fifteen minutes later with Price aboard. He jumped down into the excavation with Saffron. 'A mobile crane arrived ten minutes ago. If you want to wait, I can send it over.'

Saffron motioned him nearer and pointed at a stain in the sand at one side of the mound. Price's voice dropped. 'You don't think he's under it?'

'I don't see where else he can be.'

Price examined the twisted section of the fuselage that the digging had uncovered. 'I think you're right. The logerons snapped and doubled the engine back. So you think we'd better use the block and tackle?'

Saffron met his eyes. 'It might be better. As we have it here.'

Nodding, Price scrambled out of the pit and began supervising the erection of the block and tackle over the engine. Before the chain was lowered Saffron jumped down and scraped around the engine for an anchorage point. Seeing he was unable to find one on the top of the engine and was compelled to dig lower, Van der Merve jumped into the pit to help. He gave a start as Saffron turned on him angrily.

'Did I tell you to come down here?'

'No, Corporal. But. . . .'

'Get back to the others. That means now!'

With a puzzled glance at Saffron's drawn face, the giant Afrikander obeyed. After another minute of scraping Saffron motioned for the hook to be lowered. Attaching it, he

138

stood back and waved the men to take up their positions.

The tripod creaked as the team heaved on the tackle. When the engine remained rooted, Price joined them. The chain quivered with strain but the engine held. Spade in hand, Saffron identified the points of adhesion and gingerly prodded at them. As Price yelled for another heave, sand began falling away and a moment later, to a cheer from the men that drowned the obscene sucking noise it made, the engine began to move upwards.

With the trainees occupied with swinging the engine away, Saffron was the only one with the time to glance into the hole it had left. He met Price's inquiring glance as the officer appeared on the rim of the pit. 'We were right, sir.'

Price jumped in alongside him and drew in his breath. 'Jesus Christ!'

Saffron heard a laugh as the unsuspecting trainees over by the engine shared a joke. 'We can handle this ourselves, can't we, sir?'

Price gave him a look of respect. 'They have to learn what it's all about sooner or later, lad.'

'I know that, sir. But this is going in at the deep end with their hands tied.'

Price took another look into the hole and drew back. 'You could be right. Get them out of the way and bring me the sacks.'

'I didn't mean that, sir. I'll handle it myself.'

'Like hell you will, lad. Go and have a smoke. I'll give you a call when I want you.'

'No, sir. I must do this myself. Please let me.'

Price stared into Saffron's pale, earnest face. 'You're being stupid, lad. Can't you see that?'

'I still want to do it, sir.'

'Oh, eff off,' Price muttered. Hs climbed out of the excavation and gave an irascible yell. 'All right, you lot. You can take a rest now. Over by the transport. Stay there until I call you. You, Van der Merve. Throw the sacks over here.'

The curious men drifted away. Price's pinched face appeared again over the rim of the hole. 'Listen. We're doing this together, so no more bloody arguing. I'm ready when you are.'

Picking up his spade, Saffron began digging gingerly

around the blood-soaked hole. Price's face grew paler as he watched. It was nearly five minutes before Saffron was ready. 'Use your spade,' Price said hoarsely. 'What difference does it make now?'

Saffron found that sacrilegious. Although he hesitated a long time, he finally reached down with his hands. Insulated by the sand and the engine, the blood-stained fragment was still warm. Stumbling across the floor of the excavation, he held it up to Price. Meeting his eyes the tiny officer muttered something, then threw away his spade, and held out his arms.

The gruesomeness of the task increased as Saffron fumbled deeper into the hole. Over by the transport the laughter and chatter of the trainees died as they realized what was happening. Numbed by the work, neither Saffron nor Price noticed Van der Merve until he jumped into the excavation alongside Saffron. The irrepressible buoyancy of his voice made Saffron think of a breeze breaking into an airless tomb. 'You take that side and I'll take this, Corporal. That way we'll soon get it over.'

Before Saffron could protest, the giant had tugged out a splintered limb from the sand and offered it up to Price. His matter-of-fact manner as he turned and probed with his spade made Price nod his head at Saffron. Like some ghastly game of hunt-the-thimble the contesseration of Prentice's body continued. The climax came when Van der Merve gave a grunt of triumph and offered an object the size of a football up to Price. The small officer placed it gently into a sack, then, as the Afrikander turned away, his eyes closed tightly. Although half-blinded with horror himself, Saffron managed to reach up and grip his arm. Price took a deep breath, gave Saffron a nod of gratitude, and wiped his hands in the sand. 'All right. That'll do. Let's get back to the others.'

With the trainees apprehensively eyeing the two tied-up sacks that bounced at their feet, Price drove the transport back to the main party. The scene there was now one of ordered activity. New arrivals were clustered around the remnants of the Anson and the mobile crane was ferrying wreckage on to a transporter. With the bodies from the Anson removed by ambulance, the original arrivals were seated on a knoll eating a packed lunch. Saffron and Price had a wash in a bucket loaned them by the salvage crew, then the tiny officer began handing out sandwiches while Saffron went looking for Bickers. He found the Londoner seated twenty yards from the others. Smoking a cigarette, he looked pale and distressed. Saffron sank down beside him.

'How's it gone?'

Bickers gave a groan. 'Do me a favour in the future, mate.'

'What's that?'

'Don't do me any favours. No invitations, nothing.'

Saffron managed a wan grin. 'It didn't work out too well, did it?'

'Work out?' Bickers gave a heartfelt shudder. 'I'll have nightmares about it for the rest of my life. Do you know why that WAAF was hysterical? She says someone heard a man screaming for minutes after the Anson crashed. In that furnace.'

Saffron opened his mouth to protest, then hunched his back and plucked a blade of grass. As he toyed with it, Bickers jerked an outraged thumb at the row of eating trainees. 'You know what's in those sandwiches?'

Saffron shook his head.

'Ham. mate! Bloody red ham. You imagine it?'

Before Saffron could reply, a guttural voice made both men start and turn. 'Well, Saffron. How are you feeling?'

Kruger, hands on hips, was standing straddle-legged over them. Saffron hesitated, then climbed wearily to his feet. 'I'm feeling all right – sir.'

'I'm glad to hear it. Although I'm surprised.'

'Surprised, sir?'

'Yes. I'd have imagined that in the circumstances it would have been a shock.'

Saffron found he was suddenly trembling. 'In what circumstances, sir?'

'Surely that's obvious.'

'It's not obvious to me.'

'Then you're obviously not the sensitive type, Corporal.'

The blade of grass wrapped round Saffron's fingers snapped. 'You're disappointed I wasn't in that Hind, aren't you?'

'I couldn't care one way or the other, Saffron. But I'd imagine Prentice's wife will feel differently.'

I'm going to hit this sadistic bastard, Saffron thought in sudden panic. I'm going to smash his mouth to pulp. His legs were already in motion when there was an urgent yell.

'Saffron! Sit down!'

Eyes clearing, Saffron saw that Price and Sedgley-Jones were less than six yards away. The normally good-natured Price resembled an enraged terrier as he ran up alongside Kruger. Only Saffron, Bickers and Sedgley-Jones were near enough to hear his threat.

'Warrant Officer Kruger, you listen to me. If you make this lad feel any worse for what's happened, I'll destroy you. I mean it. Not another word of it, now or later. You got that?'

Kruger, red-faced and stiffly at attention, threw a glance at Sedgley-Jones. The fair-headed SCI, his eyes on Price's face, turned away.

'You hear me?' Price hissed.

'Yes. sir.'

'Then piss off!'

Kruger snapped up a salute, allowed himself a single glance at Saffron, then marched stiff-legged across the sand after Sedgley-Jones. Price glared at Saffron. 'You were going to hit the bastard, weren't you?'

'Yes, sir.'

'Then show some sense. That's what he wants you to do.'

As Saffron murmured something and slumped down, Price's expression changed. 'I wouldn't have blamed you, lad. I've met 'em all shapes and sizes but that's one for the book. Have a fag and then get your men together. OK?'

As Saffron nodded, Price noticed Van der Merve approaching the other trainees. The benign giant had a fistful of sandwiches and was munching them happily. With reaction calling for a victim, Price let out another yell.

'Van der Merve! Have you washed your hands yet?'

The giant was clearly taken aback by the question. 'My hands? No, sir. I didn't know we had any water.'

A strangled sound brought Price round. Saffron, his outraged stomach taking its revenge at last, was doubled up over a clump of grass.

CHAPTER 20

Bickers sniffed. 'We made a deal. Share and share alike.'

'Share alike?' Saffron said indignantly. 'This is the third Friday in a row.'

'So what? You haven't a girl to take there. You're still mooning over that Synevva woman.'

'That doesn't mean you've the right to grab the flat for yourself every time the old woman visits her relatives.'

'Once a week,' Bickers pointed out. 'That leaves you six other days. So why be so bloody mean?'

'I wanted a quiet night tomorrow,' Saffron muttered. 'Why can't you go to the girl's home? She's got a home, hasn't she?'

'Oh, sure,' Bickers said sarcastically. 'Girls' parents have a way of lending you their bedrooms. Anyway, this isn't Betty. It's Valerie. I only met her on Tuesday.'

Saffron glanced at MacFarlane who was sharing the same table in the Corporals' Mess. 'He meets her on Tuesday and beds her on Friday. Lover Boy himself. What do you do? Make out you're a fighter pilot or something?'

For a moment Bickers forgot he was asking a favour. 'I suppose an experience like yours does leave a man with sour grapes. Why not ring her and see if she'll give you a second chance? You could always stuff yourself with stout and oysters.'

At Saffron's reaction Bickers grinned shame-facedly and picked up their glasses. 'Only joking, mate. This round's mine.'

Saffron's vengeful eyes followed the Londoner to the bar. He leaned towards MacFarlane. 'Are you still friendly with that corporal in the Sick Bay?'

'You mean Nolan? Yes. Why?'

'Will he do you a favour?'

MacFarlane grinned. 'You want Bickers put down?'

'In a way.' As Saffron explained, the South African gave a horrified chortle. 'You're not serious?'

'I am. It'll teach him a lesson.' Seeing MacFarlane had scruples, Saffron offered a bribe. 'If you do it, you can be

143

with me when he comes out. It'll be better than a seat at the Palladium.'

MacFarlane's better nature succumbed to the temptation. 'You're on. I'll nip round to see Nolan before I turn in.'

Full of brotherly love towards a world that contained the delights he was soon to enjoy, Bickers gazed benignly round the bar of the Hoop and Grapes. 'You know, this isn't a bad pub. We're lucky to have it close by.'

Saffron winked at MacFarlane. 'What about another stout?'

Bickers hesitated. 'Think I should?'

'Why not? A man can't have enough lead in his pencil, can he?'

'That's true enough. But let me buy them.'

Saffron drew the euphoric Londoner back. 'It's your night, so it's my treat. Stay here and talk to Mac.'

Bickers' eyes followed Saffron affectionately to the bar. 'You know, Saffron's all right. A bit of a reactionary at times but that's his background. His heart's in the right place.'

MacFarlane grinned. 'How's the girl getting here?'

'She's borrowing her father's car. He thinks she's spending the evening with an old school friend.'

'How long have you got before your landlady gets back?'

'She usually comes in round eleven. So if we leave at 10.30 we should be OK.' Rubbing his hands with enormous smugness, Bickers glanced at his watch. 'Three hours of heaven, mate! Starting in fifteen minutes' time.'

Saffron pushed through the surrounding crowd and handed him a pint of stout. 'Try this for size.'

Bickers took a gulp and frowned. 'This stuff has an odd taste, hasn't it? I thought the last one had too.'

Saffron glanced at MacFarlane. 'You notice anything?'

The South African took a sip of his own stout, then grinned. 'It's Vitblitz.'

'Vitblitz?' Bickers asked.

'A special stout they brew in the Transkei. It's supposed to be full of vitamins. Great for this,' and MacFarlane bent up a significant forearm.

Bickers' face cleared. 'It is?'

'Marvellous, man. The best.' MacFarlane turned to the innocent-faced Saffron. 'Expensive, wasn't it?'

Saffron waved a modest hand. Touched by the gesture, Bickers drew him aside. 'There's just one thing, mate. You didn't take those things I said about you and that Synevva woman seriously, did you?'

Roaring with laughter at the suggestion, Saffron slapped his shoulder. 'Me? We're friends, aren't we? Doesn't that mean we can share a joke?'

The relieved Bickers decided it was a warm old wonderful old world. 'Be terrible if we couldn't, mate. What time's your match tomorrow?'

'Back to normal. In the afternoon.'

'Still at Wingfield?'

'Yes.'

'I might risk it and come,' Bickers said generously.

'You might? That's great.'

The two of them rejoined MacFarlane. Glancing at his watch again, Bickers downed his stout. 'I'll have to go. You two staying or moving on?'

'We'll probably stay,' MacFarlane told him.

'Great. Then I'll see you around 10.30. Don't drink too much. I won't be in any state to carry you home.' A glance in a mirror, a tug at his tie, and Bickers was ready. 'That's it then. Wish me luck.'

'We do,' Saffron said, not daring to look at MacFarlane.

Bickers went to the door where he paused to make a last-minute adjustment of his cap. Seeing Saffron and Mac-Farlane still watching him, he gave them a smirk before disappearing outside. Saffron gave an hysterical moan, 'Oh, brother,' and collapsed weakly on the South African's shoulder.

The girl, tall, blonde, and affecting an air of sophistication, giggled as she entered the austere bedroom. 'What a funny place. Do you really sleep here?'

A firm believer in making the best of one's drawbacks, Bickers rallied quickly. 'Maybe to you. But to us, used to bombshelters and fox-holes, it's a bit of heaven.'

Instead of the sympathy countless movies had assured him was his right, all Bickers received was a blank stare. 'It's the contrast, you see,' he said, trying again. 'You can't imagine what life's like over there. Bombs screaming down, ice-cold shelters, trying to snatch a few minutes sleep before you're up to fight off the next attack ... The same clothes on your back for weeks on end ... Dreaming of the girl you might never see again ... People over here can't imagine what it's like.'

The girl's somewhat long nose wrinkled fastidiously. 'I hope you change them more now you're here.'

'Change what?'

'Your clothes.'

'Clothes?'

'Yes. You said over in England you used to wear your clothes for weeks at a time. My father's always said the English aren't as clean as we are. He says some of you haven't even got bathrooms.'

The indignant Bickers momentarily forgot his objective. 'Who's your father? Goebbals?'

'Who?'

I've got a right lulu here, was Bickers' thought. 'Never mind. How about a drink?'

'You haven't asked me to sit down yet,' the girl complained.

Bickers hastily grabbed the only chair in the room, a high-backed monstrosity, and slid it beneath her. 'Sorry.'

She sank down on its plywood seat. 'It's not very comfortable, is it?'

Always the opportunist, Bickers patted the bed. 'It's softer on here. Try it while I open the wine.'

'On the bed?' She looked shocked.

'Think of it as a seat, not a bed,' Bickers suggested.

The girl hesitated, then sank with a giggle on the coverlet. 'I daren't think what Daddy would say. He'd probably have a heart attack if he knew I was out with a RAF.'

Bickers, deciding things were improving after an inauspicious start, took a bottle of sherry from the wardrobe. 'What's wrong with the RAF?'

'You must know what a reputation they've got with girls.'

With unconscious symbolism Bickers dug in the corkscrew. 'I'm glad you don't believe it.'

'Who said I don't?'

Hiding his glinting eyes, Bickers tugged at the cork. 'If you did you wouldn't be here with me tonight, would you?'

146

Proprieties appeased, the girl sank back. 'Naturally I'm expecting you to behave yourself.'

Except for this damned cork, things were coming along nicely, Bickers decided. As he took a fresh hold of the corkscrew, the girl sniggered. 'You're not very good at opening bottles, are you? What is it? Sherry?'

Bickers nodded. Leaning forward, the girl examined the label. 'It's not a very good one. My father always buys KWV.'

Scowling, Bickers braced himself and heaved. With a loud plop the cork shot out and showered his slacks with wine. As he dabbed himself with a handkerchief, the girl giggled again. 'I don't think you're used to drinking wine, are you?'

Bickers decided there was only one way to handle this situation. 'That's right. I'm not. I'm one of the licentious soldiery. Beer's my drink.' Before the surprised girl could answer he half-filled a tumbler with sherry and thrust it at her. 'Your father's right about us. Except that we're worse. All we live for is beer, women and fighting. Like animals.'

She shrank back as he dropped on the bed. Half-draining his glass, he turned and leered at her. 'Why do you think I asked you here? Because we like our women warm and in bed. That's why.'

'Stop being so silly.'

Bickers scowled. 'Who's being silly? You don't think I got you here to spout poetry, do you?' Taking the glass from her, he bore her down on the bed. Squirming, she tried to wriggle from beneath him.

Bickers took a dive at her, missed her mouth, and found himself biting her neck. As she heaved like a corvette in a heavy sea, he wondered for an uneasy moment if he could hold her. 'Relax and enjoy it,' he panted.

'I'll scream! I mean it. Let me go!'

Deciding if he was in for a penny he was in for a pound, Bickers found her lips with his mouth and pressed hard. She made muffled sounds and then suddenly wilted. A few seconds later Bickers felt her fingernails biting through his shirt. When he drew back, breathless but triumphant, her eyes were heavy. 'If you must behave like an animal, at least put the light out,' she muttered sullenly.

Staggering to the door, Bickers clicked off the light. When

he turned Valerie was slipping out of her dress. Dropping back on the bed in only bra and briefs, she stared at him defiantly. 'Well, what are you looking at?'

Remembering his role, Bickers threw himself on her again. As he pulled down her bra, he felt her tugging impatiently at his trousers. 'You're not making love to me in those, are you?'

With his lips glued to her mouth, Bickers tried to unfasten his fly buttons. The third one down was tight, and with only one unencumbered arm he struggled without success. With a cry of exasperation she reached down. 'For God's sake get them off.'

Their combined efforts got the trousers down to his knees where they stuck. Fumbling down, the girl gave a cry of disbelief. 'You've still got your shoes on.'

Legs locked together, Bickers managed to wriggle round and reach a lace. Kicking off the shoe, he fumbled down the other leg. Underneath him there was a gasp of pain. 'You're only digging your elbow in my stomach!'

Lost in the folds of his trousers, the other shoe proved obdurate and the red-faced Bickers was forced to roll off the girl and tackle the task with both hands. As his shoe thudded to the floor and his trousers followed it, Valerie gave a cry of relief. 'Thank God. You've taken long enough.'

The liberated Bickers discovered that during his travail she had removed her briefs as well as her bra. Eyes glinting at the sight he pushed her back and rolled on top of her again. Moaning, she dug her nails into his back and ran them down his spine. A few seconds passed and then her eyes opened. 'What's the matter?'

'Nothing's the matter,' Bickers said, startled.

'Don't be a fool. Of course there is.'

Glancing down at himself, the dismayed Bickers realized she was right.

'What is it?'

'I don't know,' Bickers muttered. 'Perhaps it was all that struggling to get undressed.'

'How could that affect you?'

'I don't know. But they say all kinds of things can.'

She stared up at him, then drew his hands down to her body and lifted her lips. Bickers, who was now feeling disturbingly lethargic, responded with a vigour born of desperation and the two of them threshed about wildly on the bed for another two minutes before the girl, with a cry of mortification, pushed him away.

'It's no use. Leave me alone.'

Bickers' lugubrious face was a study in embarrassment as he sat up. 'I don't understand it. It's never happened before.'

Valerie's laugh was hard with revenge. 'We've only your word for it.'

'But it's true.'

'I don't believe it. I think you're impotent.'

Bickers was aghast. 'You can't believe that.'

'If you aren't, then what other reason is there? Aren't I good enough for you?'

'Of course you are. I just don't understand it.'

Breathing hard, Valerie flung round and began dressing. 'You act like an animal and then you humiliate me like this. Don't just sit there! Get your clothes on.'

The doleful Bickers dragged on his trousers. As he reached for his shirt his desire to yawn proved irresistible. He heard the girl's gasp of anger.

'You're yawning! You're actually yawning!'

'I can't help it,' Bickers protested. 'Perhaps I'm sickening for the 'flu or something.'

Straightening her dress, the girl snatched her handbag from the chair and flung open the door. 'You're disgusting, Ken Bickers. Daddy was right about your kind. I've a good mind to tell him what's happened. If I do, he'll come after you with a sjambok.'

Bickers, deciding the affair was a dead duck, found he was too tired to care. 'Tell your Daddy anything you like. Tell him I hope the RAF drop a piss pot on his head.' Slumping down, Bickers gave a bitter grin. 'No, better still, tell him I hope he drowns himself in his bloody bathroom.'

With a sob of rage the girl turned and ran down the stairs. For a moment it seemed likely Bickers would hoist his legs on the bed and go to sleep. Instead, with a heartfelt groan, he rose and went over to the washstand. Five minutes later, a man carrying the cares of the world on his shoulders, he limped across the road to the Hoop and Grapes.

*   *   *

Bickers nodded resignedly. 'Just my bloody luck, mate. I get the room for the evening and she can't stay because her mother's ill.'

Saffron slid a glance at the grinning MacFarlane. 'But you still had forty minutes with her. Don't tell me you wasted it.'

'We aren't all animals, mate. Some of us consider a woman's feelings.'

Saffron acknowledged the rebuke. 'All the same, it can't have been easy. Not after all that vitblitz.'

'Oh, I don't know. You can't let a few drinks destroy your sense of decency, can you?'

Saffron slapped his shoulder. 'I like that. And she's sure to appreciate it the next time you meet.' Reaching through the crowd that surrounded them, he picked a full glass of stout from the counter. 'You can drink another vitblitz, can't you?'

'I don't see why not. Cheers.' Bickers took a sip and paused. 'You're sure this is vitblitz?'

'That's what I ordered. Why?'

Bickers took another sip. 'It tastes different to the stuff I had before.'

MacFarlane's shoulders were shaking. Giving him a warning look, Saffron glanced over his shoulder. Deciding the crowd was dense enough to afford protection he began backing away. His voice reached Bickers as he slipped behind a group of middle-aged men.

'Perhaps that's because it hasn't any bromide in it.'

It took Bickers a full five seconds to react. 'Bromide?'

With Saffron safely gone, MacFarlane took over. 'Saffron dosed your other booze with it.'

Some things are too wicked for a man to grasp readily and this was one. 'Bromide,' Bickers repeated.

MacFarlane was fighting off hysteria. 'You know. The stuff they're supposed to put in your tea when you join up.'

'Bromide!' Bickers said for the third time. For one touching moment his eyes showed relief. Then they flooded with homicidal rage. 'Where is he?'

The South African pointed to the street door. 'He's gone. Back to camp, I think.'

The howl Bickers released turned every face in the bar

150

in his direction. 'It's terrible! The worst thing I've ever heard! The dirty, treacherous bastard!'

As a buzz of curiosity rose Bickers gave another howl, threw himself into the crowd, and ran vengefully into the street. Thirty seconds later, when the commotion began to die, Saffron glanced cautiously from the door of the men's toilet and made his way towards MacFarlane. 'Has he gone?'

The South African was weeping hysterically. 'Hell for leather, mate. And screaming for vengeance.'

CHAPTER 21

Assisted by Saffron, Price rose to his feet and thumped a tankard of beer on the hotel table. 'All right, lads. Let's have a bit of quiet.'

Loud shushes came and elbows were knocked away. Swaying unsteadily, Price gazed at the twin rows of beery faces.

'Lads, I'm proud of you. At last we've done it ...'

A huge cheer drowned his voice. Price supported himself against the table until the noise died. 'A marvellous job, lads. I'd have been happy with a one goal win. But three ...' Another tremendous cheer interrupted him. 'Three bloody nil. I still can't believe it.'

'Nor can Wingfield,' someone shouted.

Price grinned his acknowledgement. 'Right. They didn't know what hit 'em, did they? Three bloody nil!'

As tankards and glasses thundered on the table, the street door of the large room opened and a dozen or so airmen began filing in. A mixed selection of RAF and South Africans, they were led by a huge moustached Warrant Officer who motioned them across the room in twos and threes. Sitting unobtrusively at nearby tables, they went unnoticed by the Breconfield team who were cheering Price's speech.

'It's on the house tonight, lads, so make the best of it. Don't forget there's a transport picking us up here at eleven – miss it and you could be in trouble.' Price gave a hiccup and then an impish grin. 'Three bloody nil! Marvellous. You didn't just beat the bastards, lads. You massacred 'em! Waiter! Let's have some more beer.'

A yell almost raised the roof as he sat down. As it faded and the rapturous Breconfield team turned itself on again, the big Warrant Officer stood up. 'Sir.'

Price peered round. 'Who was that?'

With a loud murmur and stir, the Breconfield team turned as one man. Saffron, as surprised as the rest, pointed at the moustached Warrant Officer. Price focused, then his tipsy face lit up. 'By the centre! MacDougall! You come to help us celebrate?'

'No, sir.'

'Then what have you come for?'

MacDougall drew himself erect. 'To tell you, sir, with respect, that your team is the dirtiest bunch of cloggers in the league. And that if you had to rely on football instead of muscle, you wouldn't make a good darts team. With respect, sir.'

With the look of a schoolboy offered a box of forbidden fruit, Price glanced at his hushed team. 'You hear that, lads? Mr MacDougall's opinion of you.'

There was a ferocious growl as the tiny officer turned back to the erect MacDougall. 'Does the rest of your team feel the same way, Mr MacDougall?'

The shout of assent from his men almost drowned MacDougall's reply. 'They think I'm being soft on you, sir. Their opinion is that you're dirty, scheming, unscrupulous and horrible. With respect, sir.'

Price's hiccup was inspired by pure delight. 'You hear that, lads? And we think that if Mr MacDougall took his team to the Windmill Theatre, they'd put bras and panties on the lot of 'em, don't we?' As men cheered, Price tore off his tunic and threw it on the table. His yell sounded like Henry V's battle cry at Agincourt.

'Three bloody nil, lads. Let's do it again!'

In two seconds pandemonium raged in the Del Monico. A tankard, smashing into a mirror behind the bar, showered the bartender with glass as he grabbed his telephone. Chairs flew through the air, threshing bodies collapsed to the floor, waiters fled for their lives. Saffron, dropping from a punch to the jaw, recovered and led an attack. With all track of time lost, he was trading punches with a useful South African at the back of the room when a yell made both men pause. 'Look out! MPs!'

152

One or two men, including Saffron's adversary, scattered. The rest fought on as whistles sounded and Redcaps came pouring through the street door. Only a few yards from Saffron, the midget Price, oblivious of his danger, was frenziedly but ineffectually butting the huge MacDougall in the stomach. Snatching his tunic from the table, Saffron caught hold of the battle-drunk officer and tried to drag him towards a back door. 'Come on, sir. You've got to get out of here.'

Price was still swinging punches. 'Three-nil! And every goal a good one, you bastards.'

Saffron managed to smother his arms and push him through the door. The corridor they found themselves in contained half a dozen hysterical members of the staff. At the sight of the two dishevelled airmen they dived for cover. Forcing Price into a run, Saffron pushed the tunic at him. 'Put it on, sir.'

The reeling Price tried to focus. 'Where're we going?'

Shrill whistles and the thud of blows followed them down the corridor. 'MPs,' Saffron panted, pausing at a street door. 'Dozens of 'em.'

'Oh, Christ,' Price muttered, momentarily sobered. Saffron, who had opened the door a few inches, saw it led into a darkened street. As another MP transport screamed to a halt at the front of the hotel, he turned his attention to Price. The midget's hair was all over his face, his nose was bleeding, his collar and tie gaped open, and his tunic was only half on. In the few seconds he dared spend, Saffron cleaned him up, then pushed him outside. Immediately Price headed for the main road. Saffron grabbed him and spun him round. 'What's the matter with you? You want to get caught?'

Whistles sounded and boots clattered as MPs searched for escapees. 'Run,' Saffron panted, pushing Price into a dark alley. As the drunken midget disappeared into the darkness there was a yell and the clatter of a dustbin lid, followed by the frenzied barking of a dog. Cursing, Saffron half-carried him to the road at the far end of the alley. There he pushed him into the entrance of an arcade of shops while he recovered his breath.

The road was well-lit, busy, and lined with shops. As he

153

gazed down it Saffron saw a taxi cross a set of traffic lights forty yards away. He grabbed Price's arm. 'Come on. We'll try to pick up a taxi on that corner.'

Price didn't move. Saffron tugged impatiently. 'Come on, sir. The Redcaps might have seen us enter that alley.'

Price let out an irascible yelp. 'How can I? He won't bloody let me.'

Saffron spun round. The arcade was dark and Price stood in a deep shadow. 'What are you talking about?'

Price, whose posture looked constrained, was trying to twist round. 'He's got his bloody teeth in my backside!'

Hearing a deep growl, Saffron gave a start and drew nearer. A huge dog was standing behind Price and appeared to have its fangs buried in the seat of his slacks. As Price fought to get away, the growl grew louder. 'Don't just stand there, Saffron. Do something!'

'It's Nuisance,' Saffron said. 'He thinks you need help.'

Cursing, Price lurched forward. There was a tearing sound, followed by the snap of teeth as the dog, as quick as a flash, transferred its hold from Price's pants to the sleeve of his jacket. Gingerly, Saffron bent over the huge animal. 'Let go, boy. Let go.'

For an answer the dog wagged its tail, bent its powerful hind legs, and dragged Price further into the arcade. A drunken yell sounded. 'Christ, what's he going to do? Eat me? Get him off, Saffron. Do you hear?'

Saffron tried again and received another ferocious growl for his pains. 'He only wants to take you to the Soldiers' Club, sir. He thinks you're drunk and need help.'

Price was hurrying faster and faster as the dog got under way. 'He's not bloody wrong, is he? Can't you kick his arse or pull his tail?'

Saffron, by no means sober himself, felt hysteria again as he fell in alongside them. 'I don't think it's wise, sir. He might take it the wrong way.'

At the arcade exit Price made a last effort to turn back and collapsed in a heap as the dog maintained its grip. 'Supposing I take off my tunic,' he muttered as Saffron helped him to his feet.

To his relief Saffron could see no sign of the MPs. Picking up Price's cap, he set it on the dishevelled officer's head. 'I wouldn't if I were you. He'd only grab your pants again and they're in a bad way now.'

Before Price could answer the dog gave a tug and sent him reeling down the street. His wail trailed back. 'How much further to the Soldiers' Club?'

Saffron hurried after him. 'Only a couple of blocks, I think.'

With cars hooting and grinning pedestrians turning to watch them, they crossed two more streets and were led towards a large building on the far side of a square. To Saffron's relief they passed no more than half a dozen South African soldiers on the way but as they neared the Club he saw three RAF NCOs talking outside the entrance. With no hope of holding the rampant Nuisance back, Saffron tried to hide Price's rank by putting an arm round his shoulders. A moment later, to the incredulous stares of the three NCOs, the dog dragged the two of them through the open entrance into the Club.

They found themselves in a brightly-lit hall. A big matronly woman in a starched WVS uniform materialized in front of them. Saffron could not decide whether her fruity, patronizing voice was aimed at him or the dog.

'So your friend's had one over the eight, has he? Sit him over there and I'll have coffee sent to him.'

Although he was now wagging his tail, Nuisance still had a precautionary grip on Price's sleeve. As the woman turned to give an order to another WVS who came up behind her, Price's drunken bark made both women spin round.

'What the hell are you walking away for? Tell this bloody dog to let go of me!'

The big woman bridled immediately. 'How dare you talk to me like that?' It was then she noticed Price's rank. 'And you're an officer too, aren't you?'

Saffron hurriedly intervened. 'He's been to a party. Couldn't you phone for a taxi? He'll get into trouble if he's found like this.'

The woman's stare was withering. 'I'm not sure he doesn't deserve it.' She spoke to the dog who released his grip and sat down with the air of one who has done his task well. Price raised his gooey, saliverous sleeve and gazed at it bitterly. 'Look at that! Ruined.'

'Look at your pants,' Saffron grinned.

Price twisted round and a dangling six-inch patch of cloth from his seat was visible to one and all. He gave the shocked woman a glare. 'Look what your bloody animal's done to me!'

She drew herself erect. 'That animal, as you call him, has helped hundreds of drunken men to find the sanctuary of this club. Instead of complaining, you ought to be grateful. Not swearing and cursing like an uneducated private in the Army.'

Price leered at her, muttered something about 'old cow', and stumbled off towards the entrance. Missing it by three feet, he collided with a chair and sat down heavily. Conscious things were deteriorating at an alarming speed, Saffron tried again. 'Won't you please phone for a taxi? I'll see he gets to camp without any further trouble.'

The woman was eyeing Price vengefully. 'He's not getting away with language like that. Not an officer. I'm going to report him.'

'You can't do that,' Saffron said in alarm.

Her irate stare turned on him. 'Can't I, young man? We'll see about that.'

'But he didn't mean to insult you.' Searching desperately for a way out, Saffron's eyes fell on the amiable Nuisance whose tail was wagging as he watched the scene. 'Perhaps it was the dog? I think it frightened him.'

'Nuisance wouldn't frighten a fly,' the woman said contemptuously. 'He's the friend of every sailor and airman in Cape Town.'

'I know that,' Saffron said, suddenly struck by a flash of inspiration. 'But Flight Lieutenant Thomas is afraid of dogs.'

'Is that his name?'

'Yes. We're from Wingfield.'

With a final just-you-wait look at the unfortunate Price, the woman came to a decision. 'Very well. Get him into my office where he's out of sight and I'll phone for a taxi. But don't think I'm not going to report him.'

The taxi arrived five minutes later and Saffron bundled Price unceremoniously into it. As it pulled away Price sat up with a jerk. 'Where's that dog?'

Saffron pushed him back. 'It's all right. We're on our way back to camp.'

156

Price relaxed and for a moment Saffron thought he was asleep. Instead he heard an exultant croak. 'Three bloody nil! We really did 'em, Saffron, didn't we? What about another drink?'

'Like hell we are. Get your head down.'

Grumbling, Price sank back into the corner. A minute later a strident howling made the cab driver turn his head. 'There's an old mill by the stream, Nellie Dean...' Price dug Saffron in the ribs. 'Open your lungs, lad. Sing!'

Saffron made the driver pull up forty yards from the camp entrance. Paying him, he led Price across the road and paused.

'I'd get to your quarters now if I were you. Can you make it by yourself?'

Price released a hiccup as the taxi headlights swung round and passed them. 'You know something, Saffron? You're all right. You're all right but for one thing.'

Saffron grinned as he urged the midget towards the camp gates. 'What's that?'

'You're mean, lad.'

'Mean?'

Price nodded owlishly. 'Dead mean. You won't tell me how you keep those bush apes of yours under control.'

Saffron's grin spread. 'I'll tell you one day.'

'When?'

'One day.'

'There you are,' Price scowled. 'Downright mean. But I'll find out, Saffron. If I have to send back to the Tower for a rack and pair of thumbscrews, I'll find out.'

Saffron pointed him at the camp gates, got him under way, and released him. The tiny figure with the square of cloth dangling from his trouser seat reeled past the sentry box. 'You all right, lad?'

The sentry was caught between astonishment and hilarity. 'Yes, thank you, sir.'

'That's good, lad. Very good.' Waving a fraternal arm, Price stumbled on. His triumphant voice trailed back a few seconds later. 'We gave 'em a hell of a roasting, lad. Three bloody nil.'

CHAPTER 22

Directly after parade on Monday morning Saffron was called into Price's office and was met with a rueful grin. 'Hell of a party, wasn't it?'

Saffron wondered how much of it Price remembered. 'Yes, sir. It was.'

'You've heard the Provost Marshal's sent in a report to the Old Man?'

'Yes. Sergeant Webber said it came in yesterday. What do you think will happen?'

'The Old Man will be as lenient as he can, but he won't be able to let us off altogether. Apparently there was a hell of a lot of damage.'

Price's use of the personal pronoun made Saffron start. 'They haven't got your name, have they, sir?'

'No. Everybody's kept mum. But how does that leave me? From all I can remember I was the ringleader.'

Saffron grinned. 'I saw you doing an enthusiastic job on MacDougall.'

Price's worried look deepened. 'There you are. So why should I get away scot free?'

'That's silly, sir. You've far more to lose than we have.' When Price frowned, Saffron delivered the ultimate threat. 'If you say anything we'll all quit from the football team.'

The midget's frown turned rueful. 'I'll say this for you, Saffron. When you threaten, you really threaten.'

'Well, it would be stupid, sir. Anyway, you didn't get off scot free. I seem to remember you losing the seat of your pants.'

'That bloody dog,' Price muttered. 'What did I say to that woman in the Soldiers' Club? I wasn't rude, was I?'

'You did call her an old cow,' Saffron admitted.

Price blanched. 'I did? Oh, my Christ. Did she get my name?'

'I'm afraid so.' As Price winced again, Saffron went on blandly: 'Flight Lieutenant Thomas. Of Wingfield.'

'Thomas?' Price breathed. 'Thomas is their team manager.'

Saffron nodded. 'You pointed him out to us before the match started on Saturday.'

An unholy grin lit up the restored midget's face. 'You're not pulling my leg, Saffron?'

'No, sir. When she said she was going to report you, I had to think of a name quickly. That was the one that came to me.'

For a moment it seemed Price might hug Saffron. 'A stroke of genius, lad! Nothing less. Tell the lads not to worry about the money. I'm going to put in all I can.'

Saffron moved towards the door. 'We'll have a whip round first. Anything else, sir?'

Price's nod made him pause. 'I'm afraid so. I'm putting MacFarlane on your course this morning. You're flying with the SCI.'

'The SCI?'

'Yes. He's playing hell again about your reports on Villiers. So he's decided to take the lad up himself to see if you're right. You're to go up with them. He wants you over at Number Two hangar at 10.00 hours sharp.'

'Number eight bomb gone, sir.' The pupil's shout sounded despondent through the intercom. The Oxford droned on for a few seconds, then banked steeply to port. Gazing past Sedgley-Jones in the pilot's seat, Saffron watched the cloud-shadowed sea wheeling beneath them. As it steadied the target appeared on their port beam. Sedgley-Jones sounded querulous. 'Are you watching it, Villiers?'

'Yes, sir.'

The practice bomb struck a couple of seconds later, on Saffron's estimate at least a six-hundred-yard overshoot. He heard Sedgley-Jones curse. 'Are you sure the sights are in line when you press the release?'

'I think they are, sir.'

'And you're sure you've got the right settings on?'

'Yes, sir. They're the ones Corporal Saffron gave me.'

'All right. Come out for a couple of minutes.' Unable to ignore Saffron any longer, Sedgley-Jones gave him a cold glance. 'Take over and make a note of the settings. I want to see them.'

As the discomforted Villiers began wriggling back out of the bomb hatch Saffron glanced at his watch. His instructions had been to leave the range no later than 11.30. Wingfield were using the range for the rest of the morning and as their Oxfords bombed from the same height the risks of collision were high unless the air space was clear. 'We've only got ten minutes left, sir.'

He received a cold stare. 'I'm aware of the time. Do as I say.'

Squeezing past the pupil, who dropped into the co-pilot's seat, Saffron wormed into the nose and checked the bombsight settings. 'These seem correct, sir.'

'I'm not interested in what they seem, Corporal. I want to see them and check them myself.'

Fishing into his overalls for a pencil, Saffron wrote the figures down on the back of a form 3073. Squirming back, he stood between the two seats and handed the paper to Sedgley-Jones. The pilot stared at them for a full minute before speaking. 'Could it be the wind that's wrong?'

Saffron shrugged. 'We've taken it twice, sir. And it couldn't account for that kind of error. But we'll take it again if you like.'

Biting his lip, Sedgley-Jones let the paper fall. 'What the hell can it be?' he muttered.

Saffron could not resist offering him the pupil's 3073. 'All eight have been overshoots, sir. And the distances have been much the same.'

Sedgley-Jones's resentment directed itself against the unfortunate Villiers. 'Get back in there again, Villiers, and this time try, for God's sake.'

Villiers wriggled back into the hatch and Saffron took his place in the co-pilot's seat. Another glance at his watch made him start. 'It's twenty-six minutes past, sir.'

Sedgley-Jones's lips compressed into a thin line as he put the Oxford into a steep bank. 'Because of your bloody-mindedness, Corporal, I've had to put urgent work aside this morning. That means I've no intention of wasting this exercise. I've still got eight bombs to drop and I intend dropping them. Is that clear?'

Saffron was aghast. 'But you can't, sir. Their Oxfords will be tracking over the target at exactly the same height as ourselves. It's asking for a collision.'

The pilot turned his head. 'You aren't scared, are you, Corporal?'

You bastard, Saffron seethed. 'As an SAI and an instructor, sir, I'm responsible that we obey the range orders, and those orders are that we leave punctually at 11.30.'

Ignoring him, Sedgley-Jones was preparing for his run in. 'See the target yet, Villiers?'

'It's at two o'clock, sir.'

The Oxford yawed and steadied. Saffron took a deep breath. 'Sir, if you won't leave the range at 11.30 then I must insist you take full responsibility.'

'I've already taken full responsibility, Corporal.'

Saffron nudged the foot of the prostrate Villiers. 'You hear that, Villiers?'

The trainee sounded embarrassed. 'Yes, Corporal.'

The glance Saffron received from Sedgley-Jones was full of cold fury. 'Are you satisfied?'

'I'm not satisfied at all, sir. I think we're taking a dangerous risk.'

The pilot's nostrils pinched white. 'I'll make a note of that. Are you ready, Villiers?'

'Yes, sir. You want to be a couple of degrees to port.'

The Oxford yawed again. Saffron's gaze was fixed on a large cumulus dead ahead. Liverish black spots had appeared against its white backdrop and disappeared again. As he narrowed his eyes they came back. He turned to Sedgley-Jones. 'There's something ahead, sir. It could be the Wingfield aircraft approaching from the sea.'

He saw Sedgley-Jones's hands tighten spasmodically on the wheel. 'If there are any Wingfield aircraft about, Corporal, the range will order them away when they see we are still bombing.'

'But the range hasn't got radio equipment. What if the Wingfield pilots think the red Very lights are meant for us and not for them? For that matter they might not even see them.'

'They can still see us, can't they?' Sedgley-Jones's mouth was tight. 'I'm warning you, Corporal. If you interrupt me once more you'll be on a charge of insubordination when we get back. Carry on, Villiers.'

Cursing to himself, Saffron dropped back into his seat. He could see only one dot ahead now but even as he watched it grew a tiny pair of wings. As near as he could estimate the aircraft was flying at the same altitude and making straight for the target on a collision course.

Common sense calmed Saffron. Sedgley-Jones was probably right. When the other pilot spotted them he would realize the Breconfield aircraft was over-running its time and would break off until it left the range. The risks Sedgley-Jones was taking were more disciplinary than physical, and Saffron ascribed them to two causes. One was the man's obsessional unwillingness to admit he was wrong about Villiers. The other was the reaction of a bully or even sadist. He believed he had discovered a way of frightening Saffron.

He wasn't wrong either, Saffron thought as he watched the oncoming Oxford. At the same time the very possibility made Saffron dig his Yorkshire heels in. The bastard could wait until hell froze over before he'd make the first move. If he sat tight, Sedgley-Jones would have to crack first and look a bigger fool than ever.

His mind made up, Saffron watched the speck ahead turn into a child's toy. Hypnotised by it, he found no time to glance at the range to see if any warning Very lights were being fired. In front and below him, knowing nothing of the drama being enacted and also fully engrossed, Villiers was giving his run-up instructions. 'It's coming into the drift wires now, sir. Left, left ... Steady. Right a bit. Right ... steady.'

Glued to his seat, Saffron no longer heard the trainee's hesitant instructions. The plane ahead, closing fast, had turned from a child's toy into a metal monster with spinning propellers and swaying wings. Tearing his eyes from it, Saffron saw that Sedgley-Jones was staring straight ahead. Then he must be seeing it too. But what was wrong with the other pilot? Was he another madman, intent on driving them off the range by pure intimidation?

Saffron's resolve was now superseded by paralysis as the combined speed of the two planes hurled them together. The wings of the other Oxford now filled the entire visor ahead of him. He could even see a grey patch near its starboard wing root. Seven seconds from eternity, six, five, four.... Breaking the spell, Saffron yelled a warning and thumped Sedgley-Jones's shoulder.

He saw the man's cheeks drain of blood and in that split second of horror knew the truth. With his mind choked with

162

frustration, dislike, and anger, the pilot had been blind to the oncoming aircraft.

It was Saffron's last cogent thought. A moment later, with Sedgley-Jones heaving back on the wheel, the Oxford shot up like a rocket. Then something struck its tail, a wing dropped, and it went into a tight spin.

The fear Saffron experienced seemed to scorch and shrink his brain. The impact must have been their tail assembly torn away. Seeing the terrified Villiers trying to squirm out of the hatch, he caught his legs and tugged. With the devilry all inanimate objects assume at such moments, the hooks of the trainee's harness entangled themselves in some part of the hatch and he could move neither forward nor back. With their parachutes secured in bins at the rear of the aircraft and the fuselage spinning like a child's top, Saffron felt the struggle to free the pupil was futile even before it began. Nevertheless he found himself trying to squeeze past the terrified man to reach the entangled hooks.

Through the perspex hatch, sea, sky, and shore lurched dizzily past. Thoughts and questions darted through Saffron's mind like swallows through a thunderstorm. In a few seconds he would be dead. Did the world continue just the same? Would there be nothing for him, not even darkness? Would he never see a flower, a tree, a girl's face again? Seconds from death, the youthful Saffron learned the divine sweetness of life and was awed that some could voluntarily surrender it.

Heaving at Villiers, he found that one of the parachute hooks had caught in a hole in an aluminium stay. Freeing it, he edged backwards, pulling Villiers after him. As something dug agonisingly into his back he had the feeling the plane's gyrations were not so violent and as he crouched by the co-pilot's seat ready to help Villiers out, the note of the engines changed and his knees bent under an increased g. Climbing into the seat he discovered the sea, less than five hundred feet below, was levelling off as the Oxford pulled out of her dive. Turning in disbelief, he could see no damage to the tail.

Resigned to death, Saffron found it was difficult to adjust to life. The ashen-faced Villiers who stumbled past him and promptly began vomiting against the side of the fuselage appeared to be having the same problem. Sedgley-Jones,

163

trembling, pale, and sweating, jabbed a finger at the sea. 'Look out for the Wingfield kite. He might have gone into it.'

Flying with care in case the Oxford was seriously damaged, Sedgley-Jones took a wide circle round the target. The suspense kept all three men quiet except for Villiers' occasional retching. When the Oxford seemed likely to hold together and they saw no wreckage, colour began to return to the pilot's cheeks. 'It looks as if they're all right. We'd better get back.'

I wouldn't be in your shoes today if they promised to make me Prime Minister, Saffron thought as the Oxford headed across the Cape Flats for Breconfield. As Sedgley-Jones brought it gingerly down, Saffron pointed to an Oxford parked near Number Two hangar with half a dozen men clustered round it. 'That's the kite. See the grey patch near the wing root?'

Looking both relieved and apprehensive, Sedgley-Jones guided the Oxford down the runway. Saffron ascribed the unusual bumpiness of the landing to the pilot's state of mind. Across the airfield the group of men had noticed the Oxford and were already making towards it. Deliberately parking well away from them, Sedgley-Jones turned to Saffron and Villiers.

'You two can get back to your classes now. I'll handle this.' His pale, vindictive eyes settled on the luckless pupil. 'I've no option but to recommend that you're grounded, Villiers. You've proved today that you're not aircrew material.'

Jumping down from the Oxford he hesitated, then made his way towards the shouting men. Skirting the fuselage, Saffron took a glance at the tail assembly. His low whistle brought Villiers, who was still retching spasmodically, stumbling towards him.

The undertail of the Oxford, bent and torn, was resting on a crooked stay, all that remained of the tail wheel. Saffron's wry comment was addressed to himself. 'Next time I grumble about my luck, someone remind me of this.'

Sedgley-Jones and the group of men had now joined forces and raised voices could be heard. I hope they lynch the bastard was Saffron's wish as he led the pupil away. Impulsively he clapped him across the shoulders. 'I wouldn't feel too bad about it, Villiers. There are plenty of interesting jobs on the ground. And you'll live longer.'

The answer he received from the shaken pupil made him start, then grin. 'Who's feeling bad about it, Corporal? After that experience it'd take a team of wild horses to get me into a plane again.'

The resilient Saffron, almost himself again, decided it was a reaction that would win Bickers' wholehearted approval.

CHAPTER 23

As Saffron entered the staff room Bickers drew him eagerly aside. 'What's happened?'

Saffron grimaced. 'It looks as if he's got away with it.'

The Londoner's face dropped. 'How, for Christ's sake?'

'Price isn't sure but he thinks Sedgley-Jones made a counter threat against the Wingfield pilot.'

'Because he didn't see you either? But the poor sod wouldn't expect to. It was after 11.30.'

'I know but it doesn't excuse that kind of negligence. I suppose when he's thought about it he's decided it wasn't worth pressing a charge.'

'But the Range must have seen what happened?'

'What can they do? The top man out there's only a corporal.'

'Gutless shower of bastards,' Bickers grunted. 'I suppose the other pilot was a junior officer?'

'Almost sure to be.'

Bickers' lips twisted bitterly. 'Same old story, mate. The system's tailor-made for the bastards.'

'Sedgley-Jones got a hell of a fright just the same. After nearly getting killed himself he thought he'd wiped out the entire Wingfield crew.'

'Let's hope the sod has nightmares.'

Saffron grinned. 'It's my guess he will.'

'Mind you,' Bickers said after a pause. 'It's not going to make him like you any better. From the way his mind works you'll be to blame for it.'

'Thanks. I can always rely on you to pull the plug out, can't I?'

'But it's true, isn't it? If you'd cancelled the report as he asked he wouldn't have needed to fly this morning.'

'If he'd acted on my report, he still wouldn't have needed to fly, would he?'

'He won't see it that way. To those two fairies you're a constant pain in the arse.'

'I'm not the only pain, am I?' Saffron said, feeling vindictive. 'They don't seem to find you one of Jesus's little sunbeams either.'

'And why? Who got me into their bad books? The least you could do was stop provoking them.'

'Like dropping my report?'

Bickers masked his shame with defiance. 'And why not? Where's all this pig-headedness got you? Only further up the creek.'

Giving him a look of dislike, Saffron dropped into a chair. Afflicted by conscience pangs, Bickers picked an AP from the table and discontentedly flicked over the pages. Half a minute later his eyes lifted. 'What're you doing tomorrow afternoon?'

'Nothing,' Saffron muttered.

Another long pause. Then: 'I'm off at one o'clock. Webber's taking my course on bomb store procedure. Feel like coming out with me?'

'Where to?'

'Clifton. I'm meeting a girl there. If I ring her, she'll probably bring a friend along.'

'On a weekday afternoon?'

'Why not? They can both make it.' Seeing Saffron's hesitation Bickers applied pressure. 'It'll do you good, mate. You've been mooning over that Synevva Helgman too long. What you want is a nice, uncomplicated woman.'

'Fourth Beach, Clifton,' the bus conductor announced.

As Saffron started to rise, Bickers caught his arm. 'Next stop, mate.'

Puzzled, Saffron sank back. The bus pulled away from the crescent of beach with its gaily-painted bungalows and entered a deserted stretch of road flanked by rocks and bushes. As it rounded a bend, Bickers picked up his sidekit and gave Saffron a wink. 'This is it, mate.'

Saffron followed him off the bus. Behind them a hillside

covered in bushes reached up to the perpendicular buttresses of the Twelve Apostles. Ahead an uninhabited coastline of rocks and shrub led down to the sea. The last bungalows of Fourth Beach were just visible three hundred yards to their right. As the fumes of the receding bus dispersed, Saffron caught the exhilarating smell of seaweed.

Bickers took a deep sniff. 'Marvellous, isn't it?' Humming, he led the perplexed Saffron across the road and down a narrow path into the bushes.

'Why are we meeting them here?' Saffron asked.

Bickers waved a blissful hand at the sunlit, breaking sea. 'Is there a better place?'

'That's not what I asked. Why couldn't we have met them in town and brought them here?'

'That's you all over,' Bickers grunted. 'You must look a gift horse in the mouth, mustn't you?'

Chastened, Saffron followed him through bushes and out-crops of granite to a stretch of sand. The beach appeared deserted but as Bickers gave a low whistle a woman appeared among a clump of bushes near the water's edge and waved a hand. A second woman came into sight a couple of seconds later. With a grunt of satisfaction Bickers started forward again. 'There they are. C'mon.'

Both of the women were wearing two-piece swim suits. Bickers had a leer in his eye as he leaned towards Saffron. 'Susie's the big one on the left. The other's yours. Her name's Marie.'

Susie was big, blonde and busty. Marie was a slimmer, dark-haired woman whose appearance and mannerisms might have been described as kittenish had she been a teenager. Now feline was perhaps more apt. As she watched the two airmen approaching she slanted a comment at her blonde companion who gave a laugh of amusement.

Saffron was showing disappointment. 'They're a bit on the old side, aren't they?'

'Old?'

'Yes. They're both thirty if they're a day.'

Bickers gave a licentious wink. 'They're experienced, mate. That's what counts.'

'I suppose by that you mean they're married,' Saffron accused.

167

'What if they are? They've still got the necessary equipment, haven't they?'

'Where do they live?'

Bickers hesitated, then jerked a reluctant thumb at the distant bungalows. Aghast, Saffron halted in his tracks. 'They live there – a quarter of a mile away? I'm up to my neck in trouble already. What're you trying to do? Finish me off?'

'You worry too much, mate. Their husbands are a couple of civvies and don't get home until after six. We've got the whole afternoon with them.'

'But what if someone walks over this way? You think their husbands won't hear about it?'

Bickers grinned triumphantly. 'That's the beauty of it, mate. Nobody will. We're on the part of the beach reserved for coloured people. Whites can't come in here.'

'Then what the hell are we doing?'

Bickers waved a hand at the deserted shoreline. 'It's a weekday. Everyone's working. We're dead safe until 5.30.'

'You mean you hope we're safe. If you have to go out with married women, can't you meet 'em somewhere else but on their doorstep?'

'Where else can we go without a car?' Bickers demanded. 'By the time we get 'em to a suitable place, it'll be time to start back again. And, as Susie pointed out, they might be seen with us in town. Whereas who's going to think they're up to anything here?'

Saffron had to admit there was some logic in the reasoning. Forty yards away the two women were showing impatience at the airmen's altercation. As the big blonde opened her mouth to call them, the slimmer woman caught her arm and glanced warningly at the distant bungalows. Feasting his eyes on the Junoesque Susie, Bickers gave a grunt of scorn.

'I never thought you were the windy type, Saffron.'

Saffron took swift and malicious revenge. 'You know what happens if you're caught with a married woman? If the husband complains, you're posted out of the country. Nearly always on active service.'

Bickers winced at the reminder, then groaned his bitterness. 'I should have known better, shouldn't I? Bring you along and you'll ruin it somehow.'

'Still want to go?' Saffron grinned.

Bickers glanced uneasily at the bungalows. From his viewpoint they appeared deserted. He was not to know that behind the lace-curtained window of one bungalow a woman of sour face and angular build had a pair of binoculars trained on him and Saffron. The sister-in-law and the long-standing enemy of Susie, the woman had long suspected the blonde was carrying on with local servicemen but to date positive proof had been lacking. Today, noticing Susie and her equally promiscuous friend Marie were not using the white area of the beach for their afternoon swim but had wandered into the coloured zone, she had been keeping an eye on their movements. Although they were now conveniently hidden from the bungalows, the advent of Saffron and Bickers had brought the woman a quiver of anticipation and a rush for her binoculars.

With the vision of active service cruelly flashed before him, Bickers was wavering for the first time. He glanced back at the two women. Disgusted by the airmen's vacillation, the voluptuous Susie had turned and was bending down to pick up her beach towel. The splendid sight that greeted Bickers swung the scale.

'The hell with 'em,' he muttered defiantly. 'I'm not passing this up. Anyway, why should active service worry you? I thought you were the guy who couldn't wait for another crack at the Krauts.'

Saffron, who had followed his eyes, was noticing how slim and shapely Marie's legs were. He was never certain whether it was sex or Bickers' challenge that brought about his capitulation. 'All right. As you've arranged it I suppose I can't let you down. Only don't go getting any bright ideas about taking them for a drink or a cup of coffee.'

Grinning his relief, Bickers patted his sidekit. 'I've got everything we need in here, mate. Just relax and live.'

He gave another low whistle. As the women saw the two airmen start forward again they glanced at one another, shrugged, and settled down in the sand. Over in the bungalow the angular woman lowered her binoculars and left the house by a side door. A few seconds later she was stealing furtively through the bushes towards Bickers' trysting place.

Saffron, wearing the briefest of trunks, stretched out and flexed his toes luxuriously. Iridescent shafts of sunlight

169

radiated from his half-closed eyelashes. The sand beneath him felt like a warm bath and the drone of insects and the wash of the sea added to the dreamlike quality of the afternoon.

The woman alongside him felt his movement and pressed invitingly against him. Lifting his head, Saffron gazed down the length of her body. Her breasts looked firm, her waist was slender, and her tanned legs felt like silk as they moved against his own. This was the life, Saffron thought as the Adam in him began to stir. This was what it was all about.

He glanced round for sight of Bickers. The Londoner and Susie had moved into an adjacent hollow ten minutes ago. They had not been seen or heard since but the occasional waving of a clump of tall grass told they were happily employed.

The slim Marie glanced up at him impatiently. 'What's the matter?'

'Nothing,' Saffron said.

She stroked his bare shoulder, then lifted her smooth feline face. 'Then why don't you give me another kiss?'

Saffron obliged willingly and his last chance of seeing the approach of Nemesis disappeared. A few seconds later the angular woman's stealthy approach brought her to the rim of the hollow in which Bickers and Susie were recumbent. The sight of the voluptuous Susie, with her huge breasts liberated, pressed up against the enraptured Bickers made the woman start in triumph before her lips compressed like a vice. For a moment she seemed undecided whether to stay and watch the proceedings or yell her findings to the four winds. In the end she chose a compromise, edging back along the path until out of earshot and then running full tilt back to her bungalow. There, pale and vengeful, she tore open the door and grabbed the telephone.

Back on the beach Saffron and Bickers were pursuing their activities in blissful ignorance of the hornets' nest they were stirring. Saffron was slipping a hand down to one of Marie's breasts. When she responded favourably, he fumbled behind her back to untie the strings of her two-piece. In the way of things, the strings became knotted and the woman had to come to his aid. Thrown a little, for he liked to think he handled such matters with deftness, Saffron drew her brassiere away.

170

A few minutes later a car driven in great haste braked in front of the angular woman's bungalow. The two men who jumped out were confronted immediately by the woman who gesticulated at the reserved area of the beach. Pausing only to drag two heavy sticks from the car, the two men ran after the woman who was already heading towards Bickers' and Susie's hollow.

The tall grasses, now waving rhythmically in the still air, betrayed the couple's exact location. Ten yards ahead of the two men, the woman motioned them to stop running. Tiptoeing forward she gave an exclamation of triumph as like some exotic mushroom the white buttocks of Bickers became visible through the tall grass. Although Susie's face could not be seen, her tanned legs were curled snugly round the lanky airman. Turning, the exultant woman waved the two men forward.

It was Marie in the adjacent hollow who prevented a total surprise. Still not divested of the lower half of her swim suit, she sat up and was wriggling to remove it when she caught sight of the three threatening figures. Her gasp made Saffron sit up sharply. 'My God! Look!'

Saffron looked and froze. 'Who are they?'

The woman's voice was sibilant with fright and anger. 'It's that old cow Phyllis. She must have tipped off Jack and Darnie.' Seeing Saffron about to shout a warning, she clapped a hand over his mouth. 'Keep quiet. They haven't seen me yet. I'm getting out of here.'

Snatching up her bra and towel, she ran down the hollow towards a stretch of bushes. The moment she vanished Saffron let out a yell. 'Ken! Look out!'

The grass ceased waving. Bickers sounded hoarse and shocked. 'What's wrong?'

Saffron was climbing frantically into his shorts. 'Two men and a woman! Heading straight at you!'

With the warning given the two men let out a vengeful howl and made straight for Bickers. Both looked to be in their early thirties. One was thick-set and balding, with a beefy, outraged face. The other was taller, with a blond beard and bulging forearms. As Saffron dived into his shoes, an apparition rose from the clump of tall grass. Stark naked, Bickers was hopping about grotesquely as he struggled to get a skinny leg into his shorts. Swinging their sticks ferociously, the two men threw themselves on him. A second later, as naked as the day she was born, the nubile Susie came bounding out of the hollow and fled towards the bungalows. As Saffron's eyes followed her, there was a gurgling yell from Bickers. 'Saffron! Where the hell are you?'

Saffron gazed around desperately for a weapon. Finding nothing he ran into the hollow. Bickers was on his feet again but the two men were in front and behind him. With the angular woman urging them on with hysterical cries, they looked incensed enough to kill. As Bickers tried to grab the man in front of him, the second man lashed him across the back of his legs and dropped him into the sand. Immediately both men were on him, flailing down with their sticks.

Had there been time to think Saffron would almost certainly have discovered that his sympathies up to that moment were with the outraged husbands. But the ferocity of their attack on Bickers made ethical stocktaking academic. Running forward, he grabbed the thick-set man and pulled him away. The cursing man's response was to swing the stick at his head. As Saffron ducked his conditioned reflexes took over and he kicked the man's shins. With a howl of pain the man dropped his stick and collapsed into the sand.

Outnumbered now, the bearded man drew back and glanced at the woman for leadership. Grabbing hold of Bickers, Saffron dragged him to his feet. 'Get your clothes on! Quickly, for Christ's sake!'

The woman's response was to run forward and try to pick up the first man's stick. As Saffron pushed her aside she tried to kick him and to reach his face with her nails. Seeing the bearded man was taking fresh heart from her onslaught, Saffron gave Bickers a yell. 'Get this woman off me!'

Bickers, who by this time had his shorts and shoes on, tried to drag the virago away. Spurred on by her cries, the bearded man swung his stick and caught Saffron high on the arm. Stung by the blow, with all rights and wrongs now forgotten, Saffron dived at him and brought him down. An elbow under the chin brought his head back and a chop across the windpipe half-choked him. Breathing hard, Saffron climbed back on his feet. At the far side of the hollow Bickers appeared to be losing his fight with the kicking woman. Grabbing her from behind, Saffron pinioned her arms. 'Got all your things?' he panted.

172

Bruised, covered in sand, Bickers bore the look of a man brought down from the heights of ecstasy to the depths of suffering in one cruel blow. Waiting until the Londoner had collected his shirt and sidekit, Saffron pushed the exhausted woman away. 'Let's get out of here,' he muttered.

A shrill whistle made both of them spin round. A jeep was halted by one of the bungalows and three uniformed figures were running down the shore towards them. Bickers let out a wail of panic. 'They've tipped off the MPs!'

Saffron pushed him towards the hillside. 'We've got to cross the main road or they'll cut us off.'

Stuffing his shirt and cap into his sidekit, the stricken Bickers led the flight through the boulders and thorn bushes. Guessing their intention the three MPs ran back to their jeep. As Bickers halted with a groan of relief, Saffron gave him a frantic shove. 'Keep going! If they get to the road first we're dead.'

They crossed the road at the same moment the jeep reached the road intersection. A slow-moving lorry trailing a column of cars delayed it long enough for the two corporals to find a way up the steep bank opposite. By the time the jeep braked below, they were fifty yards up the hillside.

The three MPs poured out of the car. An authoritative voice shouted for them to halt. Bickers glanced down apprehensively. 'You don't think they'll shoot, do you?'

Saffron gave him a look and saved his breath. One MP ran back to the jeep, the other two started climbing. 'Radioing for reinforcements,' Bickers panted. 'The bastards mean to get us.'

Drenched in sweat, the two airmen reached a high-level road half a minute later. Conscious that if any other road existed higher up the hillside they would almost certainly be cut off if they paused for rest, they crossed it and recommenced their climb. As the mountain range drew nearer, the hillside steepened. Bickers, whose back was covered with red weals, suddenly halted. 'Must ... have a rest,' he gasped.

Saffron took the sidekit from him. With less incentive to climb than the hunted airmen, the two MPs were now a good two hundred yards below them. As Saffron lit a cigarette and passed it to Bickers, an Army transport came roaring round a bend of the high-level road. Halting half

173

a mile away with a squeal of brakes, it disgorged two uniformed figures. Accelerating away it repeated the procedure below the two airmen and again a few hundred yards past them. As he recognized the red caps Bickers turned to Saffron in disbelief. 'It's a bloody man-hunt!'

Spurred by the danger the Londoner threw away the cigarette and went up the hillside like a startled jack-rabbit. As the MPs spotted him, shouts rang out. With legs aching and hearts pounding, the two corporals climbed until they reached a belt of pine trees where they plunged thankfully into the shade.

Chest heaving painfully, Bickers halted again. 'Sadistic civilians and bloodthirsty MPs,' he groaned. 'I should have known, shouldn't I?'

Saffron glared at him. 'You're not blaming *me* for this, I hope.'

'Who else? They couldn't just be ordinary husbands, could they? They have to be homicidal lunatics. Do you realize they were trying to kill me?'

'What did you expect them to do? Kiss your backside? Those were their wives we were with.'

'That doesn't give 'em the right to cripple me,' Bickers complained.

'It depends on one's point of view, doesn't it? What would you do if you found a Yank knocking off your girl friend on your doorstep?'

Bickers gave a grunt of disgust. 'Since when have you been a prude? What about the Synevva woman?'

'At least her husband was civilized. But you have to pick two women married to psychopaths. If we get caught, those two will see we're skinned alive.'

Bickers glanced round apprehensively. Sunlight, filtering through the trees, illuminated the pine needles that carpeted the hillside. The air was aromatic and the only sound the singing of birds. The Londoner looked brighter as he turned back to Saffron. 'Maybe now we've disappeared they'll all give up.'

'You're worse than an ostrich. Of course they won't give up.' Saffron pushed himself away from a tree. 'That's long enough. Those MPs looked pretty fit to me.'

Bickers followed him across the pine needles. 'You know where we're heading, don't you?' he complained. 'Straight to the top of Table Mountain.'

'It's not that high, is it?'

'How high do you call high? It's over three thousand bloody feet.'

Saffron glanced at his watch. 'Perhaps we won't have to climb it. If we can keep out of sight until dark, perhaps we can take a contour path back to town.'

A distant shout, echoing eerily back from the mountain, made Bickers jump and hasten to Saffron's side. 'They won't use tracker dogs, will they?'

'That's what I like about you,' Saffron said bitterly. 'Always cheerful and good for a laugh.'

'With a Jonah like you around, I haven't much to be cheerful about, have I?'

Saffron's teeth gritted together. 'Blame me just once more for today and so help me I'll kill you.'

'Who else is there to blame?' Bickers demanded. 'I've been going out with Susie for weeks and until today nobody gave a damn.'

An answering shout, much louder this time, made both men start. Glaring at one another, they broke into a painful run and disappeared into the trees.

CHAPTER 24

Saffron halted and pushed Bickers back. 'Hear something?' the Londoner asked nervously.

Motioning him to be quiet, Saffron drew aside a bush that flanked a path. The slope below, covered in dense bushes, dropped steeply for five hundred feet before merging into a long belt of pines. With the sun down, the impressive peak of Lion's Head was rising from the dusk as if it were an island. To Saffron's right, car headlights could be seen moving over the shadowy slopes of Signal Hill.

Saffron let the bush swing back. 'I can't see anything. Not that it means very much. There's a lot of cover down there.'

Bickers, fully dressed at last, looked apprehensive again. 'I thought we'd lost them.'

'Maybe we have. It could have been a bird or animal.'

Bickers gazed uneasily along the high-level contour path

that ran along the base of the mountain. Narrow and winding, it was flanked by vegetation dense enough to conceal a small army. His eyes rose to the massive buttresses that towered almost perpendicularly from the scarp two hundred feet above them. 'If they know we're up here, we're trapped,' he muttered. 'Even if they can't catch us themselves, they've only to send men in from the other end. We should have gone over the top when we had the chance.'

Saffron nodded bitterly. 'That's you all over! You funked it back at Clifton where it looked climbable and now you start regretting it.' He jabbed an accusing finger at the sheer 1,500 feet wall above. 'It's too bloody late now, isn't it? We'd need wings to get up there.'

Weary and aching from his beating, Bickers was in no mood for self-recrimination. 'Listen who's talking! I didn't notice you rushing to get your crampons on.'

'And why? I was thinking of you. You were moaning and groaning as if you were down for the chop any minute.'

The indignant Bickers snatched his shirt from his trousers. 'You saying I'm putting it on? Look at these bruises. If you'd a quarter of 'em you'd be flat on your back bawling for a doctor.'

'You know your trouble? You're too sorry for yourself.'

Bickers' yelp of anger echoed from the heights above. 'You've a nerve, Saffron. What about all your bellyaching about Kruger? I've heard nothing else since you arrived.'

'The nicest thing about you is your gratitude,' Saffron said bitterly. 'Have you stopped to think what would have happened down there on the beach if I'd run off and left you?'

'From the time you took, I thought you had,' Bickers hissed, suddenly remembering the need for silence.

It was too late. Dry twigs snapped and a bush threshed wildly. A second later there was a breathless, triumphant yell. 'All right, you two. You're under arrest.'

Saffron saw the man's shadowy figure ten yards back along the path and his reaction was instinctive. Yelling at Bickers to follow him, he dived from the path and went rolling down the hillside. Bickers, mentally and physically slowed down by his beating, hesitated and was lost. With a curse, the MP snatched out his revolver and levelled it.

'Don't try it, Buster. You haven't a chance.' His parade-ground yell brought pebbles rolling down from the scarp. 'I've got one of 'em, Mac! The other's run off into the bush.'

A distant shout answered him. 'OK, Les. I'll alert the others and then take a look.' The frozen Bickers heard a whistle, followed a few seconds later by the distant bleep of three more. Satisfied, the MP took a step forward. 'What's your camp, airman?'

Ten yards below the path, a sage bush had halted Saffron's fall. As he lay there he could hear the two men talking. Bickers, who had lost all hope, had decided to die defiantly. 'Don't you know a corporal when you see one?'

'Sorry, Corporal,' the man grinned. 'What's your camp?'

Saffron silently applauded as Bickers stalled off the inevitable. 'I'm not local. I'm on leave.'

'Both of you?'

'Yes.'

By this time Saffron was on his feet. Hidden by the bushes and the growing darkness he began crawling back, judging the MP's position from his voice.

'What about your name? I suppose it's Smith?'

'No. It's Jones. J. C. Jones.'

The MP let out a guffaw. 'You're a real jester, aren't you, Corporal? Good thing. It's going to be a help to you.'

Saffron could now see the man's shadowy figure through a network of twigs. He edged forward, pausing at each hiss of dried leaves. The MP motioned Bickers closer. 'Because you really are in the brown stuff, Corporal. Rolling in the bushes with married dames, clobbering their husbands and manhandling a woman witness … My guess is you'll be lucky if five years covers it.'

Afraid that if he exercised caution any longer the dry bush would betray him, Saffron took a deep breath and launched himself forward. With the bush checking him less than he expected, his shoulder struck the MP in the back and flung him forward. As the man gave a yell and tried to rise, Saffron swung a punch into his stomach and another to his jaw. Grabbing the revolver which had fallen to the ground, Saffron was half-prepared in his desperation to hit him with it but to his relief the man gave a groan and lay still.

With sweat trickling down his face, Saffron threw the

revolver into the bushes. There came a distant shout. 'Anything wrong, Les?'

Saffron did his best to imitate the unconscious MP's voice. 'Naw, it's nothing, Mac. You keep on looking for the other guy.'

Before there was time for an answer he grabbed Bickers' arm. 'Come on! Run like hell!'

Stiffened by his rest, Bickers looked aghast. 'Run? I can hardly bloody walk.'

'Les! You're sure you're all right?' The shout from below was followed by a chorus of whistles, all distinctly nearer. Saffron's fingers dug into Bickers' arm.

'You heard what he said. Five years. Think of it! Five years with bastards like that clobbering you every day.'

Bickers' eyes went round with horror. Down the path the stricken MP was beginning to stir and the Londoner noticed him. Before Saffron could say another word Bickers turned and bolted down the path into the dusk.

Saffron hurried out of the railway station, glanced around him furtively, and joined Bickers hidden in a nearby shop doorway. 'It's no good. They've called in the police as well. They're parading with MPs in front of the ticket barriers. And that thick-set character from the beach is with them.'

'So what now?' Bickers muttered.

'How much money have you got?'

Bickers fished painfully in his pockets. 'Four bob.'

'I've got two and six. So a taxi's out. We'll have to hitchhike.'

'Why not take a trolley bus?'

Glancing down the wide road lined with lighted shops, Saffron hurried him away. 'What's the point? They only go half way. And the MPs might be keeping a watch on them.'

Bickers' groan would have moved an SS Gruppenführer. 'How long do you expect me to keep going?'

'I didn't think you looked so bad since we cleaned you up,' Saffron said, following his reassurance with a grin. 'No more miserable than usual in fact.'

'Oh, funny, funny,' Bickers said bitterly.

It was over an hour since the mountain path, gradually

losing height, had deposited them in the high-level suburb at the back of the city. With Bickers complaining that he was near death, a pub had been their first priority. At the stares that greeted them, Bickers had claimed they had been set on and robbed by a gang of skollies. The outcome, free drinks and an opportunity to wash and clean up, had made Bickers smug as the whisky revived him. Although impressed by the Londoner's inventiveness, Saffron had reacted sarcastically when at last they had dragged themselves away.

'I notice you workers of the world aren't above conning one another when the chips are down.'

Bickers, still buoyed up by half a dozen whiskies, had smirked triumphantly. 'You're just jealous you never thought of it yourself.'

Bickers' alcoholic revival had been short-lived. By the time they had reached the town centre his feet had been dragging again. Now, shuffling alongside Saffron, he looked like the last survivor from the Polish Death March.

'How far do you intend walking? All the way?'

Saffron glanced back at the crossroads. 'We've only come two hundred yards.'

'Why can't we hitch from here?'

'Because we've got to get away from the town centre. There must be other MPs on the lookout for us.'

Bickers, drawing the glance of every passer-by, stumbled on round a long bend in the road without speaking. As they came opposite a large furniture shop, he stopped. 'That's it,' he announced. 'Not another step.'

Unable to urge him further, Saffron began thumbing passing cars. As first one car and then another swept by, Bickers gave a growl. 'Look at 'em! Warm and rich and safe. What the hell do they care about us poor bastards who're fighting the war for 'em.'

The words had barely left his mouth before a large Chevrolet pulled into the kerb and a cheerful Afrikander voice greeted them.

'Where do you lads want to go?'

'Breconfield,' Bickers said promptly.

'Breconfield? OK, I'll run you there. Jump in.'

The Chevrolet drew up opposite the gates of Breconfield. Saffron jumped out first, then lent a hand to Bickers who had stiffened up during the ride. The middle-aged Afrikander driver showed his concern as Saffron turned to thank him.

'Better get him to a doctor right away. And don't forget to let the police know about those skollies.'

'I'll see to it,' Saffron told him. 'Thanks for coming out of your way.'

'Glad to be of help. Tot siens.'

As the car reversed and headed back up the road, Saffron turned to Bickers. 'If a general alarm's gone out to all the camps they might put two and two together if they see you limping. So you'll have to put on a show.'

Bickers, tetchy with pain and weariness, was gingerly testing one leg and then the other. 'You think I don't know that?'

Across the road the sentry, after taking a look at the Chevrolet, had retired again into his box. Their main threat, Saffron knew, was the lighted guardroom thirty yards inside the gates. 'Ready?' he asked.

'Give me a minute,' Bickers snapped.

Saffron waited patiently. 'How do you feel now?'

'Bloody awful,' the Londoner muttered, flexing his arms.

'If we stay out here much longer we'll make them suspicious. Surely you can manage another thirty yards.'

Giving him a glare, Bickers tottered towards the gates. As they passed the sentry Saffron gave the man a wink and said loudly. 'It's a good thing you haven't a birthday every day, mate!'

A heavy-faced corporal neither man had seen before was sitting at the guardroom window as they approached. As Bickers shoved in his pass and stumbled on, the man leaned his head out suspiciously. 'What's wrong with him?'

'Smashed,' Saffron grinned.

'What's he been drinking? Meths?'

'Not him. A couple of sniffs at an empty bottle and he's away.'

The corporal sank back. 'You notice any trouble in town tonight?'

Saffron felt his heartbeats quicken. 'There were police and MPs on the station when we caught the train back.'

The corporal's grin had a touch of malice. 'It's two of your mob. Man, they're in trouble.'

'What have they done?'

'Had it off with two married women at Clifton, beat up their husbands and a woman neighbour, and half-killed a Redcap. We got the report through an hour ago.'

Saffron hid his apprehension well. 'Have they any idea who they are?'

'Not yet. But they've got witnesses.'

'What happens now?'

'Christ knows. It's up to the Provost Marshal and the police. But, man, I'd hate to be in their shoes.'

Bickers, eavesdropping at the far end of the hut, gave a groan of despair as Saffron joined him. 'You hear that? They've only got to bring those civilians here on an identity parade and we're finished.'

Saffron helped him through the darkened huts towards his cubicle. 'Maybe they won't do that. Let's take each fence as it comes.'

'I think we ought to get out while we can,' Bickers said plaintively.

Saffron stared at him aghast. 'You mean desert?'

'What else? It can't be worse than getting five years.'

He could be right at that, Saffron thought, then pushed the temptation aside. 'Don't talk stupid. Only a couple of minutes ago you were moaning you couldn't walk another step.'

Indignation momentarily rallied Bickers. 'It's easy to be a hero when you aren't in pain, isn't it? You ought to have these bruises of mine.'

'I'm sick of hearing about your bloody bruises.'

'I'll bet you are.'

'What's that supposed to mean?'

'Don't tell me you don't know, Saffron.'

They were now outside Bickers' hut. Breathing hard, Saffron pushed the door open. 'Think you can undress yourself?'

Bickers was on his dignity. 'I'll manage.'

'That'll be a change,' Saffron growled. 'All right. Get your head down and I'll be over early in the morning to see how you are.'

CHAPTER 25

Anxiety at what the future might bring plus the attention of the fleas combined to give Saffron a sleepless night and made it easy for him to keep his promise. It was 5.45 when he pushed open the door of Bickers' cubicle to find, to his mortification, that the Londoner was sound asleep and snoring. When shaking did not awaken him, Saffron was driven into pinching his long nose. There was an explosive snort followed by a yell of indignation.

'Whaaat the hell are you doing?'

Saffron hushed him. 'You've forty-five minutes before parade. So you'd better start loosening up.'

Bickers made an effort, rose two inches, and fell back with a groan. 'I can't move.'

Saffron put an arm beneath him. 'You can if you try.'

'Get the doctor,' Bickers moaned. 'I think I'm paralysed.'

'You're just stiff. It'll work out once you're on your feet.'

'And how the hell do I get on my feet?'

'Swing 'em to the floor, and work yourself round. Then lift up.'

'Bloody easy, isn't it?' Bickers complained. 'When you haven't half-a-dozen cracked ribs and aren't black and blue from head to foot. I want to see the doctor.'

'If you do, it'll be a dead giveaway. Even if you aren't on parade, someone's sure to put two and two together. Kruger must have heard about it by this time.'

Bickers gave a glare of dislike. 'So I have to go out on that parade ground even if it kills me. Which it will.'

Saffron put an arm round his shoulders again. 'You'll be all right once the stiffness wears off.'

Inch by inch, accompanied by groans and the creaking of joints, Bickers came upright. Saffron gave him a cigarette and then began hoisting him to his feet. The Londoner's groan was heartfelt.

'It'll all be wasted. They've only to send one of those civilians here and we're straight through the trapdoor.'

Yanking down his pyjamas, Saffron helped him into his slacks. 'Maybe. But we're not the only camp in these parts.

We have to play it as it comes. Put your shoes on and we'll go for a walk.'

'A walk!'

'Up and down the hut a few times,' Saffron explained.

Supporting him, Saffron led Bickers down between the twin rows of beds. The men, inured to the disturbances of service life, slept on despite the Londoner's yells of pain and his collision with a bucket. By the time the two of them had traversed the hut three times Saffron was able to withdraw his supporting arm. He watched Bickers critically as the gangling corporal headed straight back for his cubicle.

'You're walking like a pregnant woman. Can't you loosen up a bit?'

'How many aspirins is it safe to take?' Bickers groaned.

'Three. Four at a pinch.'

Bickers fumbled vindictively in his kitbag. 'Maybe I'll take the whole bottleful. Then you'll be on your own.'

Saffron grinned. 'They'd pull you round. And then give you another two years for attempted desertion.'

Bickers swallowed a handful of aspirins and sank back on his bed. 'Go away,' he muttered weakly.

With the record player blaring out its military music and the squads of men marching and counter-marching around it, the stupefied Bickers felt he was a helpless puppet in the midst of a giant clockwork toy. He was drilling his squad in front of one of the hangars and had discovered that by sending them on only twenty-yard excursions he himself was able to remain almost stationary. Ignoring the puzzled glances and comments from his trainees, he was preparing to about-turn them for the eighth time when a bark at his elbow made him stiffen.

'What the hell's going on, Corporal? You trying to make them dizzy?'

Bickers swallowed. 'They're a bit sloppy on the turn, sir. So I thought I'd give them some practice.'

Kruger's small eyes moved over him aggressively. 'They're not the only ones who're sloppy. You look like a dog's breakfast this morning. Have you had a shave?'

'Yes, sir.'

'What'd you use? A rusty bayonet? And what's the matter with your eyes?'

'Eyes, sir!'

'They look like organ stops. What were you up to last night?'

Wondering if Kruger had heard of the incident yet, Bickers felt instant panic. 'Nothing, sir. I'd a very quiet night.'

Kruger had the look of a man whose sudden suspicion was too good to be true. He jerked his swagger stick at the squad of murmuring men. 'Get those men moving! Properly this time.'

Bickers braced himself. 'Squad, by the left, quick march. Left, right, left, right, left, right. . . . As the tail of the squad passed him he gritted his teeth and started after them. He had not gone ten yards before there was a loud yell.

'Bickers! Halt your squad!'

Bickers' voice had a cracked sound as he obeyed. Before he could turn Kruger was alongside him. 'What's the matter with you, Bickers? You peed yourself?'

'Peed myself, sir? No.'

'Then why the hell are you walking like that?'

As the dismayed Bickers searched for an avenue of escape he caught sight of Saffron who had halted his squad forty yards away and was watching the confrontation apprehensively. 'I don't know what you mean, sir,' Bickers managed.

Kruger had noticed Saffron's concern and the bright glitter of his eyes suggested the excitement of a man who has uncovered gold when it was least expected. 'I want a talk with you at break time, Corporal. Prompt on eleven!'

Bickers dropped his mug and irons on the cookhouse table and with a groan sank down beside Saffron. 'The bastard knows!'

Saffron gave a start. 'How can he know?'

'He's guessed. He's seen the state I'm in and put two and two together.'

'Did he actually accuse you?'

'Not in as many words. But he knows all right.'

Saffron relaxed. 'Guessing's not proof.'

'He can soon get proof, can't he? He's only got to tip the police off that we're stationed at Breconfield and we're dead.'

'He wouldn't dare do that. It would be going right over the Old Man's head. Don't forget Mottram's a regular. They hate civilian interference, particularly when their men are involved.'

'All right, then Kruger contacts the civilians and they tell the police. What's to stop him doing that?'

Saffron took a contemplative sip of tea. 'That's looking ahead. You're sure you're not imagining all this? I mean, no one could call you the world's greatest optimist, could they?'

Before the indignant Bickers could reply, the tannoy spluttered. A second later its blare stilled the clatter of plates and cutlery.

'Attention, everybody! There will be a dress parade for all personnel at 15.00 hours sharp this afternoon. All classes and flying are cancelled and all personnel will assemble outside Number One hangar under Warrant Officer Kruger. Only men in sick quarters will be excused. That is all.'

Bickers looked numb as a buzz of speculation ran round the cookhouse. 'That's it. We're finished.'

'What do you mean – finished?' Saffron asked irritably.

'Isn't it obvious? They're holding an identity parade.' Forgetting his bruised back as he jumped up, Bickers gave a yelp of pain. 'We've got to get away. While there's still time.'

Glancing round warningly, Saffron grabbed hold of him. 'Don't be a fool. How far do you think you'd get in this state?'

The panic-stricken Bickers tried to pull away. 'We can't just go out there like targets in front of a firing squad.'

'You can't be certain it is an identity parade. It could be a pep talk by the CO; it could be anything.'

'Of course it's an identity parade. They're on to us. It's five years in the glasshouse if we don't think of something.'

'Will you belt up?' Saffron hissed, dragging him down. 'Our only chance is to brazen it out. Perhaps we can get some of the lads to say we were with them yesterday afternoon.'

The suggestion stilled Bickers' panic but only for a moment. 'When they've got three witnesses and one of them a woman? I'm not going out there, Saffron. I'll try going sick. I feel sick anyway.'

Saffron grabbed him again. 'If you go sick, Kruger'll have you in front of the witnesses before they can give you a

Number 9. It'll be a direct admission of guilt. Our only chance is to act innocent, attend the parade, and play it from there.' At Bickers' forlorn expression, Saffron managed a grin. 'Even if it is an identity parade, they might not recognize you. They only saw you in the nude and you're a hell of an improvement in uniform.'

The parade ground that afternoon looked like a khaki and blue sea. Drawn into three sides of a deep square, the personnel of No 99 Air School muttered and shuffled in restless speculation as the hot minutes dragged by. At 15.07 a staff car appeared and halted twenty yards from Kruger at the head of the parade. The first officers to climb out were the Adjutant and the CO. The last man was a large, lantern-jawed Group Captain carrying a brief case. The glance Bickers gave Saffron was graphic with alarm.

With Kruger in charge there had been no opportunity for either corporal to seek anonymity in the deeper reaches of the square. Compelled to stand at the head of their squads, they felt almost nakedly conspicuous. Kruger, all bronzed limbs and white gaiters, snapped to attention as the three officers approached him and jerked up an arm in salute. As the Group Captain responded, he turned one polished boot at right angles to the other, then crashed the second boot down alongside it. For a moment he appeared to stare straight at Saffron and Bickers. Then his massive bawl scattered a flock of pigeons roosting on the top of Number One hangar.

'Parade! Attention!'

A staccato roll of thunder echoed across the parade ground as hundreds of boots stamped down. The lantern-jawed Group Captain set down his briefcase and nodded at Mottram. Acknowledging Kruger, who saluted again, the CO led the senior officer into the open side of the square. Rotund and Pickwickian, he resembled a benign uncle forced against his will to take part in a family admonition. The Group Captain was clearly content to keep the parade at attention but Mottram turned and muttered something to Kruger who was following the two officers. Looking as disapproving as the Group Captain, Kruger did another of his absurd buck-jumps.

'Parade! Stand at ease!'

A murmur ran round the square as some of the tension eased. It died at Kruger's yell. 'Silence on parade!'

Mottram gave a cough before speaking. 'Men, you're on parade today because of a complaint the Cape Provost Marshal has made to Group Captain Sprake. The incident is extremely serious, so you'll all give the Group Captain your hundred per cent attention.'

The lantern-jawed officer acknowledged his salute and stepped belligerently forward. The nod he gave Kruger made the Afrikander's eyes gleam with approval.

'Parade!' came the bawl. 'Attention!'

Tension snapped back with the crash of boots. Saffron, unable to see anything of the three civilian witnesses, could not decide how apprehensive to feel. Ten yards away, with his lanky legs pressed together and elbows at his sides, Bickers was swallowing so hard his Adam's apple was a ping-pong ball bobbing over his shirt collar.

Thrusting out his chin, the Group Captain stared round the square of hushed men. 'Some of you might have heard of me. Others might not. So I'll put you in the picture right away. No one gives my group a bad name and gets away with it. No one. Is that clear?'

A few heads nodded dubiously. Lantern-Jaw's glare moved on round the square. 'I don't mind a bit of spirit. I don't object to a bit of fun. But, by the centre, I won't tolerate behaviour that turns the local people against us. And that's what this disgraceful affair has done.'

It looked bad, Saffron conceded, wondering again where the prosecution was hiding its witnesses. Warming to his theme, the Group Captain crashed a fist into the palm of his hand.

'I've told your Commanding Officer that if anything like it happens again to stop everyone's pass for a month. Everyone's. And that's only for starters. The offenders will serve time in the Glasshouse. You're a military unit and you'll behave like one while I'm responsible for you. Is all that getting through?'

More dubious nods. Behind the irate officer, Mottram leaned forward and whispered something in his ear. Scowling at the reminder, Lantern-Jaw faced the puzzled square again. 'You needn't look so bloody innocent – you all know what I'm talking about. You know how much we've had to pay the Del Monico for the damage done? Over a hundred pounds. And it wasn't even an inter-service fight. Do you know that half the pubs in Cape Town are thinking of closing down to airmen?'

Across the square Bickers was looking like a man reprieved from the gallows and unable to believe it. Saffron, as quick to recover from relief as from danger, was watching a huge dog that was moving in purposeful fashion across the parade ground towards the assembly. Its size and colour were familiar, and as it paused unnoticed behind the group of officers, he saw it was Nuisance.

Lantern-Jaw was now in full cry. 'And all over a bloody football match. Don't you know why we encourage you to play games? It's to forge links of friendship with other units. Not to act like hooligans and knock hell out of one another.'

Behind the officers the dog gave a massive yawn, cocked up a leg and peed against the Group Captain's briefcase. The square of men began to sway, and here and there muffled laughter broke out. As Lantern-Jaw gazed about him in disbelief, Kruger let out a yell that made a pigeon discharge in flight.

'Silence! Silence on parade!'

An anticipatory hush settled. The Group Captain was breathing heavily. 'So that makes you laugh, does it? You think behaving like hooligans is funny. I wonder if you'll think it's funny if you're all confined to camp next week.'

Hundreds of youthful faces changed expression at the threat. Lantern-Jaw nodded his triumph. 'You're going to learn, as Wingfield have learned, that I expect discipline from the men in my command. Not occasionally but twenty-four hours a day. So from now on . . .'

His voice broke off as the dog, as if deciding the moment for action had come, walked past him into the centre of the square. There, making a noise halfway between a yawn and a raspberry, it turned, settled on its tail, and stared straight at the Group Captain.

Lantern-Jaw turned to Mottram. 'Whose bloody dog is that?'

'No one here, sir,' Mottram said hastily. 'It's Nuisance.'

'I'm as aware as you are it's a nuisance. But whose dog is it?'

'It's the Navy's, sir. It's their mascot.'

'Then what the hell's it doing here?'

'It probably heard about the parade,' Mottram offered.

'Heard about the parade?' Lantern-Jaw moved closer to Mottram and lowered his voice. 'You feeling all right, Mottram?'

'Yes, sir.'

'Then what the hell did you mean by that?'

'Nothing, sir,' Mottram retracted.

He received a suspicious glance. 'Then get one of your men to move the bloody thing.'

Mottram nodded and turned to Kruger. 'Warrant Officer!'

Kruger stiffened. 'Yes, sir. Right away.'

Hundreds of gloating eyes watched Kruger approach the sitting dog. Holding out a hand he made encouraging sounds. 'Come on, boy. Come on.'

'Bite the bugger,' someone shouted. Kruger's heavy cheeks turned florid. Drawing heart from the tail that was thumping the tarmac like a carpetbeater, he reached forward and tried to grab the dog's collar. As an indignant growl made him leap back, jeers and delighted laughter rolled round the parade ground.

A loud shout from the Group Captain compounded Kruger's discomfort. 'What's the matter with you, Warrant Officer? Are you afraid of a dog?' Glaring round, Lantern-Jaw spotted two grinning sergeants. 'What the hell are you grinning at? Go and help him!'

The three men approached the dog from back and sides. Nuisance wagged his tail until they were within range, then let out a salvo of warning barks. To a great cheer all three men retreated.

Ripping out a curse, Lantern-Jaw started forward himself. As if this confrontation was the reason for his presence, Nuisance rose majestically and gave a deep, let's-have-you growl. As Lantern-Jaw halted, the dog growled again and took a few, stiff-legged steps towards him.

Immediately what had been a rebuff became a rout. As men howled with laughter and leaned weakly against their comrades, Lantern-Jaw backed up to Mottram whose Pickwickian figure was convulsed with the agony of repressed mirth. The bawl for order from Kruger was lost in the uproar. Recognizing an impossible situation when he saw it, the Group Captain snarled something at Mottram and grabbed up his briefcase. A moment later, followed by the grinning Adjutant, the two senior officers made for the car. As it drove off, Kruger, astute enough to know that when leaders retreat, subordinates are wise to follow, turned on his heels and vanished. Left the undisputed victor on the field Nuisance gave a victory bark and prepared to pad back the way he had come. Instead he was surrounded by hundreds of rapturously cheering fans.

Saffron, who looked as if his fairy godmother had granted his dearest wish, pushed his way hysterically towards Bickers. 'You see that? You see what that dog did?'

With Bickers' bruised ribs bearing the brunt of his mirth, the Londoner's sobs were a mixture of pain and rapture. 'Kruger – sorted out in front of the entire Air School. And that Group Captain's face ... Mate, isn't that dog the greatest?'

Tears were streaming down Saffron's cheeks. 'It'll go down in history. A dog wrecks an Admonishment parade and sends a Group Captain packing. We'll have to buy him a gold collar or something.'

Swept along by the general euphoria, the two men encountered the conquering hero outside the canteen at the far side of the parade ground. Tail wagging enthusiastically, he was lapping beer from a wash bowl that delighted air mechanics kept filling. Meat pies and cakes were piling up alongside him as more men crowded in to pay their homage. Reaching through them, Saffron patted the dog's flanks reverently. 'He's human! He has to be.'

Hysteria overcame Bickers again. 'A dog – making a fool of 'em all. Oh, God, stop me laughing. My ribs are killing me.'

Saffron could not resist the reminder as he dried his eyes. 'I told you, didn't I? If you'd had your way we'd be posted AWOL by this time.'

'Don't tell me you weren't surprised,' Bickers scoffed. 'Even Kruger thought it was us they were after. Didn't you notice his expression when he heard it was about the Del Monico affair?' The Londoner's attention was drawn back to the half-drunk Great Dane. 'I wonder who brought him here?'

Saffron grinned. 'You said yourself he's on the side of the

lads and always comes here when there's an Admonishment parade. Now I believe you.'

It was a full fifteen minutes before order was restored and the parade ground cleared. Marching his gleeful trainees over to the quadrangle, Saffron glanced back as he waited for them to enter. Over at the canteen Nuisance had drunk and stuffed until his belly would take no more. Now, as drunk as a sailor on shore leave, he was making his unsteady way towards the camp gates with a large meat pie bulging from his mouth.

CHAPTER 26

Knife, fork, and mug in hand, Bickers pushed open the door of Saffron's cubicle and dropped apprehensively on the bed. 'Something's brewing.'

Saffron, also about to go to lunch, turned impatiently. 'Not again.'

'It's not funny, mate. Kruger wants to see me at two o'clock. From the way he said it, he's cooking up something.'

Looking thoughtful, Saffron lit a cigarette. 'In that case you could be right!'

Bickers' unease turned immediately into alarm. 'Why?'

'He wants to see me at the same time,' Saffron told him. 'I got the message just before we broke for lunch.'

Kruger jerked a thumb at the cab of the Bedford. 'Get in!'

The two corporals glanced at one another and obeyed. Kruger climbed into the driver's seat and slammed the door. As he slid a key into the ignition Saffron broke the silence. 'Might we know where we're going, sir?'

'No,' Kruger said flatly.

A minute later the transport was heading down the road that led to Eerste Rivier. Stealing a glance at Kruger, Saffron decided he had a look of grim expectation. At his opposite elbow Bickers looked jumpy enough to leap from the cab at any moment. Perhaps for once the Londoner's pessimism was justified, Saffron thought with wry humour. Having failed to nail them any other way, perhaps Kruger intended to shoot them and bury them out in the Flats.

Deciding bold was best, he fished into his bush-jacket pocket. 'Do you mind if I smoke, sir?'

He felt rather than saw Kruger smile. 'Smoke while you can, Saffron.'

The Afrikander's compliance drew a startled glance from Bickers. When Kruger refused a cigarette, Saffron offered the packet to the Londoner. The way Bickers sucked in smoke betrayed his state of mind.

No one spoke for the next three minutes. Alongside Saffron the muscles of Kruger's bronzed legs were flexing as he turned the Bedford off the main road and guided it down a country road that ran parallel to the Cape Flats. With the road quiet and straight, the Bedford's revs began creeping up. As the transport leapt over a bump on the uneven surface and Bickers, whose ribs were still sore, gave a muffled yelp of pain, Saffron's thoughts turned whimsical again. Perhaps the bastard was trying to do a Sedgley-Jones and frighten them to death.

After a mile or more the road swung to the left. As they came out of the bend Saffron saw a large American car, backed into a farm gateway, a hundred yards ahead. Two men occupied the front seats. Taking his foot off the accelerator, Kruger halted the Bedford on the opposite side of the road and turned his head. 'Out!'

Bickers' face told Saffron that the Londoner's fears were his own. Kruger was staring at them aggressively. 'I said get out!'

Bickers jumped down to the grass verge, followed by Saffron. Kruger was already alongside the American car talking to its occupants. One look as they emerged from behind the transport told both corporals the worst. The driver was the balding, thick-set civilian Saffron had rendered hors de combat at Clifton. The other was his blustering, bearded companion. As Bickers made a choking sound, Kruger drew his head from the car window. 'All right, you two. Stand in front of the car!'

Bickers seemed about to run. Saffron caught his arm. 'Don't be a fool. It'll only make matters worse.'

They stood before the car, Saffron smoking a cigarette defiantly. The two civilians, their expressions a cross between hostility and triumph, nodded at Kruger, who shook his closely-cropped head at something the driver said to him. 'No. It's better we handle it.'

The two men began arguing heatedly. Fear that revenge might be snatched from him made Krugers' guttural voice rise. 'For Christ's sake, man, you might never have found 'em without me. And I've got more against them than anybody. They're not going to get away with it. Just the opposite in fact.'

The balding driver, glaring through the windscreen at Saffron, was clearly dissatisfied. 'Why not take 'em straight to the police?'

'For one thing, it's too risky. You know what the Courts are like. They're not South Africans, they're bloody roineks, and might get off on some technicality. But with us they'll get the full treatment.'

It was an argument that quietened the two men although the driver still sounded sullen. 'You've forgotten about my sister, haven't you?'

'You don't have to tell her right away, do you?'

The man hesitated, then glanced at his companion. 'We'll give you a couple of days. If they aren't hammered by then, we'll tell her and go straight to the police.'

Satisfied, Kruger straightened. 'Two days is long enough. You'll get a ring from me tomorrow afternoon.'

'Don't forget,' the man grunted. With a last glare at the two corporals he switched on the engine. A moment later, without any warning, the car leapt straight out at Saffron who had just time to hurl himself aside. Colliding with Bickers, he sprawled out on the road. Dust sprayed over him as the car swung round and accelerated away. As he spat out grit and sat upright, Saffron saw Kruger gazing down at him. 'It's not your day, is it, Saffron?'

Shivering with hatred, Saffron climbed to his feet. 'You've nice friends – sir.'

Kruger turned away with a guttural laugh. 'I've more friends than you'll have in the next day or two, Saffron. Get back into the transport.'

They were halfway back to Breconfield before Saffron decided there was nothing to lose by putting up a fight. 'I think you're making a big mistake. No CO likes a scandal of this size – it reflects on his command. On top of that there's a protective streak in Mottram. Yet if you give him our names he'll be forced to notify Group and the Provost Marshal. Coming after that shambles with Nuisance, which can't have put him in a good light with the Group Captain, it'll be the last thing he'll want.'

Kruger laughed. 'You mean the last thing you want, don't you, Saffron.'

The hell with it, Saffron thought and recklessly threw his hand grenade. 'You'll find out I'm right. He won't like you for it and what's more, he won't like your boy friend, Sedgley-Jones, if he backs you up.'

Bickers gave a gasp of horror. The transport swerved violently but after Kruger's glance of disbelief, a mask fell over his face. Saffron, who was braced for sterner things, felt let down. A full mile was covered before the Afrikander spoke and Saffron found more menace in his hoarse measured voice than in his anger.

'Nothing's going to help you now, Saffron. You heard that civilian. If no action's taken against you in the next couple of days, he'll give your name to his sister. And she'll see a police car's round here in fifteen minutes.'

Saffron tried a touch of bravado. 'I wouldn't mind taking my chance in Court. I've heard they're very fair over here with the RAF.'

Kruger grinned. 'You didn't believe that bullshit I gave those two civvies, did you? If you ever got to Court, those three witnesses would tell a story that'd make you sound like sex maniacs. But don't worry, you're not going to Court. Apart from the rest, you've beaten up an MP and that means the Provost boys can't wait to get their big red hands on you.'

He drove the Bedford into the camp and halted outside the quadrangle. 'You can both get back to lectures now. But remember this. You're under open arrest, so Christ help you if you try anything. Now get out.'

The two corporals watched the Bedford head for the Transport Pool. Bickers' narrow shoulders slumped. 'That's it. All he has to do now is tell Sedgley-Jones and we vanish for five years.'

Pulling himself together, Saffron shoved the Londoner towards the swing doors. 'Come on.'

'Where to?'

'We've one chance,' Saffron said. 'To tell Price everything.'

Price waved the two corporals into his office and closed the door. For once his gnome-like face wore a serious expression as he walked towards his desk. 'Well, I've had a long talk with the CO. And I can't say the news is good.'

Bickers' Adam's apple bobbed turbulently as Price turned. 'The truth is you've been a couple of damn fools. I know what it's like being a young man but all the same we are guests in this country. That means that no matter how high they lift their skirts we don't co-habit with married women, we don't knock hell out of their husbands, and we don't beat up Military Police.'

'Those civilians weren't just trying to stop us,' Saffron protested. 'They meant to cripple Bickers.'

Price scowled. 'You don't have to prove your case to me, Saffron. Legally you've still clobbered two outraged husbands, laid hands on a woman witness, and damaged the pride of the Redcaps. It's no use arguing you're not South Africans – you'd be in just as much hot water if you were in England.'

'So Kruger's won,' Saffron muttered gloomily.

Price glared. 'And whose stupid fault is that? You've played right into his hands.' Giving the seat of his shorts an agitated scratch, the midget sat down. 'Anyway, it depends what you mean by won. The CO phoned him while I was there and said that on no account was he to take any action against you without his permission.'

Both men started. 'Isn't that hopeful, sir?' Saffron asked.

'I don't see why,' Price snapped. 'On a matter as grave as this it's obvious he wants to make all the moves himself.'

Saffron's moment of hope died. 'What about Sedgley-Jones?'

'You're lucky there. There's some snag over at the range and he's been there most of the day. Kruger'll tell him when he gets back, of course, if he hasn't phoned him already, but now he won't be able to take any action without the Old Man's consent.'

Bickers broke his silence. 'What do you think the CO will do, sir?'

Price gave his backside another scratch. 'How the hell

do I know? When I left him he was phoning everyone from Churchill downwards. My guess is that he'll try to cool things outside first. If he can do that, he can punish you in his own time.'

'Do you think he'll manage it, sir?'

'How do I know that? All I know is that he'll do his best. In the meantime I've taken responsibility for the pair of you, so for Christ's sake don't let me down.'

Du Plessis coughed anxiously. 'Corporal.'

Saffron, staring moodily from the classroom window, did not move. Course 21, pencils in hand, glanced up as Du Plessis coughed again. 'Corporal!'

This time Saffron heard him. 'What's wrong?'

'I asked if I could leave the room, Corporal.'

'What for?'

De Plessis was moving agitatedly from one leg to the other. 'I seem to have diarrhoea, Corporal.'

Saffron expected a laugh as the unfortunate Du Plessis hurried out but noticed instead the curious glances the trainees were giving him. His voice rose irritably, 'Settle down. You've only got half an hour left.'

There had been an odd change in Course 21 since the afternoon tea break. Before it they had been their good-natured, predictable selves. On their return they had seemed inhibited and in spite of the test Saffron had given them – a move to keep them occupied while he pondered on the fate in store for himself and Bickers – he had heard whispers and seen glances thrown at him from all points of the classroom. Instead of wondering at the reason, he had felt only irritation that on top of everything else Course 21 would appear to be backsliding into anarchy again.

As faces lowered over exercise books, Saffron drifted morosely back to the window. In spite of his natural optimism and the knowledge that Price was working undercover to help them, this time he could see no hope of escape. As he gazed out into the quadrangle, the sound of urgent whispering reached him again. Turning, he saw Van der Merve and Moulang had their heads together. As the big Afrikander jerked back into his seat and made a great show of scribbling, Saffron moved towards him.

'That's the third time, Van der Merve. Crib once more and I'll have you in front of Price.'

The giant looked almost hurt. 'I wasn't cribbing, Corporal.'

'You're a bloody liar. Shut up and answer those questions yourself.'

Grinning sheepishly, Van der Merve bent over his desk. For thirty seconds there was only the scribbling of pencils. Then: 'Are you feeling all right, Corporal?'

This time it was Moulang. By some miracle of sunlight his hobgoblin face was looking solicitous.

'What do you mean – am I all right?' Saffron demanded.

'I thought you were looking a bit under the weather. Is there anything wrong?'

Saffron saw that the rest of the trainees were looking at him and nodding their agreement. Still not comprehending, he scowled at the slim Afrikander. 'You're what's wrong, Moulang. You and your side-kick. Help him once more and you'll both go in front of Price.' Irascible with tension, he scowled round the classroom. 'I don't know what's come over you characters this afternoon but I'm not in the mood to take it. Any more cribbing or whispering and you're in camp for the rest of the week.'

Aware he was punishing Course 21 for his own frustration, Saffron was in the act of lighting a cigarette when the door was flung open. Framed in the sunlight like some military Mephistopheles, Kruger jerked a thumb. 'I want a word with you, Saffron. Outside!'

Wondering if this was his summons to appear before the CO, Saffron threw away his cigarette and obeyed. Closing the door, Kruger glanced up and down the empty quadrangle. Pitched low his voice was hoarse with dislike. 'You didn't waste any time getting your puppet on the move, did you?'

'What did you expect? That I was going to sit back and do nothing?'

'He can't help you this time, Saffron. If the Old Man doesn't throw the book at you, those three civilians will go straight to the police. So either way you're for the big drop.'

'There's one consolation, isn't there?' Saffron taunted.

'You can't tell them yourself or the Old Man will have your guts for biltong.'

Glancing around him again, Kruger grinned. 'You don't think so? I'm waiting for just one thing, Saffron – to see what the Old Man does. If he plays it soft I'll see they hear about it. And it'll be a damn good man who can prove it was me.'

As all his problems focused down into one simple desire, Saffron suddenly felt very calm. 'You know what I'd like to do, Kruger? I'd like to break your back.'

Prurient lights glinted in the man's small eyes. 'You would? Why don't you try it?'

'Tonight?' Saffron asked eagerly. 'Out on the airfield. Just the two of us. Will you?'

For a moment Kruger appeared to consider the proposal. Then he gave another grin. 'Why should I take risks when I've already got you screwed down? I might half-kill you and what then?'

'So you're not just a bastard,' Saffron jeered. 'You're a yellow bastard too. You know something. That's the feeling I've had about you all along.'

The man's cheeks paled beneath their deep tan. 'I wish I was in that glasshouse you're going to, Saffron. I'd run you day and night until your lungs collapsed and your heart stopped beating. And if that didn't do the trick, I'd see you were beaten to death. But who knows? When I've said my piece to them, they might oblige. After all, you did beat up one of their men.'

Turning, he walked with stiff strides to the door at the far end of the quadrangle. Saffron watched him a moment before moving resignedly back into the classroom.

CHAPTER 27

Eyes rose from exercise books as Saffron entered and slumped down on the table. Moulang glanced at Van der Merve, then put up his hand. 'Corporal.'

It was a moment before Saffron responded. 'What is it? You got diarrhoea too?'

Moulang gave a fleeting, hobgoblin smile. 'No.'

'Then what?'

'There's a rumour going around, Corporal. We heard it at break time.'

'When isn't there a rumour going round? What's this one about?'

'That you're in trouble with Kruger again. Only this time it's serious.'

Saffron gave a start, then eyed the slim Afrikander warily. 'Now how the hell did you hear that?'

'That creep Steiner told Bekker and Du Toit.'

Saffron knew Steiner well. A shifty-eyed air mechanic who worked in Kruger's office and was suspected by all the trainees of being an informer. 'What did he say?'

Moulang tried to hide a grin. 'He said you beat up two civilians out at Clifton when they caught you and Corporal Bickers with their wives. And then did the same to an MP who tried to arrest you. Is it true, Corporal?'

Saffron sighed. 'I suppose it's one way of putting it.'

'Will you tell us what really happened?'

Saffron hesitated, then succumbed to a reckless bout of confidence. What the hell – it would pass the period away. When he finished he saw grins and even looks of admiration on the young trainees' faces. The sight irritated him.

'Don't look so amused. It's not something I'm proud of. Only they shouldn't have attacked Bickers like that.'

Down the classroom Moulang was conferring with Van der Merve and every other trainee in his vicinity. As the puzzled Saffron called for order, Moulang turned to him.

'Will you let us help you, Corporal?'

'Help me? How?'

'We can, Corporal.' It was the beaming Van der Merve, unable to contain himself any longer. 'We talked it over earlier and have got it all worked out.'

'Got what worked out?'

Moulang took over the reins again. 'It's this way, Corporal. A senior officer should never swear at or strike a lower rank, should he?'

Startled, Saffron threw a glance at Van der Merve but the grinning giant had never looked more innocent. 'What's that got to do with it?'

A deep chuckle ran round the class as Moulang replied. 'Everything, Corporal. It's a court-martial offence, isn't it?'

Uncertain where he was being led, Saffron walked with care. 'That depends. It can be in certain circumstances. But what's the connection?'

'I'm surprised you don't see it, Corporal. You've got Kruger over a barrel.'

'I have?' Then Saffron reacted. 'Moulang, if you've picked this time to pull some fool joke, I'll do you. I will, that's a promise.'

The loud murmur of protest from Course 21 ceased only when Moulang raised a hand. 'We're not pulling anything, Corporal. All we're doing is reminding you what happened when Kruger walked into the classroom ten minutes ago.'

Saffron wanted to pinch himself. 'What did happen?'

Never had Moulang looked more like a jinnie. 'You can't have forgotten.'

'I bloody seem to, don't I?' Saffron shouted. 'So tell me.'

Uncontrolled laughter was breaking out all over the classroom. Van der Merve's guffaw sounded above the rest. Saffron glared at him. 'Shut that big mouth and tell me what happened?'

The laughter momentarily died as the grinning trainees waited. 'He swore at you, Corporal. Called you a sod and an English bastard. And then threw a punch at you.'

There was an outburst of jeers, boos, and then a wild stamping of feet. Saffron yelled for order. 'Have you all gone crazy. Who thought this one out?'

Van der Merve's uneasy shuffling brought Saffron's wrath down on him. 'It's typical of you, isn't it? All brawn and no brain! Do you realize what would happen if you made an accusation like that? Every one of you would get the treatment. And if just one of you broke down, the rest would spend the war in the glasshouse.'

The giant's growl sounded like gravel sliding down a tin roof. 'Nobody would break down, Corporal.'

'Even though you'd all have to make a statement under oath?'

'We know all the risks, Corporal.' It was Moulang again. 'And we're ready to face them if we have to. But we don't think it'll come to that. Kruger's got his knife in you, but he's not going to risk a court-martial to bring you down. Make the threat to him and see what happens. Don't worry about us. We'll stick together.'

As Saffron cleared his throat, there was a loud cheer from Course 21. The chance to help Saffron and at the same time gain revenge on the hated Kruger was something no one wanted to miss. For a moment Saffron allowed himself the joy of indulgence. To call Kruger's cards, to hold a threat over him as he so often held threats over others ... Then, coming to earth, he shook his head impatiently.

'Sorry but it's too late. I've already spoken about it to Price and he's been to the CO.' As thirty faces dropped, he gave a rueful grin. 'It's a pity I didn't talk to you bunch of perjurers as soon as I got back to camp.'

No one looked more dismayed than Van der Merve. 'Then maybe we should speak to the CO, Corporal?'

'You mean threaten him too?' Saffron grinned.

'We could put in a good word for you, Corporal. Maybe then he'd give you a light sentence.'

'Even that wouldn't help,' Saffron told him. 'There are three civilian witnesses waiting out there in the wings. If the CO doesn't hand out heavy punishment, Kruger's going to let them know and they'll go straight to the ...'

His voice broke off in mid-sentence. Across the class-room Moulang's hobgoblin eyes had begun glowing at precisely the same moment. 'Well, Corporal.'

'That's one way it might work,' Saffron conceded hoarsely.

'You've nothing to lose by trying, have you?'

Lost in a sudden sea of calculations, Saffron pulled himself together. 'No. But you lot have.'

'Don't worry about us, Corporal. We want you to do it.' Moulang turned. 'Don't we?'

Although by this time nobody but Moulang and Saffron knew precisely what was going on, there was a loud affirmative yell. Saffron gave it thought for another minute, glanced again at the eager faces for reassurance, then hitched up his shorts.

'All right. I'm probably crazy but you've talked me into it!'

At the wild cheer that rose. Saffron hastily waved the trainees back into their seats. 'Shut up and keep quiet while I'm gone or you'll have Price in.' At the door he turned. 'Just one thing. If this camp blows wide apart in ten minutes' time, don't blame me.'

Leaving a breathless Course 21, headed by Van der

Merve, crowding round Moulang to find out what was happening, Saffron went in search of Bickers. With his instincts for self-preservation vibrant again, he was seeing new prospects opening up on all sides. Dazzled by them, he had to remind himself that with the CO already in possession of the facts, any advantage gained from them could only be marginal. But at least it might frighten the pants off Kruger and wouldn't that help to make those months and years in the glasshouse easier to bear? Saffron decided it would and continued his hunt for Bickers.

He found him taking a conversion course in Number One hangar. 'Would you like some fun with Kruger?'

Bickers, drawn and pale, eyed him suspiciously. 'You feeling all right?'

'Never felt better. Put your senior man in charge and come with me.'

'What for?'

'You'll find out. Come on.'

With Bickers trying to discover what was happening and Saffron giving nothing away, the two corporals crossed over to the Flight Offices. Glancing in Sedgley-Jones's window Saffron saw with satisfaction that the officer was still absent. With the two rooms isolated from the main block, it meant a row with Kruger would not be overheard.

Sitting at his desk, which was in a patch of sunlight, Kruger had discarded his bush jacket. As he scribbled in a notebook, sweat could be seen glistening on his thick, hairy forearms and heavy face. Black chest hair sprouted through the open neck of his khaki shirt. As he turned to light a cigarette, Saffron caught Bickers' arm and pushed open the office door.

Kruger gave a start, then his face hardened. 'Who the hell gave you permission to barge in like that? Get outside and knock. On the double!'

Saffron pulled the stunned Bickers inside and closed the door. Kruger rose sharply. 'What the hell do you think you're doing?'

Although his pulse was racing, Saffron found his voice was steady. 'I've come to talk about what happened in my classroom fifteen minutes ago.'

'In your classroom?'

'Yes. When you came in.'

'What the hell are you talking about?'

'Your behaviour, sir. The way you swore at me and that blow you struck.'

Bickers gave a loud gasp. Kruger's expression made Saffron realize that a part of him was enjoying the confrontation.

'Have you gone out of your mind, Saffron?'

'If I have, so have all my trainees. They say they witnessed everything.'

Kruger released his breath slowly and sank back into his chair. 'So that's it. You blackmailing bastard.'

Saffron jerked his head at the petrified Bickers. 'Keep it up. The more witnesses the better.'

Kruger said something vicious in Afrikaans. 'It won't work, Saffron. Not in a thousand years.'

'Are you sure?' Saffron was gaining confidence by the minute. 'It's our word against yours. Thirty-one to one. Those are heavy odds.'

'Not heavy enough. Not in these circumstances. Even a fool would recognize a frame-up.'

Saffron released his spear. 'You're forgetting how popular you are. Everyone will want to believe it.'

The Afrikander's eyes showed the thrust had gone home. 'What exactly are you saying?'

'That little creep Steiner might have done you a big favour by telling my trainees what happened out at Clifton. At first they were determined to put in a complaint to the CO. Now they tell me they're prepared to forget what happened if you forget about me and Bickers.'

'You are crazy, Saffron. What's the point of my forgetting when the CO already knows? And who told him? You – through your little puppet Price.'

'I'm talking about those threats you made me outside the classroom. If those three civilians go to the police, my thirty lads go straight to the CO, with their Bibles in their hands.'

'And how am I supposed to stop the civilians going to the police if they feel like it?'

'That's your problem. Just keep remembering this – if Bickers and I go to Court, you go in front of a court-martial.'

A cord had risen on the side of Kruger's thick throat. 'I wonder if those men of yours know what they are doing.'

Lost for the past few minutes in the satisfaction of bullying the bully, Saffron felt sudden alarm. 'I think so.'

Kruger shook his head slowly. 'No, they don't. I'll wait until the MPs take you away, Saffron, and then I'll crucify them. And it'll be your fault. You think about that.'

A sudden shiver ran through Saffron. Slipping out of his bush jacket, he threw it into a corner of the room. 'That's as much as I can take. You wouldn't come out on the airfield with me. So let's do it in here.'

The chair under Kruger slid back on the linoleum. 'You wouldn't dare, Saffron.'

'Wouldn't I? What have I got to lose?'

'Much more than you think. Violent insurbordinates get special treatment.'

'Not this one.' Having involved his pupils, Saffron decided it was all or nothing. 'You're forgetting Course 21 again. Mention a word of this and you'll be sweating it out in the ranks with the rest of us. And Christ help you then.'

As Kruger let out another thick Afrikaans curse, Saffron glanced at the sweating Bickers. 'Don't interfere unless he tries to get out.' He turned to Kruger. 'This is where we came in, remember? You knock us down and we never get up. All right. Try me.'

The man's tongue came out and wet his lower lip. The pause gave the critic in Saffron a chance to frown on his display of aggression. Wasn't self-disgust at involving Course 21 in his troubles behind it? Wasn't it also a bit childish – wouldn't he look back on it one day with distaste?

The humour that was never very far from Saffron added its own wry comment. There was the chance he might look back with more than distaste! The bastard looked as strong as a bull and even if he was yellow he'd fight as desperately as any animal now that he was cornered.

Saffron's self-doubts were forgotten as Kruger reached for his telephone. Realizing immediately he would have no time to use it, he drew his hand away and without warning came charging round the desk. As he swung a vicious boot, Saffron leapt back and kicked in turn beneath his swinging leg. With a startled grunt the Afrikander upended and crashed against the desk. Before he could recover, Saffron swung two heavy punches into his rotund stomach. As he expected the sensation was that of punching solid rubber. Kruger gave a grunt of pain but pulled away and ran round the desk. He grabbed his chair as Saffron followed him and swung it with all his strength at the corporal's head. Ducking beneath it, Saffron dived for his legs.

Standing near the window Bickers resembled a frozen statue as the two men, kicking and gouging, rolled across the floor. As Kruger came on top he tried to jab his fingers into Saffron's eyes. When Saffron jerked away his head, Kruger seized his hair and slammed his head against the floor. Jabbing his knuckles under the man's nose, Saffron forced his head back and broke free.

Gasping for breath, the two men came together again like fighting bulls. Seizing Saffron round the waist, Kruger forced him back against the desk. Throwing his weight forward, he grabbed the corporal's throat. Feeling his spine would snap at any moment, Saffron locked his arms between the man's wrists and twisted to break the throttling grip. As the hairy hands parted, he clubbed two blows into Kruger's suffused face. A desperate heave and he broke free.

Staring round him, Kruger snatched up a spike file that had fallen from the desk to the floor. Eyes inflamed with the desire to maim and kill, he advanced on Saffron. 'Jou Blikskottel! I'll have your eyes, you bastard!'

The overturned chair was six feet away. As Saffron dived for it Kruger jabbed viciously and gashed his forearm. Before the steel spike could stab again he swung up the chair and drove it at the advancing Kruger. A second thrust pinned the Afrikander to the wall with one leg of the chair distorting his cheek. Saffron was prepared to thrust again when the desperate lunge of a boot raked his leg. As he stumbled in pain, Kruger broke free and lunged with the spike but Saffron managed to turn and gain a stranglehold round his neck. Grabbing his wrist with the other hand, Saffron applied pressure with all his strength.

Like a buffalo with a cat on its back, Kruger hurled Saffron round the office in a desperate effort to free himself. Eyes closed, Saffron was flung against the wall, then driven cruelly into a corner of the desk. Blood, flowing freely from his gashed arm, splattered the walls and turned both men's faces into grotesque masks. How long the pounding went on Saffron had no idea: his one thought told him that no matter what the pain or the exhaustion he must keep that grip intact.

Kruger's massive strength began to falter at last. Face

purple from his exertions and the stranglehold, he sagged to his knees. Hardly knowing what he was doing, Saffron released his grip and drove a knee into his jaw. As Kruger swayed, Saffron smashed his knee into his face again. This time the man toppled sideways and lay still. Unable to believe the fight was over, Saffron swayed over him for a moment. Then, breath sobbing in his chest and blood pounding in his ears, he staggered across to the desk and clung to it for support.

Bickers' awed voice penetrated the blanket of silence that enveloped him. 'You all right, Saffron?'

Saffron swallowed and nodded. As his senses came back he heard loud cheering and saw jubilant faces crowding in at the doorway and window. Before Course 21 could rush in to congratulate him, the small, stern figure of Price materialized from nowhere. 'That's enough! Get back to your classroom and stay there. I'll attend to you later. Go on – move!'

The men murmured their disappointment and drew back. As Price shouted at them again they began moving reluctantly away. Walking like an angry bantamcock, Price approached Saffron. 'Satisfied now?'

Still unable to speak, Saffron gave a shamefaced nod. Price's glance wandered round the smashed, blood-stained office. 'Christ,' he muttered. Scratching his backside in agitation he moved to the unconscious Kruger. 'Is he dead?'

Bickers, his head to Kruger's chest, looked disappointed. 'No, sir. It's going like a drum.'

Price glowered at Saffron. 'No bloody thanks to you. Why did you do it?'

Saffron managed a hoarse whisper. 'He had it coming, sir. You can't say he didn't.'

'Don't tell me what I should say,' Price snapped. He snatched up Saffron's gashed arm. 'That needs attention. Get over to the Sick Bay. Only wipe the blood off your face first.'

'Yes, sir.'

'Wait!' Price went to the door and peered out. Seeing no one of consequence in the vicinity, he waved the two corporals forward. 'Out, both of you. Bickers, you get back to your course and keep your mouth shut.'

'Yes, sir.'

There was a groan behind them as Kruger began to stir.

Saffron gazed at Price in bewilderment. 'Aren't you going to do anything, sir?'

'I'll attend to him when you've gone,' Price snapped.

'I don't mean that. I mean aren't you going to do anything about me?'

The glare he received from the tiny officer was a masterpiece of deceit. 'I'd love to, Saffron. Only I've been told what happened in your classroom and I don't see how I can give you what you deserve without getting Mr Kruger into trouble.'

Saffron's bruised face almost managed a smile. 'That is true, sir. I'm glad you see it that way.'

The scowl Price gave him this time was genuine. Gritting a curse he yanked Saffron out of earshot of Bickers. 'You cocky young bastard, don't get any ideas you're fooling me. I know those thirty villains of yours are committing perjury for you, and if I wasn't delighted that Kruger has got his, I'd have your guts for biltong. Get over to the sick bay and keep your mouth shut. And if that course of yours starts chortling and spreading the news, God help 'em.'

Bickers paused uneasily outside the canteen door. 'Let's turn it in and go back. It'll be a red rag to those two fairies. And the CO and Price will take a dim view of it too.'

Saffron, who, although stiff and sore, was riding a wave of euphoria since his defeat of Kruger, tried to push him forward. 'We're not breaking any rules. We're confined to camp, not to our billets. And think of all the free beer in there waiting for us.'

Bickers' expression showed he knew his weakness was being exploited. 'What's beer? We're in deep enough as it is.'

The two men were standing outside the trainees' canteen. In spite of Price's threats there had been no silencing Course 21. With the jubilance of men announcing the fall of the Bastille, they had sent messengers to every corner of the air school and by evening Saffron was the trainees' hero. The result was an invitation to both corporals to attend a celebration that threatened to be the Bacchanalia of the year. Indignant at the way Saffron had involved him that afternoon, Bickers had refused to attend, only to falter when Saffron had shamelessly elaborated on the treat he

207

was turning down. Now, with the Rubicon at his feet, the Londoner was faltering again.

'What have we to lose?' Saffron argued. 'Condemned prisoners get a last meal, don't they? So why turn ours down?'

Bickers scowled. 'Trust you to say something like that.'

'Well, it's true, isn't it?' As Bickers scowled again, Saffron turned towards the door. 'You do as you like but I'm going to enjoy myself. It might be our last chance for five years.'

Bickers flinched at the reminder. 'That's you all over, Saffron. You dragged me into that fight this afternoon and now you'd walk out on me.'

Saffron grinned. 'I needed a witness, didn't I? Anyway, who's walking out? I'm walking in.' He clapped a hand round Bickers' shoulders. 'Come on. Let your hair down.'

Bickers capitulated with bad grace and Saffron pushed the door open. Immediately there was a deafening cheer and a headlong rush of trainees. Hemmed in by their enthusiasm and their desire to shake his hand, Saffron needed the beaming Van der Merve to extricate him. He had to bawl over the din. 'They're a bit lively, aren't they?'

The giant's protective arm almost crushed him. 'You're their guest of honour, Corporal. You can have anything you want tonight.'

Reaching the bar, the two men were surrounded by the euphoric Course 21. As first one drink and then another was pushed at them, both corporals found the edges of the evening becoming blurred. By 9.30 Bickers, who in spite of his grumbles showed no reticence at sharing Saffron's glory, was drunk enough to be both apprehensive and resigned at the same time.

'Bloody marvellous party, Saffron. Even if they do line us up and shoot us tomorrow.'

Saffron, affected differently, was gazing round the crowded mess. 'Never thought I'd see the day.'

Bickers focused on him. 'What?'

'Never thought I'd see the day when I'd be sorry to see the back of 'em.'

'Who?'

'This lot,' and Saffron waved at the South African trainees. 'Bloody good crowd. Couldn't find a better.'

'You're drunk,' Bickers announced.

Saffron turned unsteadily. 'That's a lie. Prove it.'

'I don't have to. You just have.'

Saffron prodded a finger into Bickers' bony chest. 'Sour grapes, that's all it is. Just because you don't know how to handle 'em.'

Bickers guffawed. 'Listen to him! Who used to say he'd like to string 'em up on trees? Admit it. You're drunk.'

Before Saffron could vent his reply Bickers muttered something about needing to pee and vanished into the golden mist that surrounded the bar. A moment later a balloon with Moulang's hobgoblin face painted on it swam into Saffron's vision.

'How're you doing, Corporal?'

Saffron tried to straighten up. 'Fine.'

'Your glass is empty.'

Saffron peered down. 'It is?'

Moulang grinned. 'Don't slow down, Corporal. Jannie! Another whisky for Corporal Saffron. In a big glass.'

Saffron gazed at the tumbler full of amber fluid that materialized in his hand. 'Christ!' he muttered.

Van der Merve, who had appropriated Saffron for the evening, threw an impulsive arm around his shoulders. With Saffron too drunk to resist, the giant gazed proudly round the ring of milling trainees. 'Bloody marvellous instructor. Best we've ever had. Isn't that right?'

At the drunken yell of assent that went up, Saffron hastily tilted his glass. A moment later his head flopped about like a limp puppet's as Van der Merve, delighted with the familiarity being granted him, shook his idol affectionately. 'Where'd you learn to fight like that, Corporal? You made dog's meat out of him.'

Saffron suddenly felt everything coming up. Holding his mouth he clawed for the toilet. He passed Bickers on the way but there was no time for courtesies. When the gasping and groaning were over he managed to reach the door, only for it to invert itself on its hinges and take him with it. His groan was heartfelt as he slid to the floor. 'Oh, my God.'

He neither saw nor heard the anxious Van der Merve who had followed him. At a sign from the giant, a willing squad of men picked him up and straightened his uniform before taking him outside. There, screening him from possible enemies, they carried him to his billet where he was reverently undressed and slipped into bed. Motioning for the others to leave Van der Merve switched off the light and returned to the bedside. As he stood gazing down, Saffron's bandaged arm dropped from the bed. As lovingly as a mother with a son, the giant Afrikander lifted it and placed it back between the blankets. He then tip-toed out and softly closed the door.

CHAPTER 28

Saffron was called to Price's office at 2.30 the following afternoon. As he knocked and opened the door he saw Bickers standing at the desk. Still pallid from his hangover and jittery with apprehension, the Londoner looked as if death would be a welcome release. The tone of Price's voice told Saffron something portentous was in the air.

'Close the door and come over here.'

With his own head still thudding like a Zulu drum, Saffron obeyed and trudged forward. Price eyed both men in disgust. 'Two dog's dinners! Don't worry, I heard about that damn-fool party last night. And so has Sedgley-Jones. By the centre, you two are asking for it, aren't you? And now it's happened. Don't either of you look surprised.'

Bickers swallowed. Saffron made a gallant attempt to grin. 'We had to go down fighting, hadn't we, sir?'

'You've made a right mess of things, haven't you? If you'd kept your noses clean you might have served here right through the war. Instead you break every rule in the book and I lose two good instructors. I ought to kick your arses right across the airfield.'

Saffron decided they had been kept in suspense long enough. 'What's the verdict, sir?'

The question brought a scowl from the upset midget. 'You in a hurry to drop over the cliff, Saffron?'

'No, sir. But we have been kept waiting nearly twenty-four hours.'

Price swore. 'It would serve you right if you waited twenty-four days. I've seen some stupid things since I've been in the mob but that fight with Kruger yesterday beat everything. What had you been doing – smoking dagga?'

'No, sir. It just built up.'

'Built up! Do you know he had to spend the night in the sick bay?'

'I saw he wasn't on parade this morning, sir.'

'You and three hundred others. Did the stupid buggers have to cheer like that?'

'He isn't actually popular, sir,' Saffron advanced.

'Not like you,' Price said sarcastically. 'The blue-eyed boy of the bush apes! I hope in a week's time you think it's worth it.'

The reminder brought Saffron back to earth. 'You still haven't told us what's happening, sir.'

Giving his backside an agitated itch, Price dropped into his chair. 'If you two had timed it, you couldn't have picked a worse time for the CO. After that musical comedy sketch with Nuisance and the Group Captain, the last thing he wanted was a scandal of this size. So ever since I saw him yesterday he's been phoning and pulling strings with Records in Pretoria and for all I know with St Peter in the Pearly Kingdom. Fifteen minutes ago he called me in and said by some miracle he'd got his own way.'

'What's that, sir?' The agonized croak came from Bickers.

'A bloody sight better than you deserve,' Price scowled. 'You're posted. As fast as I can get you out of here.'

Bickers was too amazed to react. 'Posted, sir?'

'Yes, posted. That's assuming, of course, that the police don't extradite you first.' Price's eyes moved to the equally incredulous Saffron. 'And with any luck, thanks to those thirty villains of yours, you should be far away before the news leaks out.'

Blood was beginning to flow again through Bickers' regenerated arteries. 'You mean we're not going to the glasshouse?'

'No, and more's the bloody shame. I can't think of anyone who deserves it more, can you?'

Saffron stirred. 'We have you to thank for this, haven't we, sir?'

'Me? You're joking, Saffron. I told the Old Man a scandal would be a negligible price to see you two buggers behind bars.'

Saffron grinned. 'Thanks anyway, sir.'

'Thanks nothing! Although you have taught me one thing, Saffron.'

'What's that, sir?'

'That bloody villainy pays,' Price grunted.

Bickers sounded fully resurrected again. 'You haven't said where we're posted to yet, sir.'

Price fished into his pockets for cigarettes. 'I haven't, have I?'

Saffron, who knew the diminutive officer better than Bickers, was suddenly eyeing him closely. 'Do you know, sir?'

'Yes,' Price said, striking a match. 'Clairwood.'

'Clairwood? Where's that?'

'Durban.'

'Durban? But there's no training school there.'

Price sounded irritable. 'Did I say there was a training school?'

Saffron gave a start of excitement. 'It's a transit camp!' He swung round on Bickers. 'You hear that? They're posting us out of the country. We're going on active service.'

Bickers, raised on wings of relief one moment and now cruelly dropped, tried to speak and failed. The excited Saffron turned back to Price. 'Where are they sending us to, sir? The Middle East or the Far East? Or are we going back to the UK?'

Price exhaled smoke. 'They haven't said. I don't even know if you're going out of the country.'

Saffron's face fell. 'After what's happened, we must be. Surely we must.'

The look Price gave him was malicious. 'Not necessarily. I hear there are training schools up in the Northern Transvaal just right for characters like you. Heat and flies and no women for hundreds of miles. They might feel the war effort is safer if you're sent up there.'

Saffron dismissed the thought. 'It's active service, sir. It has to be.'

Price's mood changed. 'I hope you're wrong, lad.' Opening a draw he took out two envelopes. 'Here are your orders and train tickets. The first train to Durban is at 19.30, so a transport's ordered for 18.15. If you want to keep out of the glasshouse, don't miss it. That's all for now. Go and get your kit packed.'

At the door Saffron turned. 'Will we see you again before we leave, sir?'

'Why?' Price asked testily. 'Do you want me to kiss you goodbye?' Before the indignant Saffron could answer, he gave his puckish grin. 'I'll be around. Now piss off and get yourselves ready.'

Bickers sank down on his bunk with a groan of despair. 'That's it. Those bastards in Pretoria have fixed us.'

Saffron lit a cigarette and impatiently tossed him the packet. 'What do you mean – fixed us? An hour ago we both expected the glasshouse. Now all we're getting is a posting.'

Bickers sat up indignantly. '*All* we're getting! Haven't you any imagination? This is a punishment posting. Don't you know what that means?'

'It means we're probably being sent on active service like a few million other guys. What's wrong with that?'

Goose pimples were standing out on Bickers' bony knees at the thought of the ordeals ahead. 'How bloody naïve can you be? Don't you know this is a world war?'

'What's that got to do with it?'

'Everything. Think of the choice the bastards have got.'

Saffron let out a guffaw. 'You think there's someone specially detailed to search a map and find out the worst place for us?'

'Why not? It's the sort of thing the bastards do.'

'Don't be a clot,' Saffron said contemptuously. 'We're getting off lightly and you know it.'

In his dismay, Bickers' imagination was running amok. 'Lightly? What about Tobruk? Or Burma?'

'What about the Solomons? Or the Russian Front? They've got some RAF out there, you know. Think of that – thirty degrees below.' Saffron chortled at Bickers' expression. 'Perhaps they might give us a couple of months in each. A South Sea Island girl one week and one of your sexy Red comrades the next. You might even have a beer with Joe while you're there. Wouldn't that be something?'

'You wait, Saffron,' Bickers muttered darkly. 'You'll be laughing on the other side of your face in a week or two.'

Saffron clapped his shoulder and moved towards the door. 'We'd better start getting packed and cleared. We mustn't miss that train.'

A sudden thought stiffened Bickers. 'What about our kit at Rondebosch?'

Saffron gave a start of dismay. Then his face cleared. 'We'll get the transport driver to call there on the way to the station.'

'But what if Price comes with us?'

Saffron's laugh as he went out brought a scowl from Bickers. 'If you're right about the Russian Front, we haven't much to lose, have we?'

Price's dumbfounded eyes lifted from the suitcase Bickers was carrying to the window of the room above. 'I don't believe it,' he muttered.

Giving him an abashed grin, Bickers slung the suitcase into the back of the waiting transport and jumped in after it. As he and Saffron gazed down at Price, the small officer, breathing hard, climbed up alongside them. 'I ought to bounce you both right over Table Mountain for this. Whose name have you been forging? Mine?'

'No, sir,' Saffron protested. 'We wouldn't do that.'

'Then whose?'

'PO Prune and Sergeant Binder, sir.'

Price goggled. 'Who?'

'Two Tee Emm characters, sir. Prune and Binder.'

Price's eyes narrowed ferociously. 'You're pulling my pisser again, Saffron, aren't you? Don't you ever know when to stop?'

'I'm not, sir. We gambled the Afrikanders in the guard-room wouldn't know who they were. And they didn't.'

'I don't get it,' Price muttered. 'Why not Smith and Jones? Or, while we're at it, Eisenhower and Churchill?'

Saffron explained. The cunning of the scheme turned Price's indignation to awe. 'You still signed the wrong names, Saffron. They should have been Borgia and Machiavelli.'

Saffron dared a grin. 'A bit too foreign sounding, sir. Prune and Binder were just right.'

Bickers had the decency to look away. Price turned back to Saffron. 'How long have you been doing this?'

'Quite a long time,' Saffron admitted.

'With Kruger and Sedgley-Jones breathing down your

214

necks? Didn't it ever occur to you what would happen if they found out?'

'They didn't, did they, sir?' Saffron ventured.

Up front in the cab the driver gave a shout. 'Are you ready to move off yet, sir?'

Price spun round. His yell made both corporals start. 'By the centre I am! And keep your foot down, Simpson! Whatever happens, these two bastards mustn't miss that train.'

The cheer that rose as the three men entered the platform drowned even the hiss of steam from the waiting train. 'Your fans,' Price said sarcastically as Saffron halted in his tracks. 'Waiting for a lock of your hair.'

There was a rush of feet and a moment later Van der Merve and his enthusiastic company ringed the three men. 'What the hell are you lot doing here?' Saffron asked.

'We couldn't let you go without saying goodbye, Corporal.' The beaming Van der Merve turned to Price. 'Thanks for the transport, sir. We'd never have got here without it.'

Price flushed irascibly at Saffron's glance. 'Don't get any wrong ideas! It was the only way I could prevent the buggers going AWOL.'

Slinging two kitbags over his shoulder as if they were filled with feathers, Van der Merve started for the train. As Saffron followed with the rest of the trainees, Price fell into step alongside him. 'I hate leaving them with Kruger,' Saffron muttered before the midget officer could speak.

'I wouldn't let that worry you too much, lad. The Old Man's known for a long time how unpopular he is and he didn't miss that cheer this morning. I got word on the grapevine just before we left that he won't be with us much longer.'

Saffron's mood lifted. 'That's the best news this week.'

Price dropped his voice conspiratorially. 'Then what about spreading the good cheer around, lad? Before the train goes.'

Saffron's look was innocence itself. 'Spreading it around, sir?'

'Don't give me that, Saffron. You know what I mean.'

Saffron was saved from answering by Van der Merve. Letting the two kitbags fall in front of a carriage door, he had taken a long parcel wrapped in brown paper from Moulang who had moved up to his elbow. Diffident now but urged on by the grinning trainees, he approached Saffron.

'There wasn't time to get you a real present, Corporal, but we had to give you something. So we're wondering if you'd like this,' and he extended the parcel to Saffron. 'It's only a little thing but . . .'

'Like hell it's little,' someone shouted. 'It's bloody big.'

Van der Merve glared round and tried again. 'What I mean, Corporal, is that it's not valuable or anything like that.'

'It would have been valuable if he hadn't been a clot and stopped us using it,' the same wag called out.

At the roar of laughter that followed the giant gave an enraged bellow. '*Bly stil* or I'll wrap it round your ear!' As the laughter died, he turned his craggy face back to Saffron. 'It's a souvenir from Course 21, Corporal.'

Saffron was feeling cautiously under the brown paper. Like a curious terrier, Price moved alongside him. 'Aren't you going to open it?'

'I know what it is,' Saffron said.

'I don't, do I? Open the bloody thing.'

Saffron hesitated, then tore off the brown paper. At the sight of the long wooden club exposed, Price's eyes widened. 'What the hell's that?'

As sharp as ever, Moulang dug Van der Merve in the ribs. 'It's a baseball bat, sir.'

'Baseball bat be buggered,' Price snapped, glaring at Moulang. 'What is it, Saffron?'

Saffron hefted it, then his face brightened. 'An Indian club, sir. You know, the things they twirl round to keep fit.'

Snatching the club from him, Price examined it suspiciously. Sensing the way the wind was blowing, Saffron pushed Bickers towards the train. 'We'd better be getting aboard. We don't want to lose our seats.'

Van der Merve grinned. 'No chance of that, Corporal. We've got two men guarding 'em.'

Saffron's eyes were on Price. 'Just the same, we'd better start moving.' Walking round the circle of trainees, he shook hands with each man in turn. The last man he encountered at the door of the coach was Van der Merve who again showed embarrassment as his massive hand closed over Saffron's.

'Thanks for everything, Corporal. The boys are going to miss you. Drop us a line from time to time, will you? We'd like to know where they're sending you.'

'Of course. Why not? Good luck on the course, Van. And thanks for . . .' Saffron's face suddenly contorted. 'Easy, for Christ's sake . . . You hear me? Let go . . .'

The startled Van der Merve showed his concern as Saffron, wringing his crushed hand, hopped up and down on the platform. 'You all right, Corporal?'

'Of course I'm not all right,' Saffron yelled. 'You've crushed my hand, you great Jarpie oaf.'

It took a minute before order and amity were restored and Saffron and Bickers were safely seated in their carriage. Outside Course 21, with Van der Merve in the forefront, were crowded round the window. Price, who had entered the coach with the two corporals, dropped into the seat beside Saffron.

'We've got three minutes before the train goes, Saffron.'

Saffron turned innocently from the window. 'We have, sir?'

Price scowled. 'Don't try that wide-eyed Betty Boop stuff with me, Saffron. You know what I want. And you still haven't told me.'

'I have told you, sir. It's just a matter of keeping on top of them.'

Giving him a look, Price glowered across at Bickers. 'Do you know?'

'Not really,' Bickers said cautiously.

'Not really? What the hell's that supposed to mean?'

Bickers made a quick decision. 'I don't know, sir.'

'You're a bloody liar,' Price grunted. As he gazed at the collection of devoted faces packed into the carriage window, a note of desperation entered his voice. 'You've had 'em eating out of your hands for weeks. And look at 'em now! If I could get the others trained like that, life would be worth living again.' In his desperation Price tried cajolery. 'I've always thought you a decent lad, Saffron.'

'Thank you, sir.'

'And in turn I've always played fair with you, haven't I?'

'Yes, sir. Very fair.'

'Then why the hell won't you come clean and tell me?'

Saffron shifted restlessly in his seat. 'You might take it the wrong way, sir.'

Price's patience blew. 'How can I take something that might save my sanity the wrong way, you stupid bastard?'

Two civilians who had just entered the compartment gave the midget a shocked glance. With departure imminent, Saffron relented. 'All right, sir. If you promise to keep it to yourself.'

'I'll promise to keep it from my shadow if I have to. Only get on with it.'

With an eye on Course 21 outside, Saffron put his mouth to Price's ear. Five seconds later the midget's eyebrows shot up and almost knocked his cap off. 'I don't believe it.'

'It's true, sir. Ask Van der Merve.'

'You did that to a trainee and no one reported you?'

'No one, sir. You see what it means?'

Price was breathing hard with excitement. 'By the centre I do. You know something, Saffron? Things aren't going to be the same without you.' He indicated the club tucked between Saffron's legs. 'Is that what you used?'

'No, sir. I used a Browning barrel. The club was for someone else.' As Saffron explained, Price gave a wicked chuckle.

'You slipped up there, lad, didn't you?'

'We all make mistakes, sir.'

A whistle sounded outside. Jumping to his feet with a flourish Price shook hands with both men. His puckish grin kept the moment light. 'Sorry you're going, lads, but it's my bet you'll drop on your feet. In fact I think I'm more sorry for them than for you.'

'Thanks, sir,' Saffron said.

Price grinned at him. 'Not a bit, lad. And don't worry. You might be leaving Breconfield under a bit of a cloud but it's my guess they'll be having an oil-painting of you up in the Officers' Mess in a couple of weeks.' Rubbing his hands, Price pointed down at the club. 'You don't need that thing, do you?'

Saffron glanced down. 'I hope not.'

The midget's eyes gleamed. 'Then hand it over, lad. You never know: I might want to do some of those Indian exercises.'

Saffron gave it to him. Looking like a gnome who has

218

just annexed a magic wand, Price gave the men a last grin and jumped down to the platform. Another whistle sounded and steam momentarily obscured Course 21 as the train began to pull away.

Saffron caught sight of them running after the carriage a moment later, with Van der Merve in the lead. Behind them, like Caligula bidding farewell to one of his conspirators, Price lifted the club in a symbolic salute. With a sprint Van der Merve reached the window. 'You won't forget that letter, Corporal?'

'I won't,' Saffron promised, reaching out for a last handshake. 'S'long, Van.'

'S'long, Corporal. Look after yourself. Tot siens!'

With a last wave, Saffron cleared his throat and dropped back into his seat. 'It's true. I'm going to miss those bastards.'

Bickers, rendered mute until now by the enormity of the disaster, stirred. 'Serve you right!'

'What did you say?'

'Serve you right. If you hadn't tried to be a bloody Baden Powell the first day you came, none of this would have happened.'

Saffron sat up indignantly. 'You're not saying that was my fault?'

'Until you arrived, everything was going fine,' Bickers said bitterly, forgetting the two civilians. 'Bright lights, booze and girls every night. And then you have to get on your high horse because Kruger makes a crack about the RAF. Who cares?'

'That's terrible,' Saffron said with contempt.

'What's terrible about it?' Bickers demanded. 'I've heard you say worse things about the mob.' His disconsolate eyes were drawn to the window where, in the dusk, the lights of Cape Town were already thinning out and falling away. His groan came from the heart. 'Think of it. All because of you we mightn't be alive in two weeks' time.'

Across the compartment the two civilians exchanged startled glances. 'Oh, shut up,' Saffron grunted.

'It's all right for you, Saffron. You're one of them. You'd love to die for Lord Salisbury or Lord Norfolk. But what about me?'

'You can die for Uncle Joe,' Saffron suggested. 'When

you do, I'll see he hears about it. You never know – he might award you a posthumous Red Star.'

'Oh, funny, funny,' Bickers muttered. For a minute there was silence as the weight of the disaster crushed him again. Then, moved by a desire to share his woes, he leaned anxiously forward.

'You're the eager beaver who always knows where the action is. Where do you think they'll send us?'

There was no reply. 'Tobruk?' Bickers asked. 'Or Burma?'

The rattle of metal wheels was the only answer. Bickers nodded bitterly. 'That's bloody typical. You get us into this mess and then haven't the decency to talk about it. I can't think why I've put up with you all this time, Saffron.'

When there was still no reply Bickers gave a suspicious start and leaned forward again. A moment later a groan of disgust was torn from him. With his legs stretched out comfortably across the compartment and a smile of oblivion on his lips, Saffron was fast asleep.